Viking

Book 15
Dragon Heart Series
By
Griff Hosker

Published by Sword Books Ltd 2016
Copyright © Griff Hosker First Edition

Cover by Design for Writers

Dedicated to Thomas and Samuel my two new grandsons both born in 2016. *Wyrd*!

Prologue

Each birth in the clan was special. It meant we were prospering and we were growing. The girls could grow to be mothers and the boys into men who would wield weapons and defend the Land of the Wolf. We had had one such birth in my hall. My new daughter, Myfanwy, had brought joy to our home. She could not replace my son, Wolf Killer but, as Kara, my eldest daughter said, "She is of our blood father. Your blood coursed through Wolf Killer and it will be in Myfanwy. Who knew what she might achieve. She and her elder sister, Erika, were the gentle side of my hall. They took after their mother, Brigid.

Kara's words had made me thoughtful. I mourned my dead son, Wolf Killer, but I still had my grandson, Ragnar and my son, Gruffyd. I would not make the same mistakes with them as I had with Wolf Killer. We would not become estranged. Both were now growing quickly. Ragnar had seen fourteen summers and was now able to go to war. He had his father's oathsworn as his hearth-weru and he had been blooded in battle. Although Gruffyd was younger he too had been in battle and had been blooded. He had not flinched from our foes. I had a new purpose in my life and that was to ensure that they were ready to leave my clan when I was gone. I was not a fool. With age came wisdom and I had lived longer than any man I had known save Old Ragnar and he had been a half blind cripple at the end. I did not think that I was doomed to endure such an end.

The last few years had changed us. Many of my Ulfheonar were now in Valhalla with my son and his son, Garth. Others had had their lives changed irrevocably. Snorri had had to kill a witch. Many now called him Snorri the Witch Killer but he did not approve of that name. We had sailed to Syllingar to atone for that act. Although the witch there had forgiven him I knew it had changed him. His hair was now turning white. He feared no man alive but a witch… that was something different. Kara was a volva and her husband Aiden a galdramenn. They had put a spell on Snorri's wolf token which he wore around his neck. Already made of gold it was already powerful but they made it even stronger. It helped but it did not drive away the demons which filled his head at night. We had all changed after fighting Eggle Skulltaker and his warband. They had been evil.

Eggle Skulltaker and his band had come close to destroying both me and my people. The fight to destroy them had been hard and they had shown cunning. I was happy that they were now gone. We had drawn even closer together. With Eden Stad and Ketil Stad to the north Windar's Mere was now the furthest west we had a settlement. Far to the south were the homes of Sigtrygg on the Lune and our ally Pasgen ap Coen at Úlfarrston. With Cyninges-tūn in the centre my land was filled with farms but beyond that was an empty wasteland. The farms which had stood there were now being reclaimed by the forests and the mountains. We were prosperous but we looked within and not without. We traded less and were warier of strangers. The attack by the Danes had made us suspicious, even of our own kind.

Aiden had read the parchments we had taken from the hall of Grimbould of Neustria. He and Egbert of Wessex had been allies and Egbert had been involved in the plot against my people. They had shown us that our enemies plotted to end our time in the north. We were too few in number, yet, to take on the mighty Wessex but it was in my mind to visit the treacherous Saxon and bloody his nose once more. His land was rich and hurting him profited us. I could not allow the hurt he had done us go unpunished.

As Gormánuður drifted to an end I saw that the leaves were now lying deep on the ground and breath began to mist in the early morn. The water of Cyninges-tūn was heavy with early morning dew, the waterfowl hidden by grey, dank fog. It would soon be the time to hunt the wolf. When the feast of Yule was over those warriors who wished to become Ulfheonar would travel into the high places and hunt that most deadly of predators. I knew not if any wished to hunt this time but I would lead hunters to take wolves. They were a threat to every isolated farm. We had learned over the years not to ignore the threat.

As I looked out over my stronghold I saw young boys practising with wooden swords, slings and bows. That was as it should be. Their play was purposeful and would make them into better warriors when they grew. Everyone else was busy preparing for the long dark nights to come. The hides from the animals we had slaughtered were cleaned and prepared. The bones which had been used for soup were now being sorted. Those which were large enough would be made into tools and jewellery. Others would be burned on the bone fires and spread on the land. Nothing was wasted. The best of the fruits which had been gathered would be stored while the poorer ones would be cooked along with the meat which had not been preserved. They would be mixed together with the precious spices from Miklagård to make our Yule feast special. Women were spinning the wool from our sheep and goats to make new kyrtles and blankets for the winter. Fish were drying on racks while others were in the smoke houses. Timber was hewn for firewood. Each day we had less sunlight and my people strove to use every moment. When winter closed in around us we would have food, warmth and safety.

I looked at the mountain that was Olaf, the old man. He watched over us still. He, along with the spirits of the Water, protected us. I touched the wolf and the dragon which hung from my neck. "Thank you, ancient ones. Soon we will start a new year and face new challenges. It is good to know that you are there."

Part One

The Clan of the Skull Takers

Chapter 1

My wife, Brigid, was a follower of the White Christ. She was not alone. There were others, mainly slaves, who chose this new religion. I did not mind for they were women and it suited them. For a warrior, it went against everything we believed. None of the men in the Land of the Wolf chose that way. It did mean, however, that we celebrated the birth of the White Christ at the same time as Yule. It seemed strange to me that the White Christ should have been born in the depths of winter. Most of our babies were born in Tvímánuður, the corn cutting month. Conceived when the nights were long that was the natural way. I did not mind the feast for my wife was happy for us to drink and to eat. She tried to get us to give gifts. So far few did so. She was a good wife and I was lucky. The two festivals seemed to meld together. My wife had her way, albeit briefly, and we could feast in the heart of winter.

The celebration this Yule was different, for my new daughter, Myfanwy, took up much of my wife's time and the feast was planned by Kara, my eldest, and the slaves. I noticed that there was more greenery brought in this Yule as well as some customs from the land of the Norse. My wife did not seem to notice.

Over the last year, we had a pair of travellers who brought us goods from the lands of the Saxons. Wighlek and Vibeke were an older couple. They both had grey hair but they were hardy for they managed to travel even in the heart of winter. Only the closed passes stopped them. They did a healthy trade with us. They brought goods which the women liked. They brought jet and amber jewellery. They used the money to buy swords from Bagsecg. They had come in early Gormánuður bringing herbs, spices and powders which Kara and Aiden needed for their magic. They also brought news. It was they who told us that King Eanred was now staying in Bebbanburgh and that Athelstan was the defender of the lands. Bebbanburgh had been called Din Guardi by the old people. I still thought of it by that name. I knew I would have to speak with Athelstan soon. His father was a frightened old man while Athelstan made sure his land was safe. He was a good ally.

Kara and Aiden's daughter, Ylva, was now coming up to womanhood. Almost twelve summers old others her age were almost ready to bear children. She was different however. She might not bear children. Ylva was a volva, like her mother. If she had children, then it would diminish her powers. Kara had waited a long time to start a family. Some of her powers had left her and gone to her daughter. Aiden had magical powers too. It meant that Ylva was special, even beyond being my granddaughter. She would be a powerful witch when she grew into womanhood. I knew that Brigid did not approve of this witchcraft but Kara had saved the clan on more than one occasion. As I sat in my chair by my roaring fire Ylva came to sit by me. She took a bone comb and began to pull it through my untidy tresses. She often did this. She would hum a tune as she did so. It was soothing and I found it made me calm but I knew not what pleasure she derived from it.

"We should use those oils that they bring back from Miklagård, grandfather. They would make you smell sweeter."

I shook my head, "Do not mind offending me, Ylva, I am just the chief of this clan. Speak your mind eh child?"

She was not put out by my mock outrage, "And that is why you should take greater care of yourself. You do not go to war in winter. You have time to look more like a chief. The people look up to you. If you take care of yourself then the other men will too. It makes the clan stronger."

She had wisdom beyond her years. She saw things that I did not and which appeared obvious to her. "You mean I do not take care of myself? Brigid would not be happy to hear such words."

She laughed, "You look like a wolf!"

It was my turn to laugh, "Then that is *wyrd* for this is the Land of the Wolf and I am a wolf warrior."

"Oh, you are impossible." She laid down her comb and spoke conspiratorially to me, "I have asked my mother if I can go to Syllingar."

The hairs on my neck prickled, "Why? It is far from here and the seas are dangerous." I had been there many times but I feared the place. We had rarely sailed there because we wished to. We had gone there because we had been summoned.

"I envy those who have met the witch there. My father believes she is a Norn. I would learn from her. She would be able to teach me how to become a powerful witch and I could save the clan. Even Snorri has met her."

"And his hair turned white as a result. Be careful what you wish."

"I would not fear her. I have spoken with the dead and they are a comfort to me." She smiled, "My first grandmother, Erika, often comes to me."

8

"She was a great woman." I still missed my wife. She lay in a barrow across the water and in the spring primroses and other wild flowers made it look alive.

"Aye and an even greater witch. She is the one who holds this land safe. It is her spirit which watches over us."

"And old Olaf?"

"Oh, he does his part but he just stands like a rock. My grandmother moves over the land and through the Water. When danger comes, she will warn us."

"And is there danger?"

She shook her head. "I have not dreamed it yet. That is why I would go to Syllingar. There my powers can become greater."

I pointed to Elfrida. She and Brigid were spinning wool in the corner away from the fire. She also had powers and had been the wife of my son, "A witch once tried to take Elfrida and make her powers greater. Ask your mother about Angharad. She nearly ended the clan for she divided us."

"I know of her. She had a black heart. She was like the witch Snorri slew. My powers will be greater and I will be able to defeat such witches. I have powers for good. There are evil witches. My mother has told me of them and I do know of Angharad. That will not happen to me."

Kara came over, "Stop bothering your grandfather. Angharad almost destroyed our family. We will not speak of her."

"But if I have tuition from a Norn then I could have even greater powers and prevent such tragedies."

"I have told you daughter, you need to be a woman first."

Ylva hung her head, "Why am I not one? I have great powers and yet I am still a child."

Aiden joined us, "That is because the Weird Sisters have plans for you. When the time is right then shall you be a woman."

"Besides, daughter, it is the Mother who makes you a woman. Each girl becomes a woman when the Mother decides that it is right. We will know when it is time for you."

Any further conversation was ended when my son, Gruffyd and Ragnar approached me. I saw my son looking at Ragnar and nodding. "Grandfather we would like to go on the wolf hunt with you when you take the Ulfheonar."

I shook my head, "I took you on one wolf hunt. The men who would be Ulfheonar need our skills to help them kill their wolves. It would not be fair to have the distraction of you two."

They looked at each other again. There was a conspiracy here. They had plotted. The two were close. The death of Wolf Killer had made them so.

"You both have a wolf skin."

9

"I know. It is not to get a wolf skin. We would not be Ulfheonar but…" Gruffyd looked at Ragnar who nodded, "Ragnar said you will not have many wolf hunts left, father. I would hunt with you."

Brigid, who had been feeding our daughter looked shocked, "Gruffyd!"

"Well it is true! You said so! You said he was too old to be hunting the wolf!"

I saw from her face that it was true. Was I getting old? The only time I saw my face was when I saw it in the Water but I knew from Haaken and the other Ulfheonar that none of us were getting any younger. I did not know my age but I had been alive a long time. I had seen kings come and go. I had buried more of my oathsworn than lived now. Perhaps my son and grandson were right. I saw Ragnar scowling at Gruffyd and I smiled, "You may be right. We all get old." A silence fell on my hall. The celebrations had been dampened. Poor Gruffyd looked embarrassed. He had not meant to be so blunt but he was young still. "But I am still the jarl of this clan. I can still ride and I can still hunt." I gave Brigid a withering look, "Despite what some people might think. I tell you what, I will ask Snorri if he can take the three of us to find the wolves. He would be scouting them anyway. If it is meant to be then we will hunt them and if not, then we can enjoy the search."

"You have no need husband! This is foolish!"

"No, it is not. I hunted with Wolf Killer. The boys are right. Wolf Killer would have taken Ragnar on a wolf hunt. When his father died, I said I would be as a father to him. It will be good to test ourselves." I looked at Kara, "Is there danger?"

She kept her face impassive, "There is always danger but if you ask me have I dreamed a death then I will answer no."

Ylva stood with her hands on her hips and said, defiantly, "Why can they do what they want and I cannot?"

"Your father has told you. When you are ready then we will know and we will tell you." My daughter had the power to bend others to her will. She stared at Ylva with eyes which pierced into my granddaughter's heart.

Ylva fought it briefly and then shook her head, "Soon I will have the more power than you, mother, and you will not be able to do that."

Kara nodded, "And then you will be ready to go to Syllingar." She smiled, "Do you see? When it is right then we will know." She turned to Ragnar and Gruffyd, "And if you two insist upon this venture Aiden and I will make you a charm. I have lost one brother. I would not lose another."

Later that night as I lay in bed with Brigid I asked, "Am I old; do you think I am?"

She cuddled closer to me. "Our son should learn to think before he speaks. No one believes you are old but it is true that you look older. When last you came back from war we feared for you. Haaken told us of the dangers you faced and how close to death you came." She sighed, "It is no secret that I wish you would not go to war as often as you do but I also know that sometimes you have to. You do not have to go on a wolf hunt."

"I know. I do not think we will find a wolf. More times than enough we do not. It is the wrong time. In fourteen nights or so it will be right to hunt and Snorri will take those who would be Ulfheonar. I need to help them to become men who will lead this clan after I am gone. I will go with them. This will be an opportunity for me to talk with my son and grandson. I also need to speak with Snorri. He has kept to himself since we returned. It is not good. The hunt is a good place to share thoughts."

"Aye, his wife is concerned too. Perhaps this is a good thing."

I smiled in the dark, "You mean it is *wyrd*? Beware, my wife, you are becoming pagan!"

The conversation was ended by the playful slap she gave me.

Snorri was happy to take us hunting. "In truth, jarl, I need to stir myself. My wife is worried that the dead witch has taken my spirit."

"That is not true; Kara told us that."

"I know, jarl, but I have not been myself. I think back to that cave and the Norn... I wake up shivering and shaking. That is not the way an Ulfheonar behaves."

"Then my son's request to go hunting may be the work of the spirits. It will be good for us. Where do we hunt?"

"Lang's Dale is still the best place to find them."

"It is a long way. We will need horses."

"If we take the high pass we can save time."

"Is it open?"

"At the moment it is but if the snows come we can return by the Rye Dale. The valley of the Lang Dale leads past the Lough Rigg."

The pass of which he spoke was rarely used. That was partly because of the spirits who dwelt there. They were not happy spirits. They were the spirits of Lang and his family. The wolves had taken them not long after we had first arrived. The pass was narrow and had little sun. If the weather closed in, then it could become impassable. Normally this suited us for it meant that we were safe from attack from that direction. Snorri was right; however, it was the quickest way. I began to look forward to this hunt. It would be a challenge for all of us. It did not matter if we found no wolves. Snorri could teach the boys how to look for sign. There would be the anticipation of a kill. Sometimes that was almost as good as one which resulted in a death.

We left while it was still dark. Ominously a wind was blowing from the north and east. They were always the coldest and brought heavy snow. It chilled us to the bone. We all wore a wolf cloak and rode a sturdy hill pony. Gruffyd had the task of holding the tether for the spare pony and bringing up the rear. However, the comments at the celebration kept him subdued. He took his present task as a punishment. We took bows and spears as well as spare food. Only Brigid and Elfrida saw us off. Brigid would fret but Elfrida seemed remarkably calm. She had the ability to speak to the spirits too. I took it as a good sign.

It was hard going up the Cyninges-tūn fell. The wind had sleet mixed in with it. Once we dropped down to the Greens Beck we had a little shelter but it was still hard going. We halted at the tarn to take on food and allow Snorri and his nose to sniff out the wolves. The wind aided us for it kept our smell from any prey and would warn us of their presence. He could not detect them.

As we watered our ponies I noticed that Gruffyd's hands were blue with the cold. I shook my head, "A warrior must look after himself. If we found a wolf now you could not hold a weapon and you would die."

"But I have to lead the pack pony and I only have two hands!"

"Hold the halter and your reins in one hand and put your other hand under your arm. When the other hand gets cold swap them over." I took the reins and halter from him. "Put your two hands under your arms now and let them get warm. I will hold these."

He did so and looked over at Ragnar, "Did you know this?"

Ragnar nodded, "I did cuz. I thought everyone did. I would have told you otherwise. I thought you were trying to prove something to your father."

I smiled. My son was learning that not everything we learned was about fighting. Much was just how to survive. Snorri returned from the head of the water. He held, in his hand, some fur. "I found this on the gorse bush. There are wolves hereabouts. We had better be alert." He looked pointedly at the two youngsters.

The sleet was now coming down harder. The black sky ahead did not bode well but it also meant we might have more chance of discovering wolves. The track twisted amongst the rocks. We saw pikes and peaks all around us. This was perfect wolf country. There was cover and there was shelter. More importantly there was game. Although most of the sheep had been brought down from the fells there were always some who evaded capture. They did not know we penned them for their own survival.

As the sky grew darker the weather worsened. The wind lessened but the rain and sleet became even more relentless. Then we heard the ominous rumble of thunder in the distance. We had just dropped down to Elter's Water. The old abandoned farm was just four ridges of rotted wood nestling beneath wild grass and reeds. Snorri turned, "Jarl, we cannot find wolves in this. Thor himself is busy. Let us find shelter."

There were no farms close by. The nearest was at the Rye Dale or the Grassy Mere. "Then let us head for Audun Thin Hair at the Rye Dale." I turned to Gruffyd, "We will need our wits about us. Give me the pony and you ride behind Ragnar."

"I can do this."

"And I am Jarl and say obey me!"

It was now a race to get to shelter before the storm hit us. I could see the flashes showing Thor was busy working in his forge. In the distance, we heard the booming, rolling, thunder. It was getting closer. The day became night. The black clouds seemed to surround us. I could barely make out the Lough Rigg. Snorri turned, "We will not make the Rye Dale, Jarl. We must head for the cave." His voice betrayed the fear of entering the cave of Myrddyn.

I nodded. This was a place which brought fear to my heart. The spirits of the ancient peoples lived here. Aiden called this Myrddyn's cave. Had Aiden been with us then I would not have felt as fearful but we had no wizard. The two boys were oblivious to any danger. They heard the word cave and thought of a sanctuary. We heard the thunder and saw the lightning as we climbed the path to the cave. Its gaping maw did not look welcoming to me but I knew that we needed to be somewhere that Thor's bolts could not strike us. The mountain would protect us.

I was thankful that Snorri entered first. His nose would warn us of animals or humans. Ragnar and Gruffyd almost threw themselves into the shelter of the huge cave. I dismounted and led the two ponies within. Even as we stepped inside the interior was illuminated by a huge flash as a lightning bolt seemed to strike above us. A few heartbeats later we heard the crack of thunder. I gripped the pommel of my sword. The sword touched by the gods did not fear the lightning. It gave me courage.

"Get the saddles from the ponies and hobble them."

"Aye grandfather."

"Snorri…"

"I know Jarl, fire. If you can find some firewood."

I knew there would be some. We had been here before and Aiden had left some. I went to the middle of the cave. Its blackness was complete. Had another

13

of Thor's bolts not flashed then I would not have spied the faggots which lay strewn about the floor. An animal had been in and disturbed the neat pile left by Aiden. That made me shiver too. Was that animal a wolf? I hurried to the wood I had seen and grabbed it. I saw the flash of flint as Snorri used the kindling he had brought. I moved swiftly to his side. The sooner we had light the better. As I dropped the pile next to him a sudden flurry of air made the flames begin to rise. Snorri took twigs from the faggots and began to build a fire. He was a master at this.

As the flames took hold the size of the cave became apparent. Ragnar and Gruffyd stared above them at the vaulted roof. "Was this made by the gods?"

"Aye." I needed them distracted so that they would not be over awed by the place. "Get the food from the pony."

"Yes father."

"Shall I get some water from the pool!"

"No!" The pool was enchanted. If Aiden had been here I might have risked it but he was not. "We will use our water skins."

Ragnar frowned at my words. What was wrong with the water? I did not enlighten him. I did not want him fearful. The less he knew about the dangers of the cave the better.

As the fire grew the full extent of the cave was revealed. I decided we would only stay here until the storm had passed. Audun Thin Hair's home was but a few miles away. It was a forlorn hope. I should have known that the Weird Sisters were spinning. Even as the warmth from the fire began to seep into our skin there was an enormous crack which seemed to be almost within the cave and then I heard a rumble. This time it was not thunder it was the Rigg itself. It seemed as though the earth itself was shaken. I felt the earth rumbled and tremble beneath my feet. The mountain was falling. The ponies whinnied in fear. There was an avalanche. The sound filled the cave. The crash, dust and debris from the entrance told me that rocks from the mountain were blocking us in. I knew that we were trapped even before Snorri confirmed it.

Snorri ran quickly to the entrance but he came back coughing and spluttering. "Jarl, we are trapped. We cannot get out that way."

I saw the fear of on the faces of Ragnar and Gruffyd. Snorri had also sounded fearful. It would not do to inflame their fear. I spoke calmly. "This changes little. We eat, we rest and, when daylight comes we see if we can be as miners and dig our way out. If the stones fell, then they can be moved. It is not as though the gods have made a door which only they can open. They have had an argument and tossed some rocks down the mountain side. We are warriors and we will deal with the problem. Ragnar, break out the food. Gruffyd lay the furs close to the fire so that they can dry. We will be cosy this night and dry."

"Are you not afraid Grandfather?"

"Even if I was would my fear get us out of this predicament any quicker? We have been set a challenge, that is all. Let us meet that challenge as men eh? The spirits of the past are in this cave. Myrddyn the Great lived here, it is said, and he is a link to my past. I do not fear my ancestors. Come, we eat."

As the boys set about their tasks Snorri said, "I fear I have brought this upon you, jarl. I slew the witch."

"No Snorri. This is the Weird Sisters and it is not a punishment. They wish us to sleep here."

"But why?"

"They wish us to dream. Or me at least."

I saw fear in the eyes of my fearless scout. He could face any number of enemies but this was a realm into which he did not wish to venture. He clutched the golden wolf which had been given a spell of protection by Kara. It seemed to comfort him a little.

As we ate I said, "This is where your father slew his first wolf, Ragnar." I pointed beyond the blocked entrance. "It was just outside there. Wolves lived in here then."

Gruffyd looked around as though a wolf might leap upon him.

Snorri smiled, "They are all long dead." Then looking at me he said, "We are ever drawn here. Perhaps we should have taken a different route."

"It would not have mattered. We were meant to come here. No matter which route we took the Norns would have made us come here. It is *wyrd*. Tonight, we watch in pairs. I will watch with Gruffyd. You two will sleep first. We must keep the fire fed. Husband the wood and make it last until dawn."

Ragnar and Snorri rolled into their furs. Outside the storm continued but the avalanche made it seemed distant, remote and it gradually faded. I kept Gruffyd busy putting wood on the fire branch by branch. It kept his mind occupied and eked out our firewood.

"Snorri is wrong, father. This is the fault of Ragnar and me. If we had not asked to hunt we would be safe at home."

"Were you not listening, my son? The Norns spin. We know not what their plans are. We are little pieces in their grand game. A man must deal with whatever they throw his way. That is what makes him a man." I turned him so that he faced me. "Tonight you may dream. Do not fear for the dreams cannot hurt you but remember every detail. When we return home, we must tell Kara and Aiden all and they will tell us what our dreams mean. Sometimes our dreams only give us a version of the truth. Kara and Aiden will divine their true meaning."

He pointed to the entrance, "But how will we get out? We are trapped."

I shrugged and pulled my cloak a little tighter around my shoulders as though the dead wolf might offer me protection as well as my sword. "I know not. Let us dream first and then see what daylight brings."

I measured time by the wood I used. I also judged it by my grandson. He began to thrash around and to mumble in his sleep; he was dreaming. Gruffyd went to restrain him. "No, my son. The spirits are making him dream. Soon he will wake and then it will be our turn."

"Snorri does not dream."

"No, for these are not his ancestors and he is not a dreamer. The blood of your grandmother courses through your veins. My mother came from the ancient people. This was her land and Myrddyn was her wizard. Snorri is lucky. He sleeps a dreamless sleep. Our family have to endure the tortures of the night."

Ragnar woke suddenly, screaming. He sat upright and his cries awoke Snorri. His terrified eyes stared at me. "I saw Danes! They came for me! I saw the skull! It was bloody and it was fierce! The skull came for me! I could not run away."

I put my hand on his mouth, "Tell Snorri your dream. It cannot hurt you now. Speaking of it will help you to make sense of it. My son and I will sleep. You are safe now."

"But we are trapped beneath a mountain!"

"Trust me, Ragnar. I do not think that the Norns wish us to end our days here, buried beneath rocks. If we are still here a week from now, then I will worry." I tried to make my voice as calm as I could but there was a little fear in me too. Perhaps the Weird Sisters had tired of me. Perhaps this was to be my doom.

I stayed awake while Ragnar and Snorri searched the cave for the last of the wood. Gruffyd had already fallen asleep by the time I rolled into my fur.

It was so black I thought that I was dead. There was no sound and nothing could be seen before me. Then I heard a steady pulsating beat. It sounded like a drum. It was in my ears and filled my head. It was my heart. I was aware of air rushing before my face. I was flying. Then I spied a light. It was a pinprick at first but I found myself dropping down towards it and it became brighter and larger. Then all went black and when I opened my eyes I saw a fog which hung on the water like a dead man's shroud. I was in the water and I swam. I could smell smoke and I swam towards the smoke. I seemed to swim for a lifetime and then I felt sand and shingle beneath my toes. I saw nothing for there was fog before my face. Then I stood and the mist vanished. I was on Syllingar. I recognised the spiral of smoke rising from the cave and I saw the grey seas surging around the island. I heard a voice and I recognised it. It was Ylva's. I headed for the cave and descended. The glow in the distance was familiar and when I turned I saw not the ancient witch but Ylva. She was older but she recognised me and she smiled. I headed towards her and her outstretched hand. She smiled and my heart soared. Her hand touched mine and suddenly it changed. It was not Ylva's soft and gentle hand it was a claw! I looked up into her eyes and saw her transform into a dragon; she had become a wyrme. I could not escape and her huge mouth opened to swallow me.

I felt no pain. I felt nothing save the cold. Was this death? Had I been shown my end? Then I heard the steady beat of a drum once more and knew that I lived still. I saw a light and headed towards it. Perhaps this was the dragon's fire and I could warm myself for I was as cold as death itself. As I moved through the dark towards it I saw that it was daylight and it was the mouth of the cave. As I stepped out the light was so bright that it blinded me. I shaded my eyes and closed them. When I opened them I saw that I was surrounded by Danes. They held axes and, from their hair, hung animal skulls. Behind them I saw a monstrous mountain of a woman with a white painted face and, atop her head, she wore a human skull like a helmet. Her eyes were red and her claw like hands bloody. She strode towards me with a seax in her hand. I tried to run but I was pinioned and without a weapon. She put her face close to mine and, as all went black, I heard her say, "Now I will have vengeance. Now will I tear out the dragon's heart!"

I opened my eyes and shivered. It was cold and the fire had gone out. Yet I could still see Snorri and Ragnar. Snorri pointed and I could see a tiny amount of light coming from the rock filled entrance. "We were waiting until you woke." Snorri looked concerned. "You were thrashing about Jarl and I was worried."

I nodded, "It is better to let the spirits decide when you wake up."

Just then Gruffyd rose with eyes wide. He screamed, "No Ylva!"

I picked him up and held him tightly, "It was a dream. Do not worry about what you saw. Aiden and Kara will explain all."

He shook his head, "But they were dead! And Ylva killed them. I saw her. She came for me."

"Did she change into a dragon?"

He looked amazed, "Aye father, how did you know?"

"Because she came to me in my dream but that was not Ylva. I am no galdramenn but I know that what we see in our dream is often a version of the truth. It is the dragon which is the danger."

"The dragon?"

"The dragon is that which we fear and cannot easily be defeated. We will not talk of that now. We need Kara and Aiden for that. Come; we will see how to extricate ourselves from this cave. Daylight will make the world seem better."

We made our way to the entrance. I saw that there were gaps through which light shone. It was daylight. Snorri climbed up to examine the gaps. "This will be hard, Jarl. If we take them from the bottom, then we risk the whole falling upon us."

"Then you and I will enlarge the hole." I turned to Ragnar and Gruffyd, "You two go and see to the horses. Give them the last of the water and see if there is any food left."

With those two safely out of the way Snorri and I began to take out the smaller pieces of stone. We laid them carefully at the bottom. It was time consuming but safer. When we had made a hole as big as our heads we felt the icy air rushing in. It brought with it hope. Perhaps we rushed a little too much for when we moved a rock the size of a piglet there was a rush of stones. I thought we had trapped ourselves but the stones tumbled outside rather than in. The hole was big enough to climb out.

"We must work down now, Snorri, so that we can enlarge it for the ponies. Ragnar, Gruffyd, come and begin to clear a path at the bottom wide enough for the animals. Do it slowly and carefully."

We finished when the sun was high overhead. We led the ponies from the tomb and found ourselves in deep snow. The sky was clear and the storm had passed. The storm had left behind a deep bed of snow whose crust would freeze as ice when the sun dipped. Mounting our horses, we hurried on to Audun Thin Hair's farm and hall. No one spoke as we rode. Each of us had a mind filled with our own thoughts and fears.

Audun's wife insisted that we stay the night. The sun was dipping behind the rigg which had tried to kill us. We would have frozen to death had we stayed out. It was a wise decision to stay. Her mutton stew was the finest food I could remember tasting. That might have been because we had gone so long on cold rations. With honeyed ale inside us we huddled together in Audun's home amongst his family.

As we wrapped ourselves in our furs Gruffyd said, quietly, "What if we dream again? I would not embarrass myself in front of these people." It was hard to live with the fact that while asleep our bodies did not obey us.

"You will not but do not worry, these are our people. They are of our clan." Audun and his family were good folk. They would keep watch over us.

And we did sleep well. I think it was exhaustion. We did not dream. When we left the next day, we saw that we had chosen the wisest course. The ground was treacherous. Had we tried to negotiate it at night then we might have tumbled to our deaths before we could freeze.

It was as we approached Cyninges-tūn that we began to talk of what we had dreamed. "Say nothing to any until we are alone with Kara and Aiden. I would not have rumour cause upset amongst my people. Aiden and my daughter will interpret these dreams." My daughter and her husband could unravel the threads which made up our dreams. I knew that there were links and there were ties but I was too close to pull them together. That would be the task of my volva and my galdramenn.

Ominously Aiden, Kara and Ylva were waiting for us at the gates to my stronghold. They had dreamed too and their faces showed that they too had been terrified.

Chapter 2

Neither Ragnar nor Gruffyd would go near Ylva. Despite my words that the dream did not mean that Ylva was the danger they did not believe me. I dismounted and took her in my arms. She was crying. I had never seen Ylva cry. Even as a small child she had remained impassive. I looked at Kara who nodded, "She dreamed too."

Turning to Snorri I said, "Thank you, Snorri. You had best get back to your wife. We will go to my daughter's hall."

"Aye Jarl Dragonheart. Suddenly my home is the only place I wish to be. I shall hold my wife and drive the demons from my head."

I knew that he would not be able to do so. The terror of the cave would remain with him. I had fallen into a cave in the land of the Cymri. That fear had never left me. Coming on top of the killing of the witch, Snorri would need his wife's care for some time.

Macha and Deidra, the two former nuns and servants of the White Christ, were waiting within with hot food and hot ale. Their furrowed brows told me that they, too, knew of the dreams.

Kara began, "Gruffyd, I wish you to tell me your dream. Tell me all and leave nothing out." She pointed to Ylva, "You will not upset Ylva with your words. Every detail that you can remember may help us to unravel this web."

20

When he had finished then Ragnar and I did the same. Kara's face showed that some of it was news to her but that she had expected most of what we had said. Ylva wept in her father's arms as she heard us tell of the terror of the cave.

"We too dreamed. Ylva was taken from us and carrion tore out our entrails as we watched. She became a dragon and she devoured the Land of the Wolf."

There was silence. To me it seemed like our world had just ended. I could fight any number of warriors as could my Ulfheonar but this was different. How could we fight the spirit world? Perhaps Snorri's killing of the witch had set all of this in motion. This, conceivably, could be the end of the Land of the Wolf. "Then what does it mean? We all saw Danes in our dreams. Are we about to be attacked? What is this dragon which comes in the form of my granddaughter?"

"We are too close to this, father. We have no answers yet. We must seek help elsewhere."

I had a sudden sinking feeling in the pit of my stomach. "Syllingar?"

Aiden nodded, "We must seek the witch's wisdom and her advice."

Shaking my head, I said, "This is not the time of year for such a voyage."

"I know and we must take Ylva. She cannot use her powers until she is a woman. We have to wait until the Mother deems it is time."

I drank the horn of ale which Deidra had poured for me and stared into the flames of the fire. It was all very well relying on the spirit world to advise but sometimes their warnings were too vague. The warriors wore skulls. There was a witch with a skull. We had killed Eggle Skulltaker. Were the spirits of the dead coming for us?

"I did not mention it to Snorri but I wondered if the witch I saw could have been the one he slew."

"Perhaps. The form of Ylva might have been chosen to warn us that there is a woman involved."

"If it is a woman then does that mean she leads warriors? I have never heard of Danes following a woman."

"Nor have I. I am sorry, Jarl Dragonheart, you have come to us for answers and you are getting none. Tomorrow we will make a steam hut by the water and the three of us will dream."

"And then you will interpret what you dream." I shook my head. "I am sorry but that is not good enough." I stood. "Tomorrow I will see Haaken and plan a visit to the land of the Danes. Prince Athelstan is a friend. I will go to him and see if he can arrange for me to visit his town of Eoforwic. There are Danes there who might have information about the Skulltaker clan. I had thought we had ended the threat of them but perhaps the dreams tell us otherwise."

" I would come, grandfather!"

21

"And me!"

My grandson and son were eager for another adventure. The terror of the cave had not dampened their enthusiasm. This was different. We would be going amongst our enemies. There would be no certainty that we would survive. "No! If there is war coming, then I need you two to be ready to be warriors and defend this land." I flashed an irritated look at Aiden. "It seems this will come down to muscles and metal rather than magic."

"That is not fair, Jarl Dragonheart!"

"It may not be but it is the truth. For all the powers in this house I cannot see what protection it affords. You cannot tell me whence the danger comes nor what the exact danger will be. I know little more now than when I woke up from my dream. I did not fear Ylva and that is the only news you have brought save that you wish to dream some more. While you dream, I will act!"

I was angry and I was about to say that which I might regret. I had made that mistake with Wolf Killer and I would not do it with Kara. Surprisingly enough she was smiling. I had hurt Aiden's feelings but Kara rose and kissed me on the cheek, "You never change father and that is why we love you. You are the rock. People say it is Olaf the Old Man but I know that it is you. The clan is all to you. You truly are the beating heart of our people. And, it seems, the mind. We will do our best; that I promise."

Her words made me feel guilty. I headed for my hall with Ragnar and Gruffyd following. As we crossed the snow covered ground I said, "I did not mean to be harsh but I am aware that we have not replaced the men who died in the last battle. It will be down to the likes of you two and other young men to defend our home."

Ragnar nodded, as we approached my door, "Much as you and Haaken did in Norway. We will try to be as strong as you were, grandfather."

Brigid had been told of the dream by Kara and I saw the concern on her face. "You were away longer than I expected. What happened?"

I shrugged, "A storm came and we sheltered in a cave. Then we stayed with Audun Thin Hair."

She smiled, "After Kara's dream I feared the worst. I am glad you were in no danger."

Elfrida gave me a curious look. "Come Ragnar, you are not too old to give your mother a hug."

Brigid laughed, "Gruffyd is younger but he does not like to say he is pleased to see his mother."

Gruffyd surprised her by throwing his arms around her. It was a clear sign that the events of the last few days had had an effect on him. As she passed me

Elfrida said quietly, "You do not wish your wife to know of the avalanche?" She had taken me by surprise. She smiled, "I too have the second sight. It will soon become common knowledge. I would tell her."

"Tonight, when we are alone. Your son dreamed. It disturbed him."

"He is his father's son."

Later, as we lay in bed, I told Brigid what had happened. Brigid did not know how to react to my news. Her religion taught her that acts of her God were to be taken stoically but the dreams and the visions were evidence of a pagan world in which she did not believe.

After tears she cuddled in to me, "But why must you go to Eoforwic. You are no longer the young warrior you were. Why anyone needs to go I know not. Our land is strong and we have warriors who can defend it. There are others who could go."

"There are and sometime in the future I can allow Ragnar or Gruffyd to take on the responsibility but for now it is my appointed task."

But why them? There are others!"

"I lead the clan. One day one or both of them will lead it too. Now silence. Let me enjoy both the warmth and you. I will be away for some time and it is time I proved to you that I am no old man, yet!"

I went about the settlement the next day seeking out those I wished to take. I would not ask for volunteers; all would wish to come. I sent for Haaken. He lived beyond our walls. The others I chose were Beorn the Scout, Rollo Thin Skin and Rolf Horse Killer. I told them what I planned and they left to gather their belongings. It did not take long for a deputation of Ulfheonar to arrive at my hall. Snorri and Olaf Leather Neck led them.

"Have I offended you Jarl? Do you not need a scout?"

"I do, Snorri, and your wife needs her husband. You need your unborn child to be healthy. It is winter. Stay with her. You have put yourself in enough jeopardy already. Now is the time of the long nights. Now is the time to prepare to be a father. You know what is coming. Enjoy your time now."

"And what of me, Jarl? I have no family to tie me to the land. Why not take me. The ones you have chosen are boys! You will need a man!"

I was glad that neither Rolf nor Rollo were there to hear Olaf Leather Neck's words. I smiled, "And I need you here to prepare warriors to meet this unknown threat. You must train more boys to become men and more men to become Ulfheonar. I will not be here to lead the wolf hunt, Olaf Leather Neck. That is now your appointed task." I saw him nod. He was mollified. "Besides this should not be dangerous. I go to meet first with the Prince of the Saxons. He is our ally and he can smooth our way. It will be more of an embassy than a dangerous mission."

I turned as Haaken galloped through my gate. He threw himself from his pony. It was when I saw him that I knew my age. Haaken had hair streaked with grey. His good eye still sparkled but the slight grimace as he dismounted showed me that he suffered the same aches and pains as I did. Unlike those around me he did not know what had happened under the Lough Rigg. I saw a slight frown replace his smile as he saw the expressions on the faces of Olaf and Snorri.

"What is amiss? Has…"

Before he could speak more I shook my head and putting my arm around his shoulders led him indoors, "Come and I will tell you all."

It took three horns of ale to give him all of my news.

"I see why you sent for me." He grinned and he was the young boy who had followed me all those years ago, "And you have made a wise choice bringing me! Although it will be a hard journey at this time of year.

"Then stay here."

He laughed, "Do not be so prickly Dragonheart! I merely meant to question that we are prepared. You have horses and not ponies? Spare mounts? Supplies and furs?"

It was my turn to smile, "Do I look as though I need my grandmother to teach me how to suck eggs? Of course, it is all planned. That is why there will be but five of us. This will need intelligence. We will have to delve beneath the onion's layers to discover the truth. It will be hints and rumours which tell us that which we wish to know."

"Good. Then when do we leave?"

"In the morning. We will travel first to Windar's Mere and then Ketil's stad."

"I shall return and tell my wife and girls the news. They will be pleased to see the back of me." He saw my raised eyebrows. "I have been like a bear woken from his sleep. I can stand the house filled with women for so long and then…" He shrugged, "It has been more than two moons. I am ready. I will bring my own horses and saddles. They are more comfortable!"

I knew what he meant. The days when I could ride all day without discomfort were in the past.

A sudden and welcome thaw meant a wet but slightly easier journey to the north and east. I told Asbjorn, at Windar's Mere what had happened. It was as well for him to be forewarned. "I will make sure that we are prepared. Our defences are better but there is always room for improvement."

Unlike Asbjorn, Ketil had stone walls for he had adapted a Roman fort. He was a rock for me. He knew the lands close to his home and protected us from both the men of Strathclyde and any Saxons who chose to disobey their Prince.

"I believe that Prince Athelstan is at Caer Ufra. It is an old royal palace on the southern headland of the Tinea."

"He is not at Din Guardi?"

He smiled, "The prince is young and the king is old. He can indulge himself away from his father's prying eyes and besides the climate is more clement there. If you wish to see him then you will find it an easier journey."

"Good. I did not relish a journey through the high lands. We have been lucky, hitherto, but I see clouds are gathering."

"Aye. I will have my men guide you over the pass of Alston. The Roman Road is still a good guide but it is hard to find beneath the snow and ice."

"Good. You will need to be on the watch for enemies. Aiden cannot, as yet, fully divine my dream but even I know that it involves a witch and Danes. Be wary of all such strangers. I would even suspect Norse you do not know."

He nodded, "We will keep a good watch. We are vigilant. Since the peace we have become closer to the Saxons. Many of my men have taken Saxon women." He chuckled, "Your warriors slew their husbands and fathers. If they want a man they choose a warrior who can defend them."

We left the next morning with Arne Sharp Eyes and Erik Long Walking, Ketil's two scouts, who took us as far as the pass of the standing rocks. We reached the col on a clear, cold day. We could see the land of the Saxons stretching away to the east. Our two guides left us and we headed north east once more. Had this been the summer I would have worried more but the cold and the snow would keep most people indoors. Our wisdom in taking horses had been vindicated as we approached the col for the drifts of snow reached our feet. On the eastern side, however, it was colder but the snow had not yet drifted as deeply.

We kept together as we rode. We were armed and we had our mail on our spare horses. We were wrapped in furs and our wolf cloaks. It was defence against the biting cold that we needed and not the barbs of weapons.

Our route had taken us slightly further south than I might have liked and we headed north for a while. As the sun began to dip over the mountains we looked for somewhere to spend the night. We spied smoke from a remote farm. It was in a dell surrounded by trees. We wound our way down towards it. There was a greenway but it looked to be little used. As we approached I saw that it was made of turf. Was it Norse?

"Do we risk it?"

Haaken said, "I am cold and I say yes. There is one farm. Unless it holds a warband I say we ask. It is made of turf. They may be our people."

Beorn shook his head, "I spoke with the other scouts. They left us at the point where there were none of our clan further east."

"We will try them."

A dog began to bark as we approached. A woman and a youth came out of the hut with a snarling dog. The youth had a bow.

"Keep your hands from your weapons." I sensed a movement to my right and saw, a hundred paces away, a hunter with two more hounds. He hurried towards us. We reined in thirty paces from the woman and the youth. I saw that the woman had a pagan token around her neck. They were not Saxons. The youth kept the hunting bow aimed at me. None of us wore helmets and our hands were in plain sight. I said nothing but the youth eventually lowered his bow. I smiled.

The hunter spoke, "What are Vikings doing here in the middle of winter? Do you hunt slaves?"

He spoke in Danish. "No, friend. We are travellers heading for Caer Ufra and we seek shelter for the night. We can pay for food and a roof."

He reached up with his arm and shook his head, "You are travellers and you come in peace. It is our duty to offer you a roof although I fear we have no stable for your horses."

"They are hardy beasts." I took his arm and then dismounted. "I am Jarl Dragonheart of Cyninges-tūn."

He nodded, "I thought I recognised the sword. I am Carr the Hunter. That is my wife Ase and the angry looking youth with the bow is Cuyler." He shook his head. "Put the bow away, son. These are now our guests. We are honoured to have the one whose sword was touched by the gods under our roof. Tonight, we will have a fine tale to enliven our supper." He held up two hares.

After we had unsaddled our horses, fed and watered them, we hobbled them and tied them in the lee of the farm. The trees afforded some protection. By the time we went indoors the hares had been skinned and gutted. The dogs greedily devoured the offal. Ase, the hunter's wife, said, apologetically, "We only have four horns for the ale."

Her husband frowned but Haaken flourished two from his leather bag. "We come prepared gammer. We each have our own horn and I look forward to the nectar you have made."

I shook my head, "Haaken One Eye is something of a poet as well as a warrior. He makes most things sound flowery."

"I have heard of you too, Haaken One Eye. Is there not a story of how you and the Dragonheart stood back to back and saved a whole village?"

Haaken nodded, "That is one of our stories. I will tell the others after we have eaten. It will pay for our supper."

The food was warming and well-cooked and the ale better than we might have expected. During the meal, we learned more about this solitary family.

"I came here thirty years since with Guthrum the Wild. I was younger then and enjoyed the life of a Viking. We came from Hedeby and liked the country. Then I tired of the wild ways of my comrades and when Guthrum was slain by the Saxons close by Hwitebi I left with my brother Cuyler and we farmed north of the Saxon town of Eoforwic. It was where I met Ase. Some wild Danes wearing skulls in their hair had captured her and enslaved her. We came upon them in the forests. She was with her sister and her sister's son. My brother was a reckless sort. Instead of seeking to buy them he charged in. I was honour bound to follow. We slew the five of them but my brother was so badly wounded that he died."

"Did you know the Danes?"

He shook his head. "This was twelve years since. There were many bands each seeking slaves and treasure."

"What happened to your wife's sister?"

"She did not want the wild woods as her home. I took her and her son to Eoforwic. We left them there and sought a new home far from those Danes who had captured them. We tried the vales by the big river to the south but there were too many Saxons who resented us. We settled here when my son was but four. It suits us. You are the first visitors we have seen in a year."

"Is it not lonely?"

"We journey, four times a year, to Eoforwic to see her sister and nephew. They have an inn by the river. She has done well. Her son is a strapping man now and he keeps his mother safe. They asked us if we wished to stay there but I like the life of a hunter."

As he spoke I saw that our steps had been guided here. "We intend to go to Eoforwic ourselves, Carr. We seek information about a band of Danes who wear skulls about their heads. I think they are called Skull Takers."

He looked up. "I know of the clan. They were the ones who took my wife or some of them were, at least. We had heard of them before we crossed the sea. They made even Guthrum the Wild fear them for they are ruled by witches with powerful magic. They are a close-knit clan. To become a warrior, you have to slay a foe and eat that which is in their skull."

I shook my head, "But why?"

"They believe it gives them powers and they are guided by their witches."

"Witches?"

"The clan is ruled not by a warrior but five witches. Each time one dies they replace her with a younger one. But they are choosy. The witch must be as powerful as the one she replaces. I can face a wild warrior but not a witch. I am pleased that I never came across them. I did not know that they had come to the land of the Saxons."

I nodded, "We fought them along the valley of the Dunum. I had thought I had slain their leader, Eggle Skulltaker, it seems I was wrong."

"Beware these witches, Jarl."

"I just need to find out their intentions. I dreamed of them in the cave of Myrddyn."

I saw him clutch Thor's hammer, "You are a dreamer and Ulfheonar?"

"I dream." I felt uncomfortable talking about my dreams and I changed the subject. "What is the name of your sister and her son? If we reach Eoforwic I would speak with her."

"Agnete and her son is Aksel. Their inn has a saddle outside."

"A saddle?"

He smiled, "It was not their choice. They worked for the owner before he died and he left it to them. It had been called the Saddle since the time of the Romans. They thought it bad luck to change it."

"Thank you." I looked over at Haaken, "I can see you are bursting to tell a tale. Which one will you give?"

"I think the story of the sword would be most appropriate."

The storm was wild and the gods did roam
The enemy closed on the Prince's home
Two warriors stood on a lonely tower
Watching, waiting for hour on hour.
The storm came hard and Odin spoke
With a lightning bolt the sword he smote
Ragnar's Spirit burned hot that night
It glowed, a beacon shiny and bright
The two they stood against the foe
They were alone, nowhere to go
They fought in blood on a darkened hill
Dragon Heart and Cnut will save us still
Dragon Heart, Cnut and the Ulfheonar
Dragon Heart, Cnut and the Ulfheonar
The storm was wild and the Gods did roam
The enemy closed on the Prince's home
Two warriors stood on a lonely tower
Watching, waiting for hour on hour.
The storm came hard and Odin spoke

With a lightning bolt the sword he smote
Ragnar's Spirit burned hot that night
It glowed, a beacon shiny and bright
The two they stood against the foe
They were alone, nowhere to go
They fought in blood on a darkened hill
Dragon Heart and Cnut will save us still
Dragon Heart, Cnut and the Ulfheonar
Dragon Heart, Cnut and the Ulfheonar

For the first time since we had entered the farm I saw Cuyler smile, "Could I hear that again?" Haaken nodded and drank some ale to clear his throat. Cuyler looked at me. "Is that the sword, Jarl?"

"It is."

"May I hold it while Haaken One Eye sings it again?"

Carr looked appalled. "Cuyler!"

I smiled, "Of course you can. But beware the blade. It is sharp."

I handed him the sword in its scabbard and he caressed it as though it was a woman. Haaken gave us a second rendition and Cuyler handed the sword back at the end. "It is truly magical, father. I felt the power course through my body. You are lucky, Jarl Dragonheart."

Carr came over to me and said, quietly, "That was kindly done. My son rarely smiles nor does he get to meet people. It is good that you came."

"Aye, Carr, it is *wyrd*."

Chapter 3

Caer Ufra sounded like a hill fort to me. When we reached it at sunset against a darkening sky I saw that it was not a hill fort after all. It stood on a headland and it was a fort but it was a Roman one with a Saxon hall in the middle of it. They had not done as Ketil had done and repaired the walls; they had just repaired the gate on the western side. There were sentries at the gates, huddled around braziers. The snow was neither deep nor widespread as we neared the coast but the wind still cut through our cloaks like a knife. We were allies of the men of Northumbria but they were wary and the guards was alerted as we closed with the royal palace.

My shield, which hung from the saddle of my spare horse, was recognised and I heard a shout which resulted in the gates opening. A mailed warrior came half way down the stairs which led from the gate house, "The prince is in the warrior hall, Jarl Dragonheart."

This time there would be stables for our horses. Leaving Beorn the Scout and the two younger Ulfheonar to see to our mounts Haaken and I dismounted and entered the hall. The Chamberlain said, "I must ask for your weapons." He shrugged apologetically, "All who enter must comply, Jarl."

I nodded, "Then watch over this with your life, Chamberlain, for this sword is Ragnar's Spirit and was touched by the gods."

He lifted it gingerly as though it would burn him. "I swear I shall guard it with my life."

The hall was lit by a few burning rushes and a large fire in the centre. There was no chimney and the roof was filled with thick smoke which hung like a fog over our heads. It would eventually seep out. It kept the wild life at bay but it left an acrid taste in the back of the mouth.

Prince Athelstan saw us and lurched over. He had been drinking and I saw that his face was flushed. He was older now than when we had first met but he was still a young man. Wolf Killer would have been of an age with him, had he lived.

"Jarl Dragonheart! This is an unexpected pleasure." He suddenly frowned, "It does not presage trouble, does it? The alliance still holds?"

I smiled and held out my arm for him to clasp," The alliance holds. I come here to seek knowledge but that can wait until the morning. Are we too late for the feast?"

He laughed, "No, Jarl. We have spent the day hunting seals in the river mouth. We are celebrating."

Haaken asked, "Is there honour in hunting seals? We just take them for their meat and their oil."

Athelstan nodded, "As do we but my men needed some diversion. We hunted them with a seax!" He proffered his arm. I saw teeth marks. "The beasts did not die easily. Tonight, we eat their flesh!"

Inwardly I groaned. I was not fond of the taste but I smiled, "Thank you Prince Athelstan! We shall try to do them justice." I gestured to the door where the other three had just entered, "There are just five of us."

"We slaughtered many! There is food aplenty and the ale is particularly good!"

It would do no good to interrogate the prince for he was not coherent. Instead we feasted with them. I did not drink as much as the others. That was mainly because I was not enjoying the food. It gave me the opportunity to observe the Saxons at close quarters. I had rarely had the chance to do so. Normally I would have been fighting them. I realised that they had much in common with my men. Although most were Christian they still had the same stories and legends which we did. Their swords were the equal of ours. I had long discussions with the Saxons around the prince's table about my sword. They were also as loyal to their leaders as were my men.

The main differences lay in what they had become. Since becoming Christian the art of war was seen as sinful. Some of the older warriors bemoaned the fact that their priests only encouraged them to fight pagans. King Egbert of Wessex would walk through this land; he paid lip service to the White Christ. It served his purpose. He was a greater enemy than we were. During my conversations with the Saxon thegns, however, I detected an unease about the Danes. Although King Eanred, through his son, had recovered Eoforwic there were still bands of Danes who caused trouble in the isolated parts of the land of the Northumbrians. It was a large land and only their burghs were secure. Even before I spoke with the prince I knew that I had done the right thing by coming east.

I woke before the others and, after picking up my sword, went to the beach. I stared east beyond the sea. There lay the land of the Norse. It was the land to which I had been taken as a slave all those years ago. It was many years since I had been taken to the land of the Norse as a Saxon slave. It was there I had been moulded into a warrior by Ragnar, Prince Buthar's father. Many things had happened since then but I still remembered those days above the fjord in that tiny hut where I had lived and served the half blind old cripple. Each time I drew my sword he was there with me and I would never forget him. I put my hand on the hilt of my sword. When Cuyler had felt its power, it had reminded me of when I had felt that power. For me it was in the heat of battle. Even as I held it I sensed the power within.

I heard movement behind me and I whirled, the sword in my hand in an instant. I saw a surprised Prince Athelstan, "I am sorry jarl. I did not mean to startle you."

I sheathed the sword, "I am sorry Prince Athelstan but I have many enemies. Assassins have tried to kill me many times."

"You have quick hands. That must come from always fighting. We do not fight as much as your people. Men like my father sit behind their walls contentedly. They do not realise that we could lose what we hold unless we are willing to fight for it." He joined me at the water's edge. "My people came from beyond this sea but that was so many generations since that I remember it not."

"As did mine but I also have the blood of the isles in my veins."

"And yet you are a Viking."

"It is not your blood that makes you a Viking it is something here," I tapped my heart.

"So, you wish to know about Danes?"

"I had a dream in which Danes wearing skulls attacked us."

"You believe in such dreams? The church frowns upon them."

I nodded, "I know and yet they have often saved us. The problem is that they are vague and ethereal like the morning mist. They are there but they do not give times or numbers. They let us men seek out those answers. I know that that there is a clan which takes skulls and I have learned that they are ruled by a coven of witches. I had thought that we had destroyed them but I was wrong. It was only some of their warriors who perished."

"Then I can tell you that we have heard of these skull takers. They do not live close by here. They would have been destroyed by me had I found them. They do not appear to have large numbers and are almost a legend. I thought they were something to frighten Saxon children. A little like the wolves from the west. I am afraid your visit has not been worthwhile."

"I would not say that and besides, it is not over yet. We would visit Eoforwic. There are still Danes there and even a rumour might help us."

"What would you have of me?"

"A letter to allow us entry to that city."

"I can do better. I will send two of my thegns there. They have to speak with the leader of my garrison in that burgh anyway."

"Then this makes our alliance stronger."

"We may have need of this alliance sooner rather than later, Jarl for we have heard that Wessex's ambitions do not stop with Mercia. He casts his greedy eye north. Now that he has almost subjugated Mercia and Corn Walum he seeks to be High King!"

"Egbert is an old enemy of ours. If he came north, then we would fight him anyway but we will serve alongside you if he does come. Tell your father that we will stand shoulder to shoulder with you."

"I fear that my father would make peace with Wessex."

"You do not make peace with such a predator. He may smile and hold out the hand of friendship but beware; in his other he will hold a knife."

"Aye I know. I am grateful for your friendship. I am training men in much the same way that you do. When I call out the fyrd my thegns will lead a well-trained army. If Egbert of Wessex comes he will find a stiffer test of his warriors than he expects."

I hoped he was right but I had fought Egbert. I did not like him but I respected his skills as a general.

We left the next day with Alfred and Asser. They were young thegns and warriors. The Saxons called their jarls, thegns and they each led a warband. Their warbands were at home. The two nobles had been enjoying the pleasures of the palace. Their homes were at Stamford and Fulford. As they were returning home the prince was using them to deliver his letters. It suited us all to travel together. In truth, they were pleasant company. Rollo and Rolf got on well with them. Their presence assured us of an easy entrance to that burgh and ensure we were accorded honour within the walls. Once through the gates we bade farewell to them as we headed for the Saddle and Ase's sister.

We saw the saddle hanging from a hook and knew we had found the right place. We were close to it when the door burst open and a Dane was hurled to the street. He was followed by a second and then a giant appeared in the doorway, "If you have no money then no ale! When you bring what you owe then you can have your swords. Until then, stay out!"

Haaken said, wryly, "I am guessing that the giant is Aksel!"

The giant glowered at the two Danes who picked themselves up and stared at him. I thought for a moment they would risk his wrath but instead they fled. Neither looked like warriors. A real warrior would not have left his sword behind. These were the hangers on who followed a warband in the hope of scraps. Leaving Rolf with the horses we followed the giant back into the ale house.

He sensed us and whipped his head around. I spread my hands, "No, trouble, Aksel. We come as friends and we have coin to pay for our ale."

His eyes narrowed. "How do you know my name? I have never seen you before. In fact, I have not seen Norse Vikings in this burgh for many a year."

I lowered my voice, "I am come from the Land of the Wolf. We met with Carr and Ase. They said we would be welcome."

His face broke into a grin. "Why did you not say so! Mother; these Vikings know Carr and Ase!"

I saw something of Ase in Agnete. She wiped her hands on her apron and came from behind the table which served as a bar. "How is my sister?"

"She is well as is her son and husband." I gestured to my companions. "There are five of us and horses. Have you rooms and a stable?"

Aksel nodded, "Aye and we will do you a good price. Mother will show you your rooms and I will see to your horses."

She led us out of the back door and into a small yard. I saw the stables off to the right and she led us left to a small hall. She opened the door and I saw that there were three rooms each divided by a curtain. "You can have two of these. I like to keep the third in case we get late visitors."

"They will do fine. Haaken, have the baggage brought around." Left alone I said, "Carr said we could trust you."

She gave me a shrewd look. "You are the one called The Dragonheart."

I was surprised for I did not have my shield with me. "Yes, but how did you know?"

"The wolf and dragon you wear around your neck warned me but that sword with the distinctive stones, there can be only one. What brings you here?"

She was a clever woman. She would need to be to survive in Eoforwic. I decided to be truthful with her. "We are seeking news of a clan called the Skull Takers. They are led by five women."

She clutched at a charm around her neck, "I have heard of them. They are dangerous. You are a great warrior but these Danes are to be feared. Their witches use magic and poison."

"I know."

She nodded, "When the inn is empty Aksel and I will tell you all that we know." She shrugged, "It is little enough."

The food was well cooked and Agnete was a fine ale wife. We sat in a corner and watched the busy inn. Patience was all. It proved useful for we saw many Danes enter and leave. Keeping to ourselves and being wrapped in our cloaks we did not merit much attention and we listened. Ulfheonar can do that; even the loquacious Haaken One Eye. We had the patience of a wolf stalking his prey. We learned much. We learned that there were many clans close to the city. Some plied the river as merchants. There was one drekar moored in the river as well. Despite what the prince had told us the Danes were back in numbers. I wondered if his master of the burgh knew of that. I felt I owed a debt to Athelstan and so I determined to find out all that I could. When we had arrived at the town gate we had seen a storm heading from the north. I doubted that we would be moving much for a few days in any case.

When the inn had been emptied, somewhat forcibly by Aksel, we sat with some fresh cheese and horns of ale. "The clan of the Skull Takers live to the south of here close by the old capital of Elmet, Loidis."

"Does not the king's man do aught about them?"

Aksel laughed, "Jarl they have five witches."

"Four," corrected his mother, "One was killed last year."

I looked at Haaken. That was the one Snorri had slain.

Agnete leaned over, "Jarl, do not take on the Skulltaker clan. They are evil. Many families have lost children to this evil coven."

"All the more reason to destroy them then."

Aksel asked, "Why the interest? Loidis is their stronghold and it is far from the Land of the Wolf."

I hesitated and then remembered I had promised to speak the truth. "I dreamed that they came and destroyed my people."

Agnete nodded, "Then you must fight them." She looked at her son. "We were taken by those who take skulls. They killed the brother of Carr. We are safe here but I can see that if they thought to have their claws in you... We will help in any way we can. We hear news in this inn. We do not rob and the ale is good. Warriors who drink too much have loose tongues. This inn is old and well frequented." She smiled and patted Aksel's hand. "My son keeps order and we prosper."

They told us all that they knew and we headed for bed. As we wrapped ourselves in our furs I said, "Tomorrow we will visit the river and see what ships are in port. Agnete hears news but there may be others who do not travel to the inn. Beorn, I would have you travel to Fulford and tell the thegn there what we have learned. They should know of the danger to the south of them."

"Will you tell the Prince?"

"Aye Haaken but that will have to wait until we are returned home. The dream was a warning but from what we have heard the threat is closer than Aiden thought."

As I curled up in my fur my mind was too busy for me to fall asleep quickly. Eggle Skull Taker had been hiding on the Dunum. We had rid ourselves of them. Now we heard they were at Loidis. Was the clan elsewhere? It seemed to me that this was a large clan. We had slain many when we had slaughtered Eggle's band. Even as sleep began to come to me I sat up suddenly. Only Eggle had had a skull atop his helmet. He had had but one witch with him. We had not even touched the main clan. As I lay back down I saw the size of the problem we faced and the threat to our lives and that of the whole clan.

It was a grey, dank day as we wandered down the quayside. There were stalls selling goods brought up the river and there were a few hardy folk buying from them but the oppressive damp which hung over the water did not invite lingering. The four of us spread out. We had coins and we bought a few items. Some of them were even useful but the most useful thing we bought was knowledge. I had hidden the tokens I wore around my neck. Agnete's sharp eyes had been a warning for me. I wanted none to know who I was. With a hooded cloak about my head I was just another Norse trader.

I spent some time talking to the Dane who had the stall close to the threttanessa. I learned that he and his companions were making their first voyage to the land of the Angles. The goods they had were from Frankia. I bought some fine pots which I knew Brigid would like. It was from him that I gleaned the most important information. I learned the name of the warrior who led the clan and the names of the four witches who ruled them. He knew of them from his homeland. The clan had left Denmark but they still traded with their homeland. The witches, it appeared, needed amber and other treasures which came from their homeland.

The Dane had been fearful and that surprised me for there were many warrior bands upon his arms. I had had to part with a gold coin taken from Neustria to loosen his tongue.

"The leader is Baggi Skull Splitter. He is the eldest of the clan. He had a younger brother, Eggle; he was slain last year. It made him angry beyond words and he slaughtered a whole village in Mercia in vengeance. It is said that they ringed his home with their skulls."

This showed me the size of the clan. If they could raid Mercia with impunity, then they had large numbers indeed.

"The power lies with the four witches. The eldest is Asta and she is ancient. It is said she has not a tooth in her mouth nor a hair on her head but she rules the clan. Then there are her daughters. There were four but one was slain. Birte Twist-Breeks is the eldest of the three. Ellesef Ship-Breast is the youngest and the third is Dagh the Second Sighted." He leaned forward, "It is said that Asta cursed the one called The Dragonheart and the people of the Land of the Wolf. Her daughter was slain by their warriors." He shivered, "I would not wish to risk the enmity of that one."

"How did you come to know so much about them?"

"One of my crew has served with them. He was blamed for the surprise attack which resulted in the death of the witch and he fled."

"Could I talk with him?"

Shaking his head, he said, "When he found out I was coming back here to this river he deserted me. He is now in the land of the Franks. He is terrified that they will find out where he is. He only escaped because it was after the battle. His hair turned white and he has seen but twenty summers."

After he had confirmed that they lived close to Loidis I handed him the coin.

"Why are you so interested in them, Norseman?"

I lied. It was not honourable but my people's lives were at stake. "We had heard of them and as I planned on travelling through the land close to Loidis I thought it prudent to know of them and their ways."

The Dane shook his head, "Avoid that land. There is little there anyway. The valleys, so I have heard, are steep and there is little to commend it. They live there for they are safe. They have hills and their stad are surrounded by wooden walls and ditches."

As I rejoined Haaken and the others I realised that it sounded like a similar land to mine. We headed back to the inn and shared what we had learned. From the others, I discovered that the clan was growing in numbers and was becoming bolder. They were making the old kingdom of Elmet their own. Taking the women of the ancient people they were growing each year. That worried me. The ancient peoples had powers. It came through their women. This was my dream. The dragon we had seen was a symbol of their new power. The sign of the Walhaz, the name the Saxons called the old people, was a dragon. When I had fought the people of Cymru I had often seen the dragon on their banners. They were not a threat but this clan was.

When Beorn arrived at the inn he confirmed some of what we had learned. "They are a problem. Asser told me that many villages had young girls stolen. They suspected slavers but as the trail always led to the land around Loidis they now believe it to be the Skull Takers. They were going to send word to Athelstan."

"Should we not scout out their stronghold?"

I shook my head, "No, Rollo. I have no intention of attacking them."

"You fear them, jarl?"

I flashed him an angry look and then shook my head. He was young and he did not lead our clan, "No my young headstrong warrior. What would we gain? We would lose warriors attacking their walls and we would not have the power to fight their magic. If they do wish us harm, then they will come to us. We are safe so long as the ground is as it is but once the green leaves emerge then there will be the need for us to be vigilant."

"You will let them come to us?"

"I will, Rolf. We have time to make our walls stronger and prepare our defences. Aiden has told us that Ylva is gaining in power. A delay helps us."

We told Agnete that we would be leaving the next morning. "The weather is not good, Jarl Dragonheart."

"We are hardy men and our horses are well rested. It will be good."

"And we will gather information. When Carr and Ase next visit we will tell them what we have learned. They come at the time of the feast of Eostre." She smiled. "We close the inn for three days and are a family once more. If you send to Carr after Eostre he can tell you all that we have learned."

I pressed a gold coin into her hand. She tried to refuse saying it was too much. "No, for you have given us something money cannot buy, friendship. Besides this is money we took from a greedy Frank who hoarded his treasure. Each time I spend a coin I feel better inside."

Just before we left, as dawn was beginning to break, Aksel said, "Jarl beware on the road. Our slave heard some Danes outside. They spied your horses in the stable. I fear they mean you harm."

Haaken said, "Good for my sword arm thinks I have forgotten how to use it. We will be ready for them."

As we entered the stable I heeded Aksel's warning. "Don your mail beneath our cloaks. Better to be ready to fight. Hang your shields from your backs. If danger comes then we fight." Once ready for a dangerous journey, we left.

The dank, damp weather of the previous day remained and hung in the air making visibility poor. We left by the north gate and headed north west towards the Dunum. I knew this road well. We would travel north on the Roman Road and cross the Dunum by the abandoned Roman fort. Then we would follow the Dunum's north bank until we came to the Force which rushed the river down from the high ground. We could cross there and be at Ketil's stad in two days.

There were many houses lining the road as we headed north, but eventually they gave way to scrubby bushes and straggly trees which had encroached since the time of the Romans. No one maintained them and soon, unless they were repaired, they would become a greenway. The dank air masked sounds but Beorn the Scout had sharp ears. He was aided by his horse which flicked its ears up. He turned and held up his hand in the signal for danger. I moved my cloak so that I could reach my sword and then donned my helmet. The others did the same, silently, and we kept moving up the road.

I nudged my horse so that I was close by Beorn's mount's hindquarters. I still held the halter for my spare horse in my left hand but I was prepared to let it drop the instant we found trouble. I heard Beorn's sword as he slid it from his scabbard and I released my horse and then drew my own sword. The Danes came at us from both sides. I whipped my horse's head to the left for Beorn could deal with the ones from his right. I brought my sword over in an arc as the Danish spear rammed at my side. My movement had made him miss. The spear head caught on my mail and then struck the rim of my shield. My sword struck him on the helmet. It was a powerful blow and the Dane crumpled, the life leaving his eyes.

In those days, we did not use the stiraps much and I slid my leg over my saddle. I would fight on foot. I drew my seax as I did so. There were four Danes facing me. Haaken appeared at my side. I did not worry about the others. They were Ulfheonar. They could handle the other Danes.

The four were armed with axes and spears. The worst thing we could have done was to wait for them to attack and I leapt forward deflecting the waiting spear with my sword. The Dane was taken by surprise. He wore no mail. Perhaps he hoped to take mine. As Ragnar's Spirit ripped into his middle he discovered that would not happen. One of the Danes who had an axe had stepped around my sword side and I felt a crack as he swung it at my back. My shield was still slung there beneath my cloak. I saw the look of surprise from behind his helmet as I turned to face him.

"You do not catch an Ulfheonar like that, Dane!" I swung my blade at head height and it bit deep into his neck. The blood spattered the spearman behind him. Even as he prepared to stab at me Rolf Horse Killer swung his own axe and hacked through to the Dane's spine. I turned and looked. Our horses had wandered a little way off but eleven Danes lay dead. They had thought that odds of more than two to one favoured them. They were wrong.

We searched them and took what little treasure they had. We searched for clan markings. They were not the Skull Takers. The paucity of their weapons had told us that. Their tokens told us they were the clan of the otter. We took the best of them and left their bodies for the carrion. In winter this would be a feast. Rollo Thin Skin had a cut cheek but that was our only wound.

As we headed north again Haaken One Eye said, "There are more armed Danes in this land than Athelstan thinks."

I nodded, "At the moment they appear to be isolated bands but it would not take much for a leader to unite them."

"You think this Baggi Skull Splitter is such a leader?"

"If they have made a stronghold in Elmet then perhaps he is. The ones we slew were looking for horses and mail. If the Skull Taker clan could offer them weapons, mail and horses then who knows. The sooner we are home and can speak with Aiden the better. He may know our news but something tells me he does not."

Rollo asked, "Why?"

I pointed at the moist and misty air around us, "If they have four witches they can hide their thoughts and actions. Aiden and Kara protect our people in the same way."

Beorn chuckled, "Sometimes, Rollo, a pair of eyes is as valuable as a galdramenn or a volva."

"Just do not say that in Kara's hearing. She would not like it." Haaken had known Kara since she had been born on Man.

Our journey to Ketil's stad was uneventful. We took shelter in the deserted Roman fort by the Dunum. It was half way to our land and we were safe there. We made a sacrifice at the shrine on the island in the river and the ancient walls protected us from the worst of the weather. Ketil had men riding the fells and they spied us as we approached.

After a night in the open the hall of Ketil was a welcome relief. We told him our news and of Carr. "He is a good man. Visit with him Ketil. He is a Dane but his heart is true. They are hardy but lonely."

"I will, jarl."

"And when the weather improves visit with Athelstan. I have no doubt that Asser and Alfred will send him news but we owe it to our ally to keep him informed. War is coming, Ketil and we must be ready!"

Chapter 4

As we were heading back to my home we met Wighlek and Vibeke. "Jarl Dragonheart, we missed you when we visited your home. We have had a good trade. We go now to see Asbjorn the Strong but we can return if you wish to trade with us."

I smiled, "Thank you Vibeke but I have no need to trade. Did my wife trade?"

The grey-haired woman laughed, "She always buys!"

"I will see you when next you visit. May the Allfather be with you." I knew that my wife would be pleased with the news of the outside world that they brought.

Everyone was relieved to see us return. We had not been away for long but, with Þorri upon us, we were in the depths of winter. We gathered in my hall. Olaf Leather Neck and Snorri joined my family to hear our news.

I saw fear on Brigid's face when I told them what we had learned but my warriors nodded. Olaf said, "You are right, Jarl Dragonheart. It would be foolish and wasteful to attack their home. Better we wait here. We can slaughter more of them."

Elfrida asked, "But what of the witches?"

I looked to Kara and Aiden. Witches were their domain

Kara said, "We must leave for Syllingar. Ylva must become a witch. With her power, added to that of Elfrida, and we two then we should be able to defeat them."

"It is a risk sailing at this time of year."

Kara smiled, "I know but you have risked more. I feel it is a risk worth taking for the clan. It is time we repaid the land for the benefits we have reaped. You were right father, we have not done enough for the clan. We begin now."

Aiden nodded, "And this will protect our daughter." He put a protective arm around her. "You said a witch died and they need five. It is a magical number. Remember Angharad when she tried to take Elfrida? Ylva is in danger until she has learned to harness her powers. Syllingar will give us the chance to make her safe."

"But who will sail you there? We cannot afford to send a longship. We need our men here."

"Then we send a knarr. Raibeart Ap Pasgen is a brave captain. He will do it."

"But can you find the island?"

"It will call to us. We have spoken with the spirits and they will guide us there."

In many ways it made sense but I was not happy about their absence. As much as I had complained that their skills did not aid the clan they had given us warning in the past. If they were away, even for just one moon, it might prove disastrous.

Once decided my daughter was like a whirlwind. Aiden was sent to Úlfarrston to arrange their passage and she began to organise the women of her hall. They were the healers for the clan as well as the ones who produced the cheese and the ale. They were vitally important to us.

While all of that was going on I spent some time with Ylva. Of all my children and grandchildren, she was the one I knew the least. That had been partly my fault for I was often away fighting but even when I was at home she was always closeted with her mother. There was a barrier between us which I could not break. "Ylva, walk with your grandfather to the Water. I would speak with you."

We wrapped up against the cold and I took her to the eastern shore. I pointed across to the mound which, in spring and summer, was topped by flowers. Now it was just a snow topped mound. "That is your grandmother, Ylva. I see much of her in you."

She nodded, seriously, "I know. She says that in my dreams." She peered at me with her huge eyes, "She says you are not to worry so much. Mother and father know what they are doing. I trust them and their judgement. When I become a woman, I shall have even more powers than my grandmother. I will save the clan."

As much as I was touched by her words I felt sad that she had not had a childhood. She had almost been forced to be grown up from an early age. Her parents had encouraged her to use her powers. "I am afraid, Ylva, that I cannot help but worry. I am the leader of this clan and many people depend upon me."

She reached up and kissed my cheek, "And when I have my powers then I can help you lead our people. You will be able to enjoy being an old man! This is meant to be grandfather. Trust me. The spirits will protect this land."

She did not mean the insult but I felt the barb. I was an old man.

To soften the blow, she cuddled in to me, "I know that I do not see as much of you as you would like but I would have you know that I feel as close to you as my parents. The spirit of my grandmother is within me and that of my great grandmother. Both loved you and were willing to die for you. I would do the same."

"I would have you live, Ylva. I have seen two of my children die. I would not see more."

They left three days later. That was the fault of the knarr. Laid up for winter it took Raibeart that length of time to make her seaworthy. I went with my family to see them off and, as they loaded what they would need I spoke with Raibeart. "Are you not afraid, Raibeart?"

"No Jarl. I am excited. The crew are too. I could have taken twice as many there were so many volunteers. I am sailing with a volva and a galdramenn. This will be my safest voyage. Do not fret Jarl. With favourable winds, we can be back in a moon. We will see a Norn and return to tell the tale."

Shaking my head, I said, "You know not how long they will spend on the island."

"Your daughter said she was keen to return here. But two months is the longest we will be away."

I did not like such promises. They were too easily broken but it was out of my hands. I embraced Kara and Ylva and clasped Aiden's arm. "May the Allfather be with you."

Aiden smiled, "He always is as well as all the spirits who watch over you and us. Fear not we will return."

I reached my hall with a heavy heart. Brigid was nursing our daughter but Gruffyd came to me with a horn of ale. "You have not told me of the visit to the Danes, father. What happened?"

Sometimes it takes a single, simple act to change events and so it was. I told my son all and in telling him I worked out what we needed to do to defeat these Skull Takers. I was now in no doubt that they were coming. There had been too many signs. We had made them our enemies. I knew that it could not have been avoided, it was *wyrd*. Now I had to make the best of it.

When I had told, him I said, "Get out the chess pieces, Gruffyd."

"We play chess?"

"No, we plan our defence!"

We did not lay the pieces out for a game. Instead I used the white ivory pieces, to represent our settlements and my warrior bands. I used the red stained ivory to represent the Danes. I was pleased that my son grasped the concept quickly. As I moved them around he made suggestions and spotted flaws. Finally, as Brigid came in with food and fresh ale I nodded, "That is how we will defend our home."

"War again!"

"Perhaps we should turn the other cheek, my love. I am sure the Skull Takers will allow some of us to live."

43

"They are Vikings like you!"

"They are nothing like us. This will not inconvenience you. Your life and that of the people within this stad will go on much as before. It is the men and the boys who will have to work harder."

She did not understand. Her people were different to ours. He religion was different. It was as though we spoke a different language.

We had had snow before Yule and the spring also began to come early. It came slowly but the ground warmed. I called my Ulfheonar together along with Scanlan and Bagsecg. The two of them were the heart of my people. I gave them the instructions for our stad. The Stad on the Eden had better defences than we did. I told Scanlan that I wanted the men in the stad to dig a second ditch and make a second rampart. The Ulfheonar would offset the gates to make it harder for an enemy to enter them. I did not stay to supervise the work. Satisfied that they knew what they were doing I left with Ragnar and Gruffyd. First, we went to Windar's Mere. Asbjorn the Strong was jarl there now. He had improved the defences at the head of the Mere but I knew that there was more to do. I spent three days with him walking around his palisade and ditches pointing out where the weaknesses lay.

As we ate in his hall I said, "You do not have enough warriors. This is not your fault. Old Windar was protected too much by my son and by me. All of your men must bear arms. I will return with my Ulfheonar at the start of Ein-mánuðr. We will test your defences and your men. I do not want to find them lacking."

Asbjorn the Strong had only been jarl since the raid which had left most of the settlement destroyed. He had been one of the few warriors who had been willing to take on the responsibility of leading the people there. Arne Thorirson had been the jarl and I had told him to improve his defences. Arne had not done as I had asked and he had paid with his life.

"I swear that this time we will be better, Jarl Dragonheart. My warriors may not be Ulfheonar but this place is worth defending!" I saw that he had made a good start and I was confident that if the Danes came they would find his walls hard to take.

My visit to Ketil was different. His defences and his men needed no improvement. Ketil was as hard a taskmaster as any, I needed to outline my plans to him and to discover his news.

"I have met with Carr. You are right, he is a good man. His son is a fine archer. I told them that if danger came they can take refuge here. He likes his independence but I think he likes our proximity. His son enjoys the company of my young men and he likes the girls. He visits at least once ever sennight."

"Good. We will need his bow before too long. And Athelstan?"

"He was disturbed by the news. His father would not stir but the prince used his own gold to hire more warriors. When the grass comes again he will take men down to Loidis to rid himself of this viper's nest."

"I pray he uses caution. From what I have heard they are a mighty clan." I did not want the young Saxon to try to fight these Danes. They were dangerous.

"He is trying to prove to his people that he can be a king like Egbert."

"When I spoke with him I learned that he sees war with Egbert as inevitable. I said we would aid him."

"Good for I like the young prince."

My last visit on this journey of my borders was to Eden on the stad. It was the easiest of my visits for it was a strongly made fortress and the river meant we could keep it supplied. Of all my stad that was the one about which I worried the least.

On the ride, south we passed through the most prosperous part of my land. The that had brought a sudden spurt of grass and my farmers used it. There were many cultivated fields and the fells were dotted with lambing ewes. Cattle grazed in the lush bottom lands. These farmers were cosseted from danger and war. Úlfarrberg seemed to watch over the prosperous little valley. Until it had been destroyed then Ulla's Water had also been prosperous. None lived there now save for one or two hardy souls. Most of the farmers around the Grassy Mere had fled from Ulla's Water. I did not begrudge them their peace. Their crops and animals were our prosperity.

As we crossed over the col into the Rye Dale all three of us looked towards Lough Rigg. I knew that my son and Ragnar still woke sweating in the night at the memory of the night in the magical cave. We could not undo it. I hoped that it would make better warriors of them.

The spell seemed to be broken as we dropped to the bubbling stream which ran towards Windar's Mere. "Do you visit Úlfarrston and Sigtrygg's Stad as well, father?"

"Aye. We will spend a day or two at home and then head south. This clement weather is good for crops but it hastens the arrival of the Danes. We need as much time as we can manage if we are to prepare."

"Can we hold them, grandfather?"

Gruffyd burst out, "Of course we can! We have a grand plan do we not, father?"

"We have a plan but let us not boast of it until it has succeeded. We need Aiden and his family back first."

I was pleased that Ragnar and Gruffyd had shown such an interest. But I feared that they would be forced to become warriors before their time. Such was the way of the clan.

When I returned home I spent two days with my wife. I was attentive and I was patient. Inside I could not wait to go to Úlfarrston and visit Sigtrygg's Stad. I needed to see my people. My son and grandson came with me along with Haaken. He had had enough time with his family. I saw Erik Short Toe and told him that we might need my drekar before summer. I was not certain that we would but a drekar needed time to prepare for sea. I sat with Pasgen enjoying a fine feast.

The next day, as I prepared to ride to Sigtrygg's stad I heard the cry of. "Sail Ho!"

Like everyone else I was curious who would be sailing into our port. We all went to the shore to watch the sail beat up towards us. I recognised the knarr. It was *'The King's Gift'*, it was my drekar. My mind raced. What had happened? Had disaster struck? I forced myself to concentrate. Speculation could not help.

It was my ship and I saw, at the stern, my daughter and her husband. Had they not found the island? Had their plans gone awry?

Gruffyd gripped my arm, "What does this portend, father?"

"Let us wait and not make up gossip and rumour."

It seemed to take an age but eventually the knarr tied up. Aiden helped Kara from the deck. I could not see Ylva, "Where is my granddaughter?"

Kara threw herself into my arms, "She is in Syllingar! The Weird Sisters have need of her. We have lost our child!"

For the first time since my wife had died, Kara wept. I let her sob and I looked at Aiden. He looked drained. "We found the cave and the witch was pleased to see us. She said that her voice had carried across the seas. We were dismissed. She said we would know when Ylva would return. We had to leave!"

"You should have taken her!" I would not have left her there.

"The witch is a Norn, jarl. She could have destroyed us. We left and boarded the ship. I am sorry. We have failed."

I felt as low as I had ever felt. Erika and Wolf Killer's death had almost been as bad but this was my granddaughter and she was lost. I had done nothing to stop this. She had entered a world in which I had no power. My sword could not save her. I had let her down. I forced myself to be strong, "We will return home and we will speak of what this means. It is not the end. It is but a pause along the way."

Ragnar and Gruffyd flanked me as we rode our ponies north through the darkening gloom. It was Gruffyd who spoke first. "Father what of Sigtrygg?"

"We will go the day after tomorrow. Another day cannot hurt and I need to speak with Kara and Aiden. Their upset was too great. I need them to be calm and reflective. I must know what happened."

"But we are ready should the Danes come, are we not?"

"We have men ready to man newly prepared walls but we have not the power, yet to face the witches. Until Ylva was lost we had three who could combine their power now we do not."

"You have my mother. She has powers."

I smiled at Ragnar, "She has limited powers. She gave up most of them when she had you. She can aid Kara and Aiden but that is all."

"My brother had power." Ragnar broke the silence.

I nodded, "I know. Kara sensed it in him. It was not as great as Ylva but he had some."

"And he was slain along with my father."

"*Wyrd*. There is little point in bemoaning what the Weird Sisters have spun. We just have to adapt." I felt myself brightening. "We will have to put our minds to this problem. The gloom about us makes us dull. Perhaps a fire in the hall will bring us to life."

We went to my hall where a surprised Brigid quickly organised food and warmed ale. I sat in my chair with my sword across my lap and listened as Kara and Aiden spoke of their voyage and their visit.

"We found the island straight away. The smoke spiralled from the top as it always did. We went down and she was waiting. She looked even more ancient than the last time."

Kara took up the story, "I was excited to meet her and I had questions racing around inside my head. She seemed to know that for she answered them all. But Ylva..." she stopped. The words were choking her.

Aiden put his arm around my wife, "She was excited. It seemed she knew the cave for while we spoke she explored and the witch did not mind. The witch told us that it was she who had sent the dreams to us. The storm and the avalanche, Jarl Dragonheart, they were the work of the Norns. That is why the dreams were as they were. We were being summoned." He took a drink of the ale. "We were hopeful and happy at that point. Then the Norn said she was grateful we had brought her acolyte and we could go."

"She just dismissed you?"

He nodded and I saw his face was contorted with the memory, "I would have faced her down but Ylva went to her side and said that she wished to stay with her." His head bowed. His voice became little more than a whisper barely audible above the spitting of the logs in the fire, "She said that she was grateful for all that we had done for her but her real work was serving Skuld."

"So, she is a Norn."

He nodded, "Kara tried to take our daughter but Skuld and Ylva used their minds. Kara collapsed in the cave and I thought her dead. I carried her hence into the daylight." He looked up at me and his eyes showed his torment and his pain. "I had to choose, my wife or my daughter. May the Allfather forgive me, I chose my wife! What kind of father abandons his child?"

I stood and put my arm around them both, "A father who has no other choice. There was naught you could have done. All that would have resulted would have been the loss of them both. We will get Ylva back."

They both looked at me, "How?"

I released them and held Ragnar's Spirit by the hilt. "This is a powerful weapon. It may be that this can defeat the witch, I know not but when the threat of the Danes is gone I swear I will take my Ulfheonar and we will rescue Ylva."

"But she is now one of them, father."

I looked at Kara, "But in her heart, she is of us. We will find that spark which is her family and we will retrieve it. Use your powers to speak with Erika and my mother. You can do nothing until you have regained your power."

"But it is hopeless. They are too powerful for us!"

My voice became stern, "When I faced enemies who outnumbered me, surrounded only by my oathsworn, did I give up? When you and your brother were taken by the Hibernians did I crawl into a hole and cry? The Norns make our lives hard but we show that we are worthy of life by fighting against it. Fight! You have one child! Is she not worth fighting for?"

"Husband you are too harsh. Your daughter needs time to grieve." My wife gripped my arm as though that act might silence me.

"No Brigid, she does not. It is not the way of our family and this clan. Grief is a luxury we can ill afford. Make a steam hut by Erika's grave and the two of you make contact. I will make preparations for this attack. Tomorrow I ride to Úlfarrston and thence to Sigtrygg's stad. The Land of the Wolf goes to war." Aiden looked at me and nodded. I added, a little more gently, "Now take my daughter to her women and sleep. You need rest. Do not despair. This is not over."

When they had gone, I turned to Ragnar and Gruffyd. "And you two need sleep. Tomorrow we head south and you will bring your hearth-weru, Ragnar. The grass may be emerging from the ground but our men must sharpen swords and not ploughs."

When they had gone Elfrida asked, "Are you so certain that war is coming?"

I gave her a grim smile. Do you think that the taking of Ylva was an accident? The Norns are spinning once more. I had thought war was threatened when I returned from Eoforwic but now I think it is imminent."

"Then we will organise the women. If the clan is in danger, then it is the duty of us all to be prepared."

I did not follow my own advice. I sat and stared into the fire. I had plans to modify and men to organise. We had only added one Ulfheonar: Aðils Shape Shifter. He had hunted the wolf. He was the son of a hill farmer, Aðgísl Svensson. Aðils' mother and father had died two winter's since and he had stayed in the hill farm alone. He had learned to be as one with the woods, the rocks and the land. He was as good as Snorri and Beorn as a scout and his skills with a bow were legendary. It was just his sword skills which needed work and Haaken could teach those.

It meant I now had sixteen Ulfheonar. I did not count those Ulfheonar who were not gesith and jarls. Asbjorn's crew numbered twenty. He would still have others to guard Windar's Mere's walls. In Úlfarrston Raibeart commanded another twenty. Although Raibeart's were not Norse they were as fine a crew as I had met. Sigtrygg's forty men were vital to my plans. The bondi in my stad were forty in number. I also had the six hearth-weru of my grandson. It meant that if the Danes came I could count on over a hundred warriors to face them. The other three stad I would leave untouched. If I withdrew men from my three other stad I was inviting disaster. A hundred of my clan would be enough.

I had finished my plans as the smell of baking bread drifted from the bakery at the rear of my hall. I went to see the slaves. Uhtric, my servant, supervised them. He frowned, "You did not sleep Jarl. It is not good. A man needs his sleep."

"Thank you Uhtric but sometimes sleep does not come."

He nodded, "I heard about the little one. You have much to bear, Jarl. I have no family save yours but I know that my heart aches at the pain you have had to endure. I know not how you do so."

I pointed beyond the walls. "I think part of me was made from the stone of this land. I have in my heart a place made of stone where none can hurt me. I go to that fortress."

"The Dragonheart!" he nodded, "You are well named."

He was right. When I had been given that name I had not thought of what it meant. Now I did. My heart had to be cold, like a fire drake. I had to be vengeful and terrifying yet a dragon could raise young and care for them. Now I saw that I had been meant to grow into my name. The dragon of which we had dreamed was me. If I did not make the right decisions, then I would destroy my own people. I had a greater responsibility than ever. I clutched my amulets and asked the spirits of all my people for help.

With all my Ulfheonar and Ragnar's Hearth-weru I was taking a large band to Úlfarrston. I was heading for Sigtrygg Thrandson's stad later than I would have wished. I did not wish to fall foul of Danish scouts. I made sure that Erik Short Toe had begun the process of preparing my ships for sea and then we headed across the river towards the enclave that was my southernmost stad.

Aðils Shape Shifter roamed ahead with Snorri and Beorn the Scout. Both were impressed with my newest warrior. As we rode south Olaf told me of the wolf hunt. "The boy had killed a wolf when he lived alone! He had the skin but he wished to follow the rules of the Ulfheonar. In all the hunts I have seen his was the most impressive. He truly is a shape shifter. He wore the skin of the wolf he had already killed and managed to approach within ten paces of the wolves before he was spotted. He killed his wolf with a single thrust of his spear and drove off the others. Snorri was impressed."

He had much in common with me. I had killed my first wolf not as a ritual but out of necessity. I had been defending Old Ragnar and myself. I took it as a good omen. I was wrong.

It was Beorn the Scout who raced back with the news. "Jarl, we have found people fleeing from Sigtrygg's Stad. The Skull Takers have attacked! The stad is lost!"

Chapter 5

The Norns were cruel. Had I left when I had planned I might have reached Sigtrygg but the return of my daughter and Aiden had changed my plans. Inwardly I cursed but I kept an impassive face. "We ride hard. Perhaps we can save more of our people. I care not what happens to the horses. We ride as though our lives depended upon it. Our people are in danger."

We were all well mounted and we had good horses. The ground was undulating and we made good time. We galloped hard. After a short time we began to pass huddles of women and children who cowered at our approach. They saw mailed riders; we could be Danes. We shouted that we would return. They would be safe for any Dane would have to get through us to get at them. I knew that Snorri and Aðils Shape Shifter would be seeking out Sigtrygg and any survivors of this attack. We could ride hard knowing we would not be ambushed. We passed thirty or so survivors. None were warriors. I knew that other refugees would have headed due north towards Windar's Mere. These might not be the only ones who had escaped. I hoped that Sigtrygg, although he might have lost his stad, might still survive. He and his warriors were stout. It would take many men to defeat him.

We were still some way from the stad when Snorri appeared from behind a tree, "Hold, Jarl. They are over the next rise. Sigtrygg and his oathsworn have formed a shield wall and are singing their death song. They have not long to live."

"Then we ride to war!"

I kicked my lathered horse hard as I drew my sword. As we crested the rise I saw that the band of Danes had the eight warriors surrounded. Aðils Shape Shifter had dismounted and was loosing arrows as fast as he could. A half dozen Danes turned to run towards him. I reined in next to him and threw myself from my saddle. I ran at the Danes. I did not even bother to pull my shield around. I was angry. The Norns had tricked me again! The Danes would pay the price. I drew my seax and sword, hurling myself at the six surprised Danes. They had expected me to wait for their attack. I saw that each had an animal skull on either their helmet or around their necks. They were Skull Takers. I moved so quickly that they barely had time to react. I flicked the spear away with my seax and rammed my sword into the stomach of the first Dane. My speed had taken them by surprise and the second Dane watched as my seax tore across his throat. I felt a blow on my back as one of the others swung his sword at me. The sword cracked off my shield; hidden beneath my wolf cloak. Then there was a cry as Haaken One Eye ended his life.

Leaving the other three for my warriors I ran, recklessly, towards the ever-shrinking shield wall. I could hear them singing.

"Sigtrygg Thrandson's warriors fight
Come you foes into our night
Sigtrygg Thrandson's oathsworn's end
Brother to brother friend to friend"

Their death song made me reckless. "Skull Takers! Jarl Dragonheart comes to end your lives!" My roared challenge made some turn and that gave the survivors the chance to hold on until more help came. A tall warrior with a two-handed axe and a large skull on his helmet ran at me. I saw that he had two smaller skulls hanging from his hair. If this was intended to frighten me he failed. He wore mail and I would have to get inside his swinging strokes. I had the experience of forty years behind me. He was younger than I was and saw the flecks of grey in my beard. It made him overconfident. He laughed, "You will die, old man!"

In the time it took for him to speak those words I threw my seax at him and swung my shield around from my back. A seax does not throw well but I was lucky. My sharpened blade ripped across the back of his right hand and he began to bleed. It angered him and he swung hard at my head. I ducked and lifted my shield. The edge of the axe caught the boss on my shield. It jarred. I thrust blindly with my sword underneath my shield. It tore into the mail at his side. Although I did not strike flesh I weakened his mail and as I stepped back I saw that there was now a gap there.

All around me were the sounds of metal on wood and the cries of the wounded and dying for my men had now joined the battle. The arrows which fell on the Danes told me that Aðils Shape Shifter was still using his bow well. I prayed to the Allfather that Sigtrygg and his oathsworn would survive.

I had now warned the chieftain that I had some skill and he came at me with feet wide apart to give him balance. He swung his axe so that it was hard for me to get inside it. I decided to take a risk. As he swung I punched the boss of my shield at his hands. I struck his left hand. He reeled backwards a little and I slashed my sword at his knee. I struck it below his byrnie and felt it scrape along the bone. As I tore it back I saw his shield arm drop a little. I had torn tendons. I stepped back to assess what damage I had done. As I did so I saw that there were just three warriors standing with Sigtrygg. I had to end this. I feinted with my sword at the Dane's good leg and he tried to step back quickly. His weakened leg could not take the weight and he fell backwards. I stepped on to his stomach and rammed my sword into his neck. I was moving towards the beleaguered Sigtrygg even as I pulled it out.

"Ragnar's Spirit!" I smashed my shield and sword into the backs of three Danes. One fell winded and my sword caught the side of a second. The third whirled around to face me. He was so close that I pulled back my head and butted him in the face. He had an open helmet and his nose blossomed like a ripe plum. As he was toppling backwards I brought my sword against his side and ripped him open to this ribs.

As I looked up I saw that there were just three warriors left and Sigtrygg was not one of them. Ignoring the three at my feet I stabbed one of the remaining Danes in the back. I used so much force that the blade came out of his front. A Dane next to me shouted in triumph as he started to swing his sword at my unprotected side. The arrow from Aðils Shape Shifter's bow hit him in the side of the head and killed him instantly.

There were no Danes left around the last stand of Sigtrygg Thrandson's hearth-weru. My Ulfheonar had slain them. There were three wounded warriors left and they knelt around their jarl. I dropped my shield and leaned over him. He looked up as one of his men took the helmet from him. He had many wounds, to his face, his legs, his arms and his body. I saw that his cheek had been laid open to the bone looking down I could see the contents of his stomach. He was dying. "Thank you for coming Jarl Dragonheart." He winced and his eyes closed briefly. His bloody fingers gripped my arm. He spoke urgently for he knew his time was come. "They knew our passwords and our routines, Jarl! I have failed you." He arced his back as pain coursed through his body. I said nothing. I could talk later. These would be Sigtrygg's last words. "Watch over my people; those that survive. We had a good home here but I fear…" He died. His hands were on his sword.

I stood and looked up to the skies, "Allfather, welcome a great warrior and an Ulfheonar. Sigtrygg Thrandson was never foresworn and was a true warrior. This was his father's land and he made it his. Prepare a place for him in your hall and I will see him ere long. Sigtrygg!"

His oathsworn raised their swords as did the Ulfheonar who stood around us, "Sigtrygg!"

I stood and saw that the Danes we had not slain were now fleeing. "After them! Let none escape!"

This was not just an act of vengeance. I wanted none to return so that they would wonder what happened to this warband. We had been caught napping but I believed we could turn this disaster to our advantage. I picked up my shield and joined in the chase. Ragnar, Gruffyd and Ragnar's hearth-weru were younger and faster than almost all of the Ulfheonar. Along with Aðils Shape Shifter they began to catch the Danes. The Danes who were fleeing had no mail. They should have been faster but there was grim determination in my men. They disappeared over a rise and as I followed I saw a wounded Dane. He had lost an arm and was bleeding to death. He was reaching over with his left hand to try to reach his sword. I picked it up and held it by the blade.

"You are dying Skull Taker. Do you want this and then you can go to Valhalla?"

He grunted and a tendril of blood seeped from the corner of his mouth, "And what is the price?"

"Who led you?"

"The warrior with the axe that you slew, Baldrekr The Wild." It was not the chief, Baggi. I had hoped it was.

"How many more men are there at Loidis?"

His eyes widened. I had surprised him. Then he laughed, "More than we brought today! Do not worry Ulfheonar, Prince Baggi will come and when Asta tears your soul from within you I will be waiting in Valhalla!" He held his hand out. I had learned all that I could and I gave it to him. He looked up at the sky and cried, "Odin!" Then the light went from his eyes.

It was getting on to late afternoon and a chill was spreading from the east by the time my hunters returned. Gruffyd and Ragnar both had blood spattered mail and their swords were notched. Einar the Tall said, "None escaped Jarl." He nodded towards Gruffyd and Ragnar. "They did well."

"You are both blooded. I fear this will not be the last Danish blood your swords taste. Collect the weapons and the mail. We shall need it before long."

It was late in the night by the time we reached Úlfarrston with the survivors of the attack. We would have reached there sooner but we had our dead to honour and to bury. They deserved that. Olaf Leather Neck took some of my men and they burned Sigtrygg's stad. If he could not have it then no one would. The smoke had billowed in the sky as a marker for our former outpost. We had lost Elfridaby and now Sigtrygg's stad. We were losing our land. Soon the blackened lines would be all that remained of Sigtrygg's stad. That did not hurt but to lose our warriors tore out my heart.

We used the horses to carry the wounded and the women. I spoke with Nagli the Swift. One of Sigtrygg's oathsworn he had a wounded leg and he rode my horse. "Tell me, Nagli, what happened?"

"We had scouts out. We always did. The jarl was careful. When two scouts did not return, he became worried and sent Arne Jorgenson with ten warriors to find them. He then prepared our defences. Arne was just leaving the stad and the gate was open when two warriors appeared. They gave the password to Arne. He turned to speak and then more Danes rose from the ground and the ditch where they had hidden. They burst through the gate before we could react. Jarl Sigtrygg shouted for any who were not warriors to flee. Arne and his men slowed down the advance but there were many Danes and Arne and his men were slaughtered but they bought time. The jarl ordered the women and children to flee. He knew there was treachery. They had known our passwords. The women and children fled and the jarl formed a shield wall to allow our people to escape. We had but twenty-four warriors left and the Danes had many more than we did. We retreated out of the other gate. We paid a heavy price for the land we surrendered. Three Danes fell for each one we lost. We wondered if we might manage to extricate ourselves and reach Úlfarrston and then a second band cut off our retreat. We formed a shield wall. You came upon us soon after. Had we not been surrounded then we might have reached you." I saw his head droop. They had been so close.

"It was not your fault." I told him of the Norns and their web. He shook his head and grasped his amulet.

Sigtrygg's death had not been in vain. I now saw their cunning. They had lured his men out of the gate to gain entry. They had had spies too who had learned of Sigtrygg's passwords and routines. Our new offset defences would stop that but they had also used a second warband. I had to work out how to stop that. My first problem was Úlfarrston. That was now isolated. It would take some time for Baggi Skull Splitter to realise that his warband were all dead. I guessed he would send scouts to see what had happened to them. They would find the burned out stad and the corpses of their dead. What would he do next?

I knew that Aiden and Kara would need to seek guidance from the spirit world but that would not give me an accurate account. I would have to use my three scouts to watch for them. I worked out that we had a month at most to finish our preparations. He would expect a messenger back from Baldrekr. It was six days to Loidis. We would use each moment well.

Pasgen ap Coen made the refugees welcome and housed my men in his warrior hall. I sat with Olaf, Haaken, Raibeart and the headman of Úlfarrston.

"The Danes will be coming. The only question is where will they strike? Here? Windar's mere or Cyninges-tūn?"

Olaf Leather Neck shook his head, "It could be anywhere Jarl. They showed us that they are cunning. The ploy they used was effective. Sigtrygg was a good jarl and he was prepared yet he fell."

"The nights are getting shorter. They used the darkness to hide themselves in plain view. They will find that harder here. You have cleared the land well. The estuary and the river are a better boundary than Sigtrygg had."

"Aye and we have made our walls higher. Still I fear for my people. We are not as hardy as your folk. Could we withstand an attack?"

I did not know. Already I feared that the Danes would use an attack on Úlfarrston to draw me from behind my walls. "Then you must have riders ready to fetch us if your scouts and your ships see anything."

"We will."

"And Raibeart, if we succeed in thwarting this attack I have need of you."

"Aye jarl, what?"

I would have you pilot '*Heart of the Dragon*' to Syllingar. I would rescue my granddaughter."

It was as though an icy wind had suddenly whistled through the well-lit hall. They all shivered and clutched amulets. "But this is a Norn, jarl. Aiden told me as much when he returned."

"Could you find the island again?"

"I know the waters where it should lie but…"

"That will do. All I need you to do is prepare Erik. I will have to return quickly to Cyninges-tūn. We have much to do. You will have less than a month to prepare for any attack. And remember they have had spies. They knew how Sigtrygg and his men defended their stad. Change your routines and passwords and be wary of all strangers. Better to be inhospitable than to die by a knife in the night. Find some time to speak with Erik. You are both captains."

Haaken said, "You know what you do, Jarl Dragonheart? Snorri's hair is testament to the horror of the cave. You would go down that hole and beard the Norn?"

"I would but I ask no man to come with me. When I face the beast, I will do so alone."

Haaken shook his head, "I have stood at your side since we were boys. I will not abandon you now."

"We will see. I may not survive this attack of the Skull Takers."

Olaf Leather Neck snorted, "I relish the attack of the Danes. Let them come and we will slaughter them. Facing a witch in her den? No. I have not courage enough for that."

We reached Cyninges-tūn by noon the next day. We had taken it slowly for we had many weary women and young children. Everyone wished to stay with us. My presence and my warriors made them feel safer. Word spread as we headed up the Water and by the time we reached the gates Brigid had organised food and shelter.

"Where is Kara?"

"She and Aiden have been in the steam hut since you left. I did not want to disturb them."

"Good for we shall need them with all of their powers. Sigtrygg and most of his warriors are dead. These are the only survivors. The Skull Takers are coming here."

Brigid gripped my arm, "Can you defeat them?"

"Time alone will tell but I hope so." I pointed to Gruffyd who was helping one of the women from the back of a horse. "Our son did well. He is a warrior."

"And that does not please me husband yet I know that we will need every warrior no matter what age they are."

Over the next seven days my people threw themselves into the work on our defences. While there was daylight they dug and they built. The new fighting platform was completed and stakes sharpened on both palisades. The new, staggered entrance was finished. It made entering the stad more difficult but we all knew it was a price worth paying. Fish and meat were salted and smoked. We had already begun to prepare for the hard times but we now did so with greater urgency. Bagsecg worked well into the darkness turning the metal we had taken from the Danes into arrow and spear heads. The ditches were seeded with spikes and filled with water. My Ulfheonar rode to my three stad to tell the jarls of Sigtrygg's fate. He had been a redoubtable warrior and his death was a warning for all. They passed the message that there were Danish spies in our land.

I also had a secret way made out of my stad. It went under the north wall. There the ground was higher and I had a gate made in the bank of the outer palisade. We disguised the entrance. This was not for escape, it was to allow my scouts and my Ulfheonar to leave unseen. When war came, there would be eight men guarding our secret passage.

Kara and Aiden had exhausted themselves in the steam hut but it had all been in vain. They had seen nothing. They knew of the disaster which had befallen Sigtrygg but only as a cry from the spirits of the dead. They had had no warning.

"We may have lost our powers, or some of them, at least. Perhaps Ylva had more power than we realised. You are right, father, this is all part of the Norn's web."

I shook my head. "You have lost confidence that is all. The loss of Ylva has sucked the spirit from you. I was the same when Wolf Killer died. You must keep working. Your powers will return and I hope that it is in time to save the clan."

It seemed I was beset by problems. We would have no warning of the Danes; at least not from Kara and Aiden. I needed to know their approach so that I could meet them sword to sword.

I now had the problem of finding another forty warriors. I was forced to the conclusion that it would have to be my farmers and those who lived in my settlement. The bondi would have to be our shield wall. I had Karl One Leg divide them into groups. Some would use bows while most would be trained to use spears. Those who had some skills already were given axes. The Danish shields we had taken and their helmets meant that we had well-armed men. The problem would come if they had to face hardened warriors inside my stad. We had to hold them outside.

On the eighth morning I sent out six of my Ulfheonar in pairs. They were sent to watch the approaches to our land. You cannot hide an army and it would take an army to defeat us. Their orders were clear. They were to watch and then report back. I wanted the enemy to be unaware that we knew of their approach. They had killed Sigtrygg's scouts and used that to destroy Sigtrygg. They knew of his passwords. We changed ours so that only my Ulfheonar and sentries knew them. They changed every three days. I wanted them to approach blind. I wanted them to seek out my scouts and not find them. All of the farms which lay on the Danish path were warned that they might have to flee quickly. I gave them horses to aid their flight. Most of the farmers sent their women to the settlement. They had the courage to stay and work their farms but they would not risk their wives, daughters and mothers. They worked but with a sword strapped to their waist.

It was Snorri who brought news of their approach. He and Rolf had been camped by the Grize Dale. They hurried back and told us of the approach of the Danes. "There is a large warband. There are a hundred and fifty or so warriors. We saw their approach and we scouted their camp. They have forty mailed warriors."

"Are there witches?"

"We saw none."

"Then go and find the other scouts and then trail them. I need to know where they are heading."

Haaken and Olaf Leather Neck joined me as we looked at the map I had made of my land. "I think they are coming here."

"It could be Windar's Mere." Haaken pointed a finger at the southern end of the Water. "Until they reach here they could be heading for Úlfarrston too!"

"I know. I want you to go to Raibeart. I want his warriors in the woods to the south of Torver. If the Danes head through the woods, then they can delay them while they send a messenger to me. If they come here, then he can follow them."

Olaf nodded, "And if it is Windar's Mere?"

"In many ways, I hope it is. Asbjorn has good defences and we can reinforce them from the Rye Dale and across the Hawks Head Ridge."

"But you believe it will be here."

"I do. They seek to hurt me here in my home."

We were on a war footing. My warriors all wore their mail from the moment they climbed from beneath their furs. Every man wore his helmet and strapped on a sword. Gone were the days when women went alone into the forests and woods to collect berries and mushrooms. Armed men escorted them. My fishing boats on the Water now collected not only fish but information. They watched for the sudden flight of birds which would tell them that men were moving through the woods.

My new entrance had a pair of towers. The base was made of stone but their tops were wooden. The climb, up the ladder, was not easy but when I reached the top I was more than ten paces above the ground. I spent much of each day there. Gruffyd and Ragnar would follow me. With the watchman as a fourth it was a tight fit but I could see almost to the farm of Torver. We had arrows ready stacked in each tower. The watchman was not a warrior but an archer. All of them were young and had sharper eyes than I.

"This waiting is hard, father."

I nodded, "A warrior needs patience. A battle lasts a heartbeat and ends with a sleep but a good warrior knows how to watch." I pointed to the eastern shore of the Water. "There my six scouts hide and eat dried meat and drink fell water. They suffer the rain and the cold but they do not move and when they spy our foes they will tell us."

Ragnar asked, "And if they suffer the same fate as Sigtrygg's scouts?"

"I hope that will not happen. Sigtrygg was taken unawares. Snorri and the others know the cunning of these Danes. Three of my scouts are the best that I have ever seen. They will survive and they will give us warning." I looked at Ragnar. He wore his new mail and his helmet hung from his pommel. He now looked like a warrior. "And your hearth-weru, they are ready?"

When we had last fought the Danes Gruffyd and Ragnar had become isolated. Einar the Tall and the hearth-weru had forgotten their duty in their eagerness to pursue the Danes. Luckily Ragnar and Gruffyd had emerged unscathed but I had berated Einar.

"My hearth-weru are ready, grandfather."

"And you Gruffyd, you will not stir from my side. You hold the banner of the wolf." With so few Ulfheonar left I had given the banner to my son and Leif the Banner would now fight in the shield wall. It would be a great responsibility for my son. A warrior who held a standard could not use a sword. His only defence was a shield.

He grinned. I had told him his new duties often. "Aye father. I stand behind the Ulfheonar. When you go forward so do I and I listen for your commands so that I may use the wolf to signal."

"It is not something to be taken lightly, Gruffyd. Men will watch for the signal and I will only give you the command once."

"I know. And I have two boys who are ready to stand by me."

Bagsecg had brought two young boys who were not quite old enough to become warriors but had shown some skills with a short sword. Edil and Leif were both keen to impress me. Armed with a sling as well as a small shield they would stand by Gruffyd to give him some protection. With just a leather helmet it would be a fiery introduction to war.

I had just descended to the ground when the sentry shouted, "Jarl, I see Beorn the Scout. He is heading across the Water."

I headed towards the Water and spied the fishing boat heading from the eastern shore. Our fishermen had instructions to watch out for our scouts as well as Danes. He was with Alf Jansson. I waited until they neared the beach and then they leapt ashore.

I said to the fisherman, Arne, who had brought them, "Have all the fishing boats drawn up on the beach and go into the stad. I fear Beorn brings ill news."

"Aye Jarl."

Beorn nodded, "You are right, Jarl." He came to the point. He pointed to the south. "Jarl they approach Torver. Snorri and the others watch them. They have spent the last few days searching the farms for those who lived there. They found none. They built traps to catch us but they did not. We told those who lived at the southern end of the Water to leave. Already they are heading up the road here."

"Will the Danes come here or go to Úlfarrston?"

He looked me in the eye, "They come here. Aðils Shape Shifter managed to get into their camp and he heard them speak." He shook his head, "Even Snorri could not do what he does. The Danes are not just Skull takers. There are other clans there with them. We saw clan of the bear and clan of the dog tokens. The leader of the warband is Ráðvarðr the Bald. He rules them with an iron hand. He had one who argued with him gutted like a fish and his body hung from a tree. Aðils heard him tell them that they had to be patient if they wished to take the stad." He paused and said, ominously, "They come for Ylva."

Ragnar said, "But she is not here!"

"They do not know that." I nodded. "This explains why the witches are not here. They wish to capture Ylva and then they will be complete once more. Perhaps the Norns have planned all of this to save Ylva." I saw my son and grandson take in the importance of Beorn's words. "Beorn you and Alf head back down the greenway on the western side of the Water."

"Aye."

"Gruffyd, go and summon the Ulfheonar. When you have done that have the men pour water on the far side of the ditch!"

"Aye Father."

"Ragnar, warn Karl One Leg that they are coming. Then ride with your hearth-weru. Fetch Asbjorn and his men."

I strode towards Kara and Aiden's hall. They both stood in the doorway. "They come here."

I was not surprised that they knew. They could read our thoughts as easily as I could the weather. "Aye and they come for Ylva."

I saw in their faces that they had not expected that. "Then the Norns took her for protection!"

"Perhaps but when this is over I still go to fetch her back."

"No, father, you cannot! She is too powerful. Ylva lives and has been saved. This is all *wyrd*."

"No daughter, that is not good enough. She is of my blood and I will fight any who tries to take her." I waved my hand as though to dispel the words which hung in the air. "There will be a time for that. There is no witch with these Danes. You must use your powers."

Aiden nodded for Kara had withdrawn into herself. "We will use our minds to confuse them. If there is no witch with them then they will be susceptible to deception. We will make a fog in their minds."

"Good. I intend to make them bleed upon my walls."

"They will try tricks as they did with Sigtrygg."

"And I have my own tricks already. Asbjorn will be here by nightfall and Raibeart and his men will follow behind the Danes. Their witches might have spotted such tricks but their warriors will not." I looked up at the Old Man. The sun shone on the eastern side and I could almost see old Olaf's face. "We have

Olaf to watch us this day." He would have approved of our actions. He had died defending his own hall on Man.

Chapter 6

Asbjorn and his men arrived after dark and entered the gates unseen for a fog had descended upon the Water. This was not of Aiden's doing. He smiled at me, "I think this is the work of the spirits who control this land. The Danes are unnatural. From what you told me they kill their own. The taking of skulls is not natural. They have made a mistake not bringing their witches with them. They have no protection from the earth. The Mother adds her protection to that which we have built."

"We need to be alert. Sigtrygg told me that they knew his passwords. They have spies in the land. Watch everyone."

I made sure that all ate well and that we had more sentries on the walls than normal. I had fires lit beyond our walls. They would not burn all night but they would light our ditches. With our scouts watching I knew they would not be able to hide close to our walls as they had done before.

I was in the tower before dawn. Wrapped against the cold I watched the light appear from the east. The last of the fires had died not long before I reached the towers. Even as I stood and watched, I sensed movement. I hissed, "Stand to!"

The words were passed down the wall so that the walls themselves seemed to speak. I peered at the land to the south. It was not pitch black. Gruffyd had good eyes, "It is Aðils and Beorn."

I saw my scouts appear. It meant only Snorri and Rolf remained at large. I said, "Open the gate." Turning I said, "You two stay here and watch."

As I reached the bottom of the ladder I saw the two boys, Edil and Leif, standing with my furled banner. They did not look nervous but were excited at the prospect of going to war. I waited with them as both sets of gates were hauled open. Beorn said simply, "They are in the woods beneath the Old Man. We waited until they camped before we came back. Snorri and Rolf watch them. They said they could do more harm outside the walls."

Aðils said, "We would have stayed with them but Snorri said we would be of more use in here."

"And so you will. Your bow, Aðils, can slay many more from my walls than in the woods where you could be hunted. Get food and then join me on the walls."

My Ulfheonar all joined me. There were two outside the walls but the rest were ready to do battle. Asbjorn and Karl One Leg were in attendance too. "They come. You know your places. Today we do not fight as the Ulfheonar, we fight as the men of Cyninges-tūn. I have spread you out so that there are captains amongst those for whom war is new. Today you are all leaders."

Haaken nodded, "The plan is unchanged? We hold them until they are weak and then sally forth?"

"Aye we let Snorri and Raibeart do their work in the woods and we hold them here." As they left to take their positions I said to Edil and Leif. "And now is the time for you two to take your place with Gruffyd. Watch my son. Today will see if you are worthy to become warriors of Cyninges-tūn."

"We will not let you down."

They climbed the ladder to the fighting platform above the gate. Olaf Leather Neck would be there with six men from the stad. I shouted up to them, "Gruffyd, Ragnar, take your places." I saw Haaken leading his thirty men to the outer palisade. It meant we had double the bows to thin them as they approached and they would have enough time to enter the gate if things went ill. Our new defences at the southern end allowed Olaf and his men to release their arrows and send their stones over the heads of Haaken and his men.

Gruffyd joined the two boys and Ragnar went to the other tower with his hearth-weru. I returned to my tower just as light began to spill from the east. I took one of the bows which stood in the corner and strung it. I turned to the sentry, Einar Siggison, "Let us see who can send an arrow the furthest, eh Einar?"

He was a farmer of thirty summers. His home nestled beneath Olaf's gaze. His wife and young son waited below. This would be the day when he defended them. He had sailed with me once but here his fight would be for his clan and family. I saw the determination in his eyes, "Aye jarl. They may destroy my farm but they will pay for that with their blood!"

A nervous air descended on my walls. We all peered to the west and the woods beneath Old Olaf. All now knew that the enemy were there. Kara and Aiden were in their hall making a fog in the minds of the Danes but we all knew that they would come.

When they came, it was almost noon. Three women and two children fled from the woods with two men behind. The men were armed and kept looking over their shoulders as though they were being pursued and then we saw them. The Danish warriors burst from the woods and were just two hundred paces behind them.

I heard Haaken shout, "Prepare to open the gate!"

"No!" I was not convinced that this was all that it appeared.

My voice made every head turn.

Einar peered at the refugees, "It is Thora and her family. They farm the valley on the far side of mine." I was about to shout, open the gates when Einar prepared an arrow. "But they are not her family! Those men are Danes!"

His arrow flew straight and true and pitched one of the men to the ground. I shouted to Aðils "The other man is a Dane!" His arrow struck the second Dane between the eyes. I cupped my hands and shouted, "Thora, take your family and board a boat! Sail across the Water!"

My clan were hardy and Thora waved to me as, like a mother hen, she shepherded the group towards the beach. They would have more chance to survive on the Water. The Danes were less than a hundred paces behind and if we had allowed them into the gates then they would have won.

Haaken shouted, "Release!"

Olaf shouted, "Release!" and fifty arrows soared into the air.

The Danes were ready and their shields came up but, even so, four warriors fell. I heard a command and the Danes formed a shield wall. Thora and her family would be able to reach the boats. The warriors had to halt. Even as they huddled beneath their shields Aðils sent an arrow on a flat trajectory to strike a mailed warrior in the face. My archers stopped releasing when the solid wall of shields surrounded the hundred men. It would be a waste of arrows. The Danes had a ditch or a bridge to cross. The bridge had been designed to take a horse and a man only. If more tried to cross, then it would break and they would find themselves in a wet, stake filled ditch.

I drew my sword and shouted, "Ráðvarðr the Bald, I know your name! You have no witches here to protect you but I have mine and the three of them will work their spells against you! You are all dead men walking!"

I knew that when a warrior relied on witches he was even more fearful of other witches. I wanted them to believe that Ylva was still within our walls. His silence was eloquent. Their subterfuge had failed and the fog in his mind was evidence that there was magic at work.

"We do not take skulls but your heads will be spread across the land to warn all such as you of the perils of the Land of the Wolf!"

He answered that. I heard his guttural voice as he growled, "And I will have your head and your sword before the day is out. Your witches are weak and your numbers are small. We are the Skull Taker clan and this will be our new home! We will take your woman and give them real men!" I saw that his helmet had a red painted skull upon it and his shield had the same emblem painted on its leather covered front.

His men began chanting, "Skull Taker! Skull Taker!"

They began to edge towards the ditch. I saw some of the famers, metal workers and miners looking up at me for orders. I heard Olaf snarl, "Watch the Danes not the jarl. The time is not yet right to hurt them!"

He was right. They had overlapping shields and spears protruded. Our stones and arrows could not harm them…yet. We could have used stone throwers if we had had them but other than that there was nothing which could damage them. Our inaction appeared to encourage them. They moved a little faster. They were heading for the bridge. I heard orders shouted and they started to change to a wedge. That was a tricky manoeuvre at the best of times but being so close to the ditch meant that, inevitably, three or four slipped. Two plunged into the ditch where they screamed as stakes tore into them. The other two were pierced by arrows and they lay dead. It forced the rest to become even tighter.

As they headed towards the bridge I readied my bow. The Danes were forced into a column just four warriors wide. They could not cover their bodies as well and arrows struck arms and legs. They were tough men and they did not fall. The first four rows had mounted the bridge and all were mailed when there was a creak and then a crack as the bridge broke. The leading warriors fell into the stake filled ditch. My arrow struck a warrior in the neck as others were hit by many arrows. The ones behind also slipped and fell towards the water. From the woods I heard a horn and the Danes formed their shield wall again and began to back towards the woods. Some of the wounded from the ditch tried to clamber out to join them. Arrows sprouted from their backs. By the time the Danes had reached the safety of the woods they had left over thirty men on the field. Some, in the ditch, were not dead. We did not end their suffering. Their moans and cries would hurt their comrades. They would die, eventually.

We could not leave by our main gate; not, at least, until we had made a new one. The bodies which remained in the ditch would enable them to cross over; if their chief could rally them. We had hurt them but we had yet to defeat them. We had not suffered a single wound.

I descended to the ground and sought out Kara and Aiden. They both looked tired, "You did well. You hid our intentions from them."

"Aye father but it took much from us. Without Ylva we have lost some of our power. If the four witches come…"

"Then we will deal with them. Do not despair. We have hurt them. Have Deidra and Macha organise the women to take food to those on the walls. I will not relax our guard."

Kara nodded, "Elfrida has already begun to organise that. She said she could not sit around doing nothing while her son stood a watch."

I went all the way around my walls. I feared an attack from the rear. It would not be an easy approach for an enemy; the ground was both high and rough but if they were desperate then who knew? The defenders there had heard the cries of battle but seen nothing. "What happened jarl? We heard the cries."

"They lost many men and broke the bridge. They will have to find another way over."

By the time I reached the main gate again it was past noon. Olaf shouted down. "We have seen movement but they have not shown their faces."

I nodded, "Food is coming. Have one man in two relieved to eat and to drink. If they need to make water, then use the ditch."

Olaf laughed, "They will enjoy that! It will annoy those in the woods if they see us pissing on their dead!"

I went to the lower palisade to join Haaken. He had laid his helmet down and was tearing pieces of bread and smearing them with runny sheep's cheese. "They will not come until dark."

"You have the second sight now?"

He laughed, "I do not need it. They showed when they attacked Sigtrygg that they are cunning. Our arrows cannot hurt them at night for we cannot see them. We cannot light the fires for we have no means of crossing the ditch. Listen."

I cupped my ear. I could hear the sound of wood striking timber, "They are making a ram or bridges."

"Aye. They will come tonight."

"Then Snorri and Raibeart will give them a surprise." I shouted. "One man in two rest. For those who watch use your ears as well as your eyes."

"And make sure you eat too, Dragonheart."

I took his advice and went to my hall. Brigid was feeding Myfanwy. My daughter had just begun solid food although the porridge she was playing with was not what I called solid food. Brigid looked concerned, "Well?"

"They came and we slew many. None of ours was hurt."

"Thank God for that." I smiled. I did not think her god would help pagans. "Is it over?"

"They will come tonight. Do not fear they will not cross our walls."

"And our son?"

"He is unhurt." I hesitated. I had not told her the full story of his blooding. "He is a warrior. He killed Danes when we went to Sigtrygg's stad."

"But he is a boy!"

"No, my love, boys are the ones who cannot stand alone. When a Viking boy stands on his own two feet then he is half way to becoming a warrior. Our son will soon be a man!"

I ate and after speaking with as many of my people as I could, returned to the wall as darkness was falling. The forest had grown silent. They had cut what they needed. We had killed many but their leader must have had enough men for him to be confident. This would be a test of my clan. I was just grateful for the sprinkling of Ulfheonar who would hold together the bondi who had yet to face such a foe. Olaf Leather Neck had gone around and issued javelins and spears. When we saw the Danes, they would be close. A bow was not the weapon to use.

Aðils came to me, "Jarl I can be more use beyond the walls. I am like Snorri. They will not see me. Trust me."

I knew that he was right. I nodded. "Use the secret passage at the north end."

"Aye Jarl. When you hear the cries, it will not be me!"

He was a young warrior but I had the utmost faith in him. As night fell I stared into the dark. They would come. The clouds made the night blacker than ever. I listened but I heard nothing. I knew that my hearing was not what it had been and I hoped that the young warriors would hear the enemy. Suddenly the night was riven with a scream. A heartbeat later and there was a second. I did not know which of my men it was but they were making life difficult for the Danes. This was the world of Snorri and Aðils. Even Raibeart was familiar with the forests. The Danes were not. The shouts, screams and movement continued for some time and then went silent.

Einar had returned to duty having eaten. He asked, quietly, "Are those our men. Jarl?"

"They are."

"Why is it now silent? Have they fallen?"

Einar had been on one voyage and had not fought on land. I shook my head, "No Einar they have withdrawn. They are pulling Danes away from our walls. They will take them deeper into the forest hunting them. They know not that it is they who are being hunted."

As if to prove my point there was a distant cry.

"So, the Danes will flee?"

"I do not think so. They serve witches who do not take failure well. This will merely make them keener to get to grips with us. We are an easier enemy than the warriors in the woods. You can face a man you can see but the knife in the night is terrifying."

Ragnar whistled from my right. I peered into the dark. I thought I saw movement but I could not be sure. "Stand to!" I did not shout it but it was passed on from warrior to warrior. I heard the sound of warriors ascending ladders to retake their places on the wall. I hefted my javelin. This would not be sword work.

I heard Haaken, three paces beneath me say, "Be ready to strike at anything which moves. We have spears aplenty!"

Haaken and his men at the lower palisade would be the first to come into contact with our enemy. The silence of the night was broken by the sound of an arrow and a scream as one of Haaken's sentries was slain.

"Shields!" They had been complacent and a warrior had paid with his life. I held my shield before me. They knew where our palisade stood and they could send arrows towards us. More arrows thudded into the walls or shields. Some soared over us. I saw Haaken raise his spear and hurl it. There was a shout in the dark. They were close.

A figure appeared below me on the fighting platform next to Olaf Leather Neck. I saw a glow and realised that it was Aiden. He handed something to Olaf who whirled it around his head. The black of night became daylight as the pot of oil shattered and fire spilled out. I saw the Danes. They were laying logs across the ditch. The light took them by surprise. They held logs and not shields. My men took their chances and hurled spears at them. The slingers sent lead balls in their direction. One of the Danes was quick thinking and threw his cloak over the fire but by then we had slain ten and we knew where they were.

Aiden handed another pot to Olaf and he threw it further to his left. As the light illuminated our attackers I saw that they were close to the outer palisade. I threw my javelin at the head of the warrior who was trying to pull himself over the top of the sharpened stakes. I missed his head but pinned his hand to the stakes. Before he could free it, a slinger had slung a stone and it cracked into his head. He hung there by his pinned hand.

The Danes threw one of their dead on the burning oil and darkness enveloped us. I knew we would have to withdraw from the outer palisade soon. There were not enough men manning the wall. I handed my spear to Einar. "Keep them at bay!"

I descended, "Ragnar, fetch your hearth-weru." As they appeared next to me I shouted, "Gruffyd, tell Haaken to abandon the outer wall." Turning to Einar the Tall I said, "We open the gate and hold it for Haaken and his men."

"Aye Jarl." Two of the hearth-weru lifted the bars on the gate.

I stood flanked by Ragnar and Einar. I heard Haaken's voice as he ordered them to fall back. We were aided by the fact that the gate which led outside was thirty paces to our right. When the Danes came through they would be disorientated. My men knew where to run and they did.

I saw a flash of light as Olaf threw another pot. Screams and shouts told me that my men had deterred the enemy. The first of my men from the walls poured past us. The three of us held our shields before us as the other hearth-weru held their shields above our heads. The outer gate burst open and the Danes ran over the bridge. Like the outer one it was not intended to take a great deal of weight. I held my shield out to block the blow from the first Dane across and rammed my sword into his middle. As he fell back Einar brought his sword sideways across the neck of a second and Ragnar cleverly dropped to one knee to hack across the leg of a third. The three bodies fell backwards as more Danes tried to cross. The bridge cracked and split asunder with the sudden weight. This ditch was dry but was filled with stakes. As Danes spilled over from both sides even their mail could not stop them being pierced.

As Haaken passed me he shouted, "I am the last. Only the dead remain!"

Olaf's voice sounded above me, "Jarl! Stand clear and close the gate!"

We stepped backwards as one. I saw Danes massing to race across the bridge of bodies. As we stood in the gate Olaf and Aiden hurled two pots of burning oil. They struck the bodies and flared up making an impenetrable barrier. The heat made me flinch.

"Close the gates!"

I sheathed my sword and clambered up the ladder. As I reached the top my nose was assaulted by the smell of burning hair and flesh and my ears by the screams of men being burned alive. Olaf and his men were now hurling more and more pots of burning oil. Even as I watched the Danes were being forced back.

It proved too much. Their best warriors were now dead and the rest fled back into the dark. We had beaten them off again but at a cost. I looked down and saw Haaken having his arm bound. "How many?"

"We lost ten of our men, jarl."

We had won the exchange but we had fewer men to lose. As the last of the burning Danes died I heard cries from the woods. Raibeart, Snorri and Aðils had resumed their work. We waited until dawn for the Danes to return. They did not. It was not a bright dawn. The sky was grey. The acrid smoke from the dead hung in the air. As we watched the light brighten the walls I saw my own dead. Fewer than the Danish dead they lay on the fighting platform of the lower palisade testament to their courage. The outer wall had done its job, as had they. It was harder to estimate the Danish dead for the bodies lay contorted and blackened in the ditch and across the bridge.

I saw a movement from the woods. "Stand to!"

Then Gruffyd shouted, "It is Snorri! It is our men, father!" It meant we had won and the enemy had fled.

While our dead were cleared, I had another bridge thrown over the ditches. I had horses readied for us to pursue the Danes. "Einar, do not forget Thora and her family. Fetch them over."

"Aye Jarl."

I saw that Snorri had a wound. His arm was bloody. As soon as I could I crossed to him. "Is it serious?"

"No Jarl but I did not wish to hold them up. Raibeart is leading the pursuit. There are many dead Danes in the forests."

"You did well. Your terror of the night must have torn the heart from them."

"It did. Aðils Shape Shifter is a terrifying warrior. I can hide but he is invisible. I fear I am no longer the scout I was."

"You have proved your worth again this night. Go to Aiden and have your wound bound."

Gruffyd brought my horse and I mounted. I led my Ulfheonar and Asbjorn's men. We headed down the Water. The Danes would flee home and that was east. We would find them. This was a hunt but a hunt of men. We rode down the Water quickly and used our road. When we reached the bottom end then we spread out in a wide line. The Danes would make for Grize's Dale. The tangle of trees and bushes there was a breeding ground for biting insects of all kinds. It took a determined man to concentrate on anything when they began to bite.

I held a spear loosely at my side. It was not easy hunting from the back of a horse but the spear would give me the advantage over any fleeing Dane. Our pursuit was not purely vengeful. The more we slew the fewer would return. Aiden's fire had taken the heart from them but their leader remained. I wanted him.

I heard a shout from my left. One had been caught. I heard his screams as my men ended his life. I kept riding with Haaken beside me. Gruffyd and Ragnar were behind. As we headed up the rise towards the wood I caught the glint of a helmet. The sun was in the west and illuminated this eastern ridge. I kicked my horse in the ridge and he began to gallop. I am a good rider and I used my knees as well as my left hand to guide the horse towards the glint of metal. As soon as the Dane began to climb the ridge he slowed. He also made the mistake of turning. As he did he slipped. His leg caught on a sapling as he fell and twisted him around. I hurled my spear from six paces and pinioned him to the earth. I slowed my horse and, twisting the spear, withdrew it. A tangle of entrails erupted with the head. I continued up the slope.

I now heard more cries to my left and right as my men found Danes. They had not stayed together or those that we followed had not done so.

Snorri was close by and he shouted, "I see their trail, Jarl. Many of them are heading for Satter's Waite."

I nodded and turned my horse to the left. It made sense. The moor and fell to the south of us was open and desolate. They would be spotted. They must have come this way and knew of the abandoned farm which had belonged to Satter and his family. The ground had been cleared around the farm and it would make easier going. They would also have the refuge of the farm. They had run a long way and they would be exhausted. My men followed me although they still maintained their line. The occasional cry and shout told me when an enemy had died.

A band waited for us at Satter's Waite. I reined in for they had a shield wall. I dismounted and tied my horse to a tree. This would need men on foot. As my warriors joined me I counted them. I saw that there were no more than thirty of them. The front rank had men wearing mail. I could not see the chief, Ráðvarðr the Bald, who had led them. There was no helmet with a red painted skull but there were three warriors who had a similar design upon their shield.

As I waited I shouted, "Where is Ráðvarðr the Bald? I will fight him now, man to man!"

A voice shouted, "He waits for you in Valhalla! He will pay you pay for the dishonourable way you fought! He thought you had honour but you do not. You fight from behind walls and use fire! You are not a man! You are a nithing!"

I heard my men growling behind me. I held up my hand, "I do not bandy words with a snake who takes skulls. I am Jarl Dragonheart and I wield the sword that was touched by the gods. You will all die this day!"

My men were already forming up on me. I heard Haaken say, "Ragnar, Gruffyd, stay in the second rank. This is work for Ulfheonar!"

The Dane was brave and he shouted back, "We all die, Ulfheonar! We will take some of you with us. Our Jarl is dead and we are oathsworn."

Haaken could not resist a jibe despite my instructions for silence, "Is that why you ran, Dane? If you had been oathsworn then your bodies would lie with Ráðvarðr the Bald!"

"Enough!"

Haaken ignored me and began banging his shield. My men took up the chant. I lifted my spear and we marched in time to the chant. It was like the drum of doom beating the time to the Dane's death.

Ulfheonar, warriors strong
Ulfheonar, warriors brave
Ulfheonar, fierce as the wolf
Ulfheonar, hides in plain sight
Ulfheonar, Dragon Heart's wolves
Ulfheonar, serving the sword
Ulfheonar, Dragon Heart's wolves
Ulfheonar, serving the sword
Ulfheonar, warriors strong

Ulfheonar, warriors brave
Ulfheonar, fierce as the wolf
Ulfheonar, hides in plain sight
Ulfheonar, Dragon Heart's wolves
Ulfheonar, serving the sword
Ulfheonar, Dragon Heart's wolves
Ulfheonar, serving the sword

They had no archers and so the men in the second rank did not need to cover us with their shields. The spears of Ragnar and Gruffyd rested on my shoulders. I headed for the three warriors with the red skulls upon their shields. Their spears were shattered but they held swords and axes. Behind their helmets I saw eyes that held no fear. They knew that death was coming and they were prepared to die. That made them a dangerous enemy. I determined to strike swiftly and true.

I held my spear overhand. I was taller than the Dane and I would use my height to my advantage. As we closed with them we all punched our shields on the word '*sword*'. The Dane struck with his own sword at the same time and shield and sword clattered together. I stabbed down with my spear at the same moment. There was a gap between his byrnie and his helmet. My spear found it. His shield was slow to rise and the spear head hit an artery. The blood spurted like a fountain in Miklagård! It sprayed to the side. The Dane who was showered with the blood could not see and Haaken's spear was rammed so hard into the Skull Taker's head that it smashed out of the back. With the two men dead Haaken and I stepped through the gap.

As I had expected those in the second rank had no mail. A huge Dane in the second rank had no time to bring his sword up but he tried to head butt me. He was the same height but I managed to bring up my shield. His face struck the boss of my shield. I was too close to use my spear and so, while he was stunned, I brought my knee up hard between his legs. He shouted in pain and lost his balance. As he fell back into the next man I thrust my spear into him. I stabbed too hard and my spear head stuck in the ground. I drew my sword. Even as I was drawing it a Dane saw his chance and a sword swung towards my right side. Two spears from behind struck him at the same time. As he fell I glanced behind and saw that my son and grandson had saved my life.

It was the last act for the Danes lay dead or dying. Two of Asbjorn's men were also dead but my Ulfheonar all lived. "Asbjorn, take your men and pursue them to the borders of our land. Then return to your stad. We will send your share of the treasure."

"Aye jarl. We will take our dead with us and bury them with honour by the Mere." He nodded toward their cloak covered bodies. "They were new warriors but they died well. I have much to do to train my men for war."

"They did well."

"Is this over, Jarl?"

"No Asbjorn the Strong; they will come again. They seek Ylva as do we. Be on your guard and continue to make your home as strong as you can. You saw that mine was not as strong as it should have been. We have more work to do."

"Aye jarl!"

We stripped the bodies of their mail, weapons and helmets. Some had treasure with them. Then we piled their bodies in the ruins of Satter's home and burned them. Satter had been a good warrior and he would have understood. We did not want carrion to grow bold having tasted human flesh. Besides which the last shield wall had fought well. They had earned the right.

Part Two

Chapter 7

Ylva

As we rode back I spoke of our defences to Haaken. "The ditches worked but we lost the wall."

He nodded, "We did not have enough men. We were just lucky that they did not try to attack at more than one place."

"We cannot make men, Haaken."

"No but we could use more boys and old men on the upper fighting platform. They could use bows and stones. And we could make the sides of the palisades slicker. They were able to clamber up too easily. The offset gate helped."

I lowered my voice. "Next time they will bring the whole clan and the witches. We have beaten off two smaller bands. It has cost them dear. They will either give up or bring everyone in the clan to defeat us. Ráðvarðr the Bald said that they wished to take our land. You have been to Loidis; it is a harsh land. This would seem like paradise by comparison. And they have brought other clans too. The witches draw warriors as does the promise of this golden land. The Skull Takers come for Ylva but the other Danes come for our land."

"And you still intend to go for Ylva?"

"I do. I will just take the Ulfheonar and Ragnar's hearth-weru. We need not go to war but I would have protection for my drekar."

"And Kara and Aiden?"

"I leave them here." He cocked his head to look at my face. "They are under the sway of this witch and I am not. They would be a distraction at best and at worst might side with the witch. They can stay here. The Land of the Wolf still needs watching."

The smoke we saw spiralling into the sky as we headed up through the late afternoon showed us that the bodies of the dead Danes were already being burned. Bagsecg and Scanlan had begun work on the repairs to our walls. They needed no orders from me. The corpses of the Danes were terrifying, even in death. Their limed hair hung with animal skulls, painted faces and filed teeth showed my people that we were facing our most terrifying foe.

Scanlan said, "Jarl I thought to have the bridge retract up to the walls. It will add to the defence of the gate and stop them crossing."

"They could cut the ropes."

Bagsecg shook his head, "I will use the poor mail and weapons to make two chains. They will not cut through that."

"Good."

Bagsecg said, quietly, "Is it over?"

"For a time, yes. The survivors will reach Loidis and their witches and this Baggi Skull Splitter will realise that they have neither Ylva nor my head. They will return again but they will need time to recover. I will sail south and recover my granddaughter."

Both looked shocked, "But she has been taken by a witch!"

"I know, Bagsecg. If she was yours would you worry who held her?" He shook his head, "I would face a dragon to fetch her home."

"You are a brave man."

"No Scanlan, I am a father and a grandfather. There is nothing more important to me than my family."

I went, with my son and grandson, to the Water. This was a ritual now. We shed our armour, padded byrnie and kyrtle and then we immersed ourselves in the Water. I squatted down beneath its surface and opened my eyes to peer into the chilly icy water. I had, occasionally, seen the spirit of my dead wife, Erika, but this time I saw just the stones on the bottom. I did not worry. It calmed me to be there and know that her spirit was close by. When I thought my lungs would burst I rose to the surface.

Ragnar shook his head, "How do you stay under so long?"

"Practice. When you are Ulfheonar you need many skills. Holding your breath under water is just one of them."

"Father, do we come with you when you go to bring back Ylva?"

I nodded, "I will need warriors who are not afraid. Ylva is family and I know that you will face whatever terror there is."

Gruffyd added, quietly, "And do we go into the cave?"

"I do not know. I will go and I will decide who accompanies me, if any, while I am there."

Ragnar said, "I would go with you, grandfather for I know that my father would. I will try to be my father for you."

"No, Ragnar, a warrior should be himself. You can never be someone else. Your father was never me and I am certainly not my own father. The gods want us to be true to ourselves and our own nature."

Feeling refreshed we went into my hall where I would have the task of telling my wife what I intended. Surprisingly she seemed resigned to it. "She is of your blood. You cannot leave her there. I know she is not a Christian but she should not be with a witch."

Of all the people in my stad she was the one who did not believe in the power of witches. Even Macha and Deidra accepted that volva had powers but my wife was convinced they were tricks. She did not fear me facing a witch.

Kara and Aiden were less happy and they tried to persuade me to take them. "You had your chance and you left her with the witch."

"But you need us father! We have powers that you do not."

"No, Kara, your powers cannot defeat the witch. You sent Ylva there because you wished to gain power you could not give. It needs a warrior. I am not afraid. You forget that the blood of your grandmother came directly to me. I will descend into the bowels of the earth and I will find my granddaughter."

"She may not wish to return!"

"Then I must persuade her." I was resolved. I did not know how I would bring her back but I was Ulfheonar and I would find a way.

I waited only until my Ulfheonar had said goodbye to their families and word had reached me that Erik Short Toe had the drekar prepared for sea. Brigid was more concerned about our son. Elfrida, too, shed tears. Kara and Aiden gave them both charms to ward off the power of the witch. They would not work; the witch was all powerful. Magic could not defeat her.

As we headed out to sea, on the evening tide, I wondered if I would ever see my home again. I was not afraid of the witch. I was not even afraid of failure for if I failed then I would be dead. My fear was of leaving Ylva in the witch's clutches. With so few warriors even my son and grandson had to take an oar. I smiled as I saw them straining to keep up with the Ulfheonar. They would not have to row for long for Erik knew the currents and the winds better than any. My crew rowed until we could catch a favourable wind.

Even though they did not row far their hands were raw when they had finished. Snorri took pity on them and used some of Aiden's salve to ease the pain. I stood by the steering board with Raibeart, Haaken and Erik.

"I know the sea where the isle should be, Jarl Dragonheart. Like Raibeart I know the rough position but I am not sure that it will be there when we reach it."

I nodded, "I have thought about that. The island is always there. It is just that it remains hidden from us. I have a plan to find it so long as the two of you can place us where it should be."

I had them puzzled but I had delved deep into my dream. I thought I saw a way. Only time would tell.

The winds were in our favour but they were not strong winds. It took all night to reach the isle of Mona. As dawn broke we passed the western cliffs. The Saxons who lived there now saw us as we sailed by. They could not harm us. We beat towards the island of the puffins and passed that by the middle of the afternoon. We sailed on into the dark but pulled in close to the hour of midnight into a small bay on the north coast of Wessex in the land which had been Corn Walum until Egbert had captured it.

"Why have we pulled in, Father? Is this not the land of Egbert?"

"It is, Gruffyd, but the coast is treacherous south of here. It would be too much of a risk to sail the ship in the dark. Better we try it in daylight. Syllingar is but a good day's sailing from here."

However, when we woke there was a thick fog lying all around the drekar. We dared not move. I saw some of my Ulfheonar looking worried. "What is the matter, Karl Karlsson? Have you never seen fog before?"

"Aye Jarl but this came up so suddenly that it looks like a Norns' web!"

"Perhaps it is. Can we do anything about that? Perhaps turn back?"

"I did not mean that, Jarl."

Haaken said, "It delays us that is all, Karl." My oldest friend was as determined as I was to see this through to its bitter end no matter what obstacles the Norns put in our way.

We prepared to sail although as there was no breeze we would have to row. Suddenly the fog lifted as thought a giant had swallowed the grey mist. There was bright sunshine. As Erik gave orders for the crew to row I spotted a huddle of horsemen on the cliff top. We had been seen. They were the men of Wessex. I recognised their banner. If they had seen us sooner, then we might have had trouble. I felt happy that we were away and we headed for the dangerous tip of land which marked the end of Britannia.

The men sang as they rowed for there was still not a breath of breeze. They sang Finni's song. His death was still fresh in our mind and we would do him honour.

The Danes they came in dark of night
They slew Harland without a fight
Babies children all were slain
Mothers and daughters split in twain
Viking enemy, taking heads
Viking warriors fighting back
Viking enemy, taking heads
Viking warriors fighting back
Across the land the Ulfheonar trekked
Finding a land by Danes' hands wrecked

Ready to die to kill this Dane
Dragonheart was Eggles' bane
Viking enemy, taking heads
Viking warriors fighting back
Viking enemy, taking heads
Viking warriors fighting back
With boys as men the ships were fired
Warriors had these heroes sired
Then Ulfheonar fought their foe
Slaying all in the drekar's glow
Viking enemy, taking heads
Viking warriors fighting back
Viking enemy, taking heads
Viking warriors fighting back
When the Danes were broke, their leader fled
Leaving his army lying dead
He sailed away to hide and plot
Dragonheart's fury was red hot
Viking enemy, taking heads
Viking warriors fighting back
Viking enemy, taking heads
Viking warriors fighting back
Then sailed the men of Cyninges-tūn
Sailing from the setting sun
They caught the Skull upon the sea
Beneath the church of Hwitebi
Viking enemy, taking heads
Viking warriors fighting back
Viking enemy, taking heads
Viking warriors fighting back
Heroes all they fought the Dane
But Finni the Dreamer, he was slain
Then full of fury their blood it boiled
Through blood and bodies the warriors toiled
With one swift blow the skull was killed
With bodies and ships the Esk was filled
Viking enemy, taking heads
Viking warriors fighting back
Viking enemy, taking heads
Viking warriors fighting back

It was late afternoon when we finally found a wind and the exhausted crew were able to ship oars. I went to the dragon prow to stare out at the grey sea which stretched to the horizon. Somewhere out there was an island and now we had to find it. We spent the last hours of daylight seeking the mysterious isle. As darkness fell we furled the sail and dropped an anchor. We had searched but not found it. There were islands and there were rocks. They were dotted all around but none was the island we sought.

We ate cold rations and slept on the deck while we waited for dawn. We awoke to a grey day; a dank day. Once again the crew had to row. I stood with Raibeart at the prow.

"I am sorry Jarl. I have let you down. I have not found the island. I am certain it was close to this part of the ocean."

"You have nothing to apologise for. I did not think it would be easy. We will find it."

Raibeart pointed ahead, "Not today, jarl. Look at that fog bank!"

I heard Erik Short Toe shout, "Ship oars."

As I peered ahead I remembered my dream. I was seeing that which I had seen in my dream. I sniffed. I turned and shouted, "Aðils!"

Aðils Shape Shifter hurried next to me. "Yes Jarl?"

"I need your nose."

Haaken and Ragnar, along with Gruffyd, had followed my youngest Ulfheonar. Haaken asked, "His nose?"

"What can you smell?"

I could see that he was confused but he was obedient and he stood up and, closing his eyes, sniffed. "I smell the resin of the prow." He sniffed again, "The sea and seaweed." He turned and opened his eyes. "What am I supposed to smell, Jarl?"

"Just tell me what you smell."

He shrugged and turned back, "The sea." There was silence. I could almost hear my men's breath. Then suddenly he said, "Smoke! I smell smoke!" He pointed to the steerboard side.

I turned and said, "Take your oars. Erik, to steerboard! Watch my hand!"

What we were about to do was madness. We were sailing in a fog in an ocean filled with submerged and semi submerged rocks yet Erik Short Toe did not hesitate. "Row! But row slowly!" His voice betrayed his fear.

The men hurried to their oars. I restrained Aðils, "Stay here and use your ears as well as your nose."

I could not smell the smoke but I had an old nose. There were too many conflicting smells. I listened and I remembered my dream. I heard only the sound of oars cutting through the water. Then Aðils Shape Shifter shouted, "I heard water breaking on the shore."

I clambered up and stood leaning over the dragon prow. I stared at the water rushing beneath us. I saw rocks ahead and I waved Erik to sail further to steerboard. Then I saw the white foam of water breaking on rocks. "Hold! Up oars!"

The oars came out of the water as one. *'Heart of the Dragon'* kept moving and then I felt a slight shudder as her keel ground on to sand. It was an alarming moment but then we stopped. There had been no tearing sound. The seas had not burst through our strakes. We were aground but we were aground on sand.

"Aðils, bring your bow and come with me." I shouted, "Haaken, take charge!" I jumped into the sea. The water came up to my waist. My young Ulfheonar joined me. He stood next to me. I think he feared this island which none had thought we would find. This was a witch and Aðils was young. "Which way?"

He sniffed again and pointed directly ahead. Our last sudden shift of direction had turned us further to steerboard. The water became shallower until it was only ankle deep. I waved my hand to slow my young companion down. As I did I turned. I could no longer see the drekar. This was magic. I had to trust that the ship had not disappeared. It was just that I could not see it. The spell was one meant to hide. As I stepped on to the sand I could smell the smoke although I could not see it. I knelt on the sand and picked up a handful. It was speckled with green and orange grains along with the occasional sparkle of a translucent white stone. It looked like the sand of Syllingar.

"Go back to the drekar and tell them that I have found the island."

"I cannot leave you, Jarl!"

"I order you to go! I will be safe. They will need your eyes to guide them back to me. Fetch Haaken and Beorn the Scout."

As he disappeared into the fog I felt suddenly alone. I drew my sword and took comfort from the feeling of power which surged through my body. "Allfather I need your help this day. I trust in your power. Help me to find my granddaughter and defeat this spirit." The witch might have her magic but I had the power of the sword. I clutched my amulets. I hoped that it would be enough to do what I planned. I seemed to be alone for an age and I fleetingly worried if Aðils Shape Shifter and my ship had disappeared. When I heard splashing and saw the grey shapes appear through the fog I knew that the Allfather had not deserted me. Ragnar and Gruffyd were with Haaken and Beorn, along with Ragnar's hearth-weru.

I shook my head, "You should have stayed on the drekar!"

Gruffyd said, defiantly, "We said we would help you father and so we shall."

"Follow me then. Haaken, stand by my side. You have been here before." I had not asked Snorri to come for I knew that this was a place of terror to him. Haaken had merely been afraid and not terrified.

We moved further up the beach. I could not see a path and so I picked a way through the rocks. We climbed. I was dimly aware that the fog appeared to be thinning. Haaken said, triumphantly, "The path! I have it!"

I looked down and saw a well-worn path. We made better time and the fog gradually dissipated so that by the time we had turned two more corners it had gone and I spied the cave ahead. I stopped. "We are here."

I turned to look back down the beach. I could make out the shore but the drekar was just a large shadow to the west. I took off my cloak. "I will enter the cave."

"We will come too."

"No Ragnar; you and my son will stay here. That is an order."

Haaken smiled, "Besides, boys, Jarl Dragonheart does not need you. Haaken One Eye will go with him."

I meant it. I was risking my life but Ylva was not Haaken's family. Would this be his doom as well as mine? "You do not need to!"

He nodded, "I know but I want to go. I have stood at your side since we were young warriors. I have never shirked my duty and I will not start now. If our journey is to end this day, then I would do it together. I would do it with a friend. I will watch your back when you face this witch. If I am to die, then this will make a good end." He grinned at Gruffyd, "You have a talent with words Gruffyd, son of the Dragonheart. If I am to die, then you will tell the tale and men will sing of it."

I shook my head, "Do not kill me just yet, Haaken One Eye." I clasped his arm. "Come then!" I turned to the others, "Farewell. We may not return quickly. Time stands still in this cave. When the fog clears have the men come ashore and set up camp." I clasped Ragnar's arm and then Gruffyd's. "You will both be great warriors. I believe I will return but if I do not then I leave my land and the clan in safe hands. May the Allfather be with you." I watched their faces fill with fear and I turned to head down into the cave.

I entered the black maw that was the cave. This was not like Myrddyn's cave. That had a wide entrance and a high roof. This one felt like you were descending into a tiny grave. It was hard to put one foot in front of the other but I somehow managed it. There was a glow but it was not as bright as it normally was. The smoke I could smell was old and it was dead. Perhaps they had gone. I had to watch my footing for the stones were slick. As I turned the corner I saw that the fire had not been doused. It was a soft red glow. I took a breath as I stepped around and peered into the dark.

Although I was expecting to see her I was taken aback when I saw the witch. She was now almost an emaciated skeleton. Behind her sat Ylva and her face was as a stone. She had changed. She looked like a woman now. The witch had even painted some cochineal on her lips. It stopped me. Even as I stepped around the corner the witch hurled a handful of something in the fire and the cave was filled with a red acrid smoke as the flames leapt into the air. I stared at her and saw hate fill her eyes. Her voice, when she spoke, seemed to not only fill the cave before me but behind me too. It was as though I was inside the witch.

"You are a brave warrior, Dragonheart! You are foolish but you are brave! You dare to come into the lair of a Norn and try to take from her that she has taken as her own."

"She is not yours! You have taken her by force and I am here to take her home."

"You will die as will your one-eyed friend who stands behind you, afraid to even move."

I spoke softly and looked beyond the witch to the statue like Ylva, "Ylva come back to me. Come back to the light." I closed my eyes and pictured my dead wife, Erika.

As I opened my eyes I saw the briefest flickers of light in Ylva's eyes and then the witch screamed. It was so loud that it hurt my ears. It sounded like the scream of a hunting bird as plunged to the kill. I saw her eyes turn red and grow. The smoke began to change colour to yellow and green. The emaciated skeleton grew before my eyes. Her nose appeared to become longer and the empty mouth filled with teeth. A smell of sulphur and pumice filled the cave. The witch was turning into a dragon. All that I could see were the red and yellow reptilian eyes which seemed to grow before my eyes.

"I will fight you, witch, even though it means my death."

The smoke was so thick now that I could barely see anything but I found it hard to breathe and the red and yellow eyes bore into me. I felt the heat of the dragon's breath. I suddenly remembered my sword. I forced my hand down to the hilt. Something stopped me from touching it.

"Ragnar! I need your help once more. I fight for my family and you are the only one who can help me." My words sounded thin and reedy in the cavernous smoke filled hall but I felt a new-found strength and my hand touched the hilt of my sword. As soon as my fingers touched it I felt as though I could breathe once more. As I drew it forth it seemed to glow both blue and cold in the smoky cave. "Ragnar's Spirit! This is the sword which was touched by the gods and born of blood and death! I defy you witch! My blade has never failed me and will not fail me now!"

The dragon's head seemed to grow and its mouth gaped wide. The smell was almost unbearable and I saw savage teeth coming for me. I knew that this was magic and yet it appeared real. That gave me hope. If the dragon was real, then I could fight it. I pulled back my arm and thrust it hard at the dragon's chest. My sword and my hand disappeared into the billowing smoke. My eyes filled with smoke and I could see nothing. Yet, amazingly, I felt my sword strike something and I pushed. I heard a primeval scream. I did not know if it came from me, the dragon or the witch. My arm became numb and pain coursed through my body. I forced my body to push my numbed arm forward. The scream grew so loud that I thought my head would burst and then all went black. Darkness enveloped me.

I was on the Dunum wading in the waters and looking for the salmon net. I saw the prow of a drekar as it nudged towards me out of the fog. Looking up I saw the helmet of a Dane and from his helmet hung a skull. It was the skull of a child. Hair still clung to the lower part. I turned to run but could not move. The warrior landed in the water and strode towards me.
As I turned I saw my mother. "That is my child! Touch him at your peril, Viking!" She was standing by the river bank and her hands were held out to me, "Come Garth! I will protect you! Trust in me and come."
I forced my legs through the water. My hand had almost touched my mother's fingers when there was a blow to my back and all went black once.

Chapter 8

"Jarl, come back! Dragonheart!"

I opened my eyes and saw, in the blackness of the cave, Haaken as he stood over me. "The dragon, where is the dragon?"

He shook his head. "I saw no dragon. You and the witch disappeared into the smoke. I heard you cry and the witch scream. I could not move. I tried to reach for my sword but my hand would not obey me. This was powerful magic. It has taken some time to find you."

I took his arm and pulled myself up. I could feel my right hand once more and I still held the sword. The cave was just black now. The smoke had gone and I saw nothing. Where the fire had been there was now just a darker patch of sand. I put the sword before me and a blue glow glistened on the edge of the blade. As I stepped towards the back of the cave I was alert for danger. Where was the witch? I felt Haaken's hand on my back as we edged deeper into the cave.

I heard Erika's voice in my ears. She was singing a lullaby. I stopped and peered into the dark. I saw nothing and the lullaby grew louder. I looked down and there, at my feet, lay Ylva. It was as though she was sleeping. I knelt next to her and put my ear to her mouth. She breathed.

"Haaken, pick up my granddaughter. Let us leave this pestilential hole."

I think Haaken was just grateful to be able to do something rather than just watching. He picked up the slight form of Ylva. I turned and headed back whence we had come. As the floor began to rise I knew that we were heading out of the cave and I sought the light that would guide me to the outside. It was just black. I determined that it must be night and I kept walking.

"Aðils! Ragnar!" My words bounced back from a wall of rock and my sword rang off stone as it clattered into the wall. The cave had been sealed and we were trapped. This was Myrddyn's cave all over again.

I turned, "There must be another way out. Stay close behind me."

"Aye Jarl. I thought my end would come in battle not trapped in a cave by a witch!"

"We are not dead yet. We are in a world of tricks and illusions. We are warriors and we can face anything so long as we are true. Ragnar's Spirit will protect us."

I stepped past him and walked back down towards the cave proper. I thought of the way Aðils Shape Shifter had found the island through ears and eyes. I was Ulfheonar. I would use the skills of the wolf. The memory of Myrddyn's cave came back to me and I remembered that Myrddyn's cave had gone further back than I had thought. Perhaps this one did too. I closed my eyes and used my other senses to guide me. My eyes would see just blackness. As I moved I felt air before me. The air was not as heavy and I moved in that direction. Haaken's hand kept contact with my back. Even as I moved into the cave I swung my sword before me. Even with my eyes closed I could sense the glow from its magical blade. It was reassuring. I wanted its protection against the witch. If she remained, then my blade would end her life. My senses told me that the roof was shelving and, just in time, I put my left hand up. "Bend, Haaken, the roof slopes."

Now I had the sense of touch as well as smell. I could smell the sea. The cave's roof kept getting lower and I wondered if it would reach the floor. I was bent almost double. Then the roof levelled out but it turned to the left and then the right. Although Haaken was carrying Ylva his left hand kept contact with my back. I wondered how long I could walk bent double. Then I realised that I could no longer smell smoke. More than that the air smelled strongly of the sea. The floor began to rise and, opening my eyes, I found that I was walking in sand. I could see my whole blade. I stopped and glanced behind me. I could see Haaken's face.

With renewed hope, I strode on and saw light from the end. It looked like the glow of a fire. Was this another trick of the witch? Had I walked in a complete circle? Then I heard voices. I pushed Ragnar's Spirit before me and strode towards the glow. I stepped out into the night. The cool air felt refreshing after the cave. To my right, by the sea, I saw the fire and in its light the faces of Ragnar and Gruffyd. Our trial had finished. We had escaped the witch's clutches.

"Father!"

Ragnar's hearth-weru leapt to their feet. Ragnar said, "You have Ylva!"

"Aye, where is the ship?"

"Moored yonder."

I turned, "Haaken, lay her down. Gruffyd, fetch water or ale."

As Haaken laid her down I saw that his hair had turned completely white. His eye looked huge in his whitened cheeks. He gave me a wan smile. "I have my saga jarl but have I the words to tell it?"

"We have not escaped her yet, Haaken." I pointed out to the water and the fog was creeping across the sea rising higher, even as we watched. "Einar the Tall go and tell Erik that we return. I would board as soon as we can."

Gruffyd was gently holding Ylva's head and dripping water into her mouth. He said sombrely, "She seems more dead than alive."

"We have taken her from the witch's clutches but she is not yet delivered from the spell nor have we found a way out of her domain."

Ragnar asked, "Will she die?"

Shaking my head, I replied as I sheathed my sword, "She is not of this world and she is not as we are. You cannot kill a Norn. I was lucky or perhaps chosen for she found a magic she could not defeat. The sword was well made by Bagsecg and was touched by the gods. The Allfather and Ragnar guided my hand and I defeated her. It drove her shadow hence. We have bought time."

I looked up as the prow of my drekar emerged through the rising mist. I reached down to help Haaken lift her. Gruffyd supported her head and we walked towards the sea. As we did I heard a wail from below the earth. It sounded as though the earth itself was being torn apart. The wail grew and I saw Ragnar's hearth-weru look around in terror and clutch at their amulets.

"Forget the noise. It is the Norn and she is angry. We must hurry. Help us carry my granddaughter to the drekar."

Eager hands waited to lift her aboard. As we were pulled up Olaf Leather Neck said, "It has been two days, Jarl, we thought you dead."

I clasped his arm as he helped me over the side of the drekar, "It was close Olaf but we are not done yet. We need to sail away from this island and reach the open sea."

"But we cannot see beyond our hands!"

He was right. He was close to me and his face was in a fog. I hurried to the steering board. "Erik, we must leave."

He waved a hand around him. "In this fog we will rip out the keel of the drekar, jarl. We should wait for it to go."

"It is not natural, Erik. This is supernatural. If we stay, then we are doomed to die here. We will trust our ship and hope that Bolli made her well. Aðils Shape Shifter, go to the prow and shout out directions."

"Jarl?"

"Use your nose and your ears. Feel with your heart. You have been chosen to be the one who sees through the mists. I know it in my heart."

I saw that he was unsure if he ought to believe me but he nodded resolutely. "Then I will do this."

Erik shouted, "Take your oars."

"Gruffyd, cover Ylva with a fur and hold her hands tightly." I took out my sword. "Put her hands on the hilt and hold them there. Let the power of the sword and the gods save her." I saw him hesitate, "You have some of the powers which Ylva inherited. They are not as great for you are a man but use them. Close your eyes and seek the spirits. Stay with your cousin." Ylva was only a year older than Gruffyd. They had played together as children and were close. I hoped that he could keep her safe until we reached the Land of the Wolf.

My crew all looked at me. I stood before them and smiled, "Today we go on a voyage none has undertaken before. We sail into the unknown. We are all the warriors of the wolf and we can face any enemy no matter what form they take."

Haaken nodded, "Aye, Jarl! We are the clan of the wolf and follow the Dragonheart!"

Erik shouted, "Back water!"

We slowly backed out of the bay. From the prow we heard, "Steerboard!"

Haaken shouted, "Stroke" and Erik moved the steering board. It seemed an age before we moved. There was silence from the bow.

Then Aðils' voice sounded, "Centreboard! Slowly!"

Haaken did not need to speak for my crew were as one and they all slowed. We edged into the fog. I tried to picture the water we had sailed into. I could not remember it. I hoped my newest scout could. I glanced down at Ylva. She had yet to open her eyes but there was a little more colour in her cheeks and she appeared to be breathing a little easier.

"Steerboard!"

I looked up. Were my eyes playing tricks? The fog was a little lighter or it appeared to be. I could see the mast. It seemed an age for we were moving slowly but we slowly emerged from the mist. At first the day was grey but, as we rowed slowly and carefully west, the sky brightened and then a breeze sprang up. It was from the north and east but Erik could still use the wind to rest the rowers. They were not exhausted but the tension of the past few days had taken their toll.

As the ship's boys took over the duties of lookout, Aðils Shape Shifter walked down the centreboard to the sound of hands banging in the deck and his name being called. That was the day he would never forget. He had been an Ulfheonar the shortest of times and yet he had already become a legend. He had guided a drekar through the fog and mist of a witch's spell. I could see Haaken already composing the verse in the saga of the dragon and the Dragonheart.

I knelt by Ylva. "How is she Gruffyd?"

He did not answer me at first and then he smiled. "I di das you asked, father. I held her hand and closed my eyes. I saw her and she was with a woman I did not recognise but who looked familiar. Feel her hand. It is warmer."

I did as he had asked and felt the blood in her hands. She was coming back to us. "That was your grandmother who came to her. You have done well."

Erik said, "This wind will aid us until we have to turn north, Jarl, and then we will need the men to row."

"Cnut Cnutson organize the food."

Haaken joined me as I sat next to Ylva. He said, quietly, "What happened, jarl? I saw the dragon and Ragnar's Spirit and then suddenly the dragon was gone. Where did the Norn go?"

"The dragon was an illusion. It was not real. It smelled and looked real but it was not. I called upon the power of the sword and the Allfather helped us. I think that my mother and my wife aided us by filling Ylva with their memories. As for the witch?" I shrugged. "She was like a spider. That was her nest and she had many ways in and out. We found a second one. There may have been a third."

Ragnar was thoughtful, "We have made an enemy of a Norn, grandfather. That cannot be good."

"Warriors make enemies all the time. We will fight them the way we fight any enemy. We will hold fast and fight together. The power of the clan will prevail." Ylva stirred a little. "But we need to get this little one home. Her healing is beyond us. That lies with her parents."

The men ate and drank and I held Ylva's tiny hands around the hilt of my sword. They seemed so delicate compared with my rough and gnarled warrior hands. How could we even be related? They felt cold but, as we sailed so they seemed to warm. I took a cloth and wiped the cochineal form her lips. I wanted my little girl back. The drekar seemed to be barely moving. I was aware of the passage of time by the warriors who passed me to make water at the steering board. I wondered if we were being held by some sort of spell.

Erik's voice brought me from my thoughts, "Take to the oars. We must come about and beat against the wind."

The men had been rested. "I will take a turn at the oars."

Gruffyd said, "You are Jarl!"

"And I can row. Stay here with your cousin and I will exorcise my own demons." I joined Ragnar. We had the two oars closest to the prow. When we were fully crewed, there could be up to three men on each oar. Now we were single oared. We could make headway with the sails even sailing so close to the wind but the oars were needed to give Erik more control over our direction.

I smiled at Ragnar, "Let me see if I can keep up with a young warrior such as you." I shouted, "Haaken One Eye, a good song!"

I heard him laugh, "Until I have composed my new one there can be but one."

The storm was wild and the gods did roam
The enemy closed on the Prince's home

89

Two warriors stood on a lonely tower
Watching, waiting for hour on hour.
The storm came hard and Odin spoke
With a lightning bolt the sword he smote
Ragnar's Spirit burned hot that night
It glowed, a beacon shiny and bright
The two they stood against the foe
They were alone, nowhere to go
They fought in blood on a darkened hill
Dragon Heart and Cnut will save us still
Dragon Heart, Cnut and the Ulfheonar
Dragon Heart, Cnut and the Ulfheonar
The storm was wild and the Gods did roam
The enemy closed on the Prince's home
Two warriors stood on a lonely tower
Watching, waiting for hour on hour.
The storm came hard and Odin spoke
With a lightning bolt the sword he smote
Ragnar's Spirit burned hot that night
It glowed, a beacon shiny and bright
The two they stood against the foe
They were alone, nowhere to go
They fought in blood on a darkened hill
Dragon Heart and Cnut will save us still
Dragon Heart, Cnut and the Ulfheonar
Dragon Heart, Cnut and the Ulfheonar
And now the sword has fought the Norn
By a Viking Jarl but Saxon born
His sword was strong and his heart was true
Sent away by Ulfheonar two
The Jarl and Haaken will save us still
The Jarl and Haaken and the Ulfheonar
The Jarl and Haaken and the Ulfheonar

It was the saga of the sword save that Haaken had added two extra lines. I heard Olaf laugh as Haaken sang the last refrain alone. "I see you put yourself in this one, Haaken One Eye!"

"And why not? It was just the two of us in that black hole!"

The song helped us and after four more renditions we were all familiar with it. I saw that Ragnar was grinning even though his hands were red raw. "Why are you happy? Your hands must be giving you great pain."

He shook his head, "I feel no pain. I rowed with the Ulfheonar. These men would die for you, grandfather. That speaks well of you. Einar and the others would have died for my father. I now see what I must do to earn such loyalty and

90

I relish the opportunity. Thank you for allowing me to accompany you. I know I am honoured."

"Wait until we see Úlfarrston before you are so grateful."

I watched the coast of Corn Walum as it slipped slowly by. Erik was keeping us close to the coast so that the wind did not take us further west. This was the shortest route. When we struck the Sabrina, he would be able to turn to larboard and the wind would aid us once more.

It was as we were passing the bay where we had sheltered when Guthrum Arneson shouted, "Ships to steerboard! They are Saxons! They have the wind!"

I suddenly remembered the watchers on the cliff when we had left the bay. My ship was well known and Egbert would love the chance to get his hands upon me and my ship. Was this the work of the Norns? I had thought we were lucky to escape the bay when we had headed south. Now I was not so sure.

Erik Short Toe shouted, "Olaf Leather Neck, up the beat!"

This time there was no song. Olaf was the strongest of the crew and I watched his mighty shoulders as he pulled on his oar. We all had to keep pace with him. I turned to Ragnar. "When you can row no longer then tell me. We have to lift our oars together else we will lose way."

He shook his head, "I will row as long as the others!"

"You have not the strength. A good warrior knows his own limitations. Your pride is not what concerns me. It is the drekar and the crew. There is no shame in not being able to row as long as Ulfheonar."

In truth, I needed to be at the steering board. Erik was a good captain but he was not a tactician. I needed to see the Saxon ships and try to outwit their captains. I could not see them but I knew what kind of ships they used. They relied more on sail than we did. They would be aided by the fact that the wind was coming directly from behind them. They had the wind gauge and could surround us. They would be fully crewed and we had half a crew. Even so Olaf's spurt made us fly and the fact that Erik turned us to sail north and west meant that the sail billowed full.

I watched as Ragnar's strokes became slower. Soon he would catch Alf Jansson's oar. "Now Ragnar, up oar!" He looked at me. "That is an order. One, two, three!" On three we lifted them. "Good. Now lay them down the centre board and then don your helmet. Soon we go to war."

I walked down the centreboard. I saw that my men were tiring. Ragnar's hearth-weru were almost done in. They did not have the levels of fitness the Ulfheonar did. I went to the steering board. Erik nodded to the crew, "They are tiring, Jarl."

"I know. They can either row or fight. They cannot do both and if they row to exhaustion then the enemy will catch us. Where are they?"

He pointed to steerboard. They were a couple of thousand paces from us. The sea swell hid them and then revealed them. They are half the length of our drekar but were low in the water. They were laden with warriors. Whoever commanded them knew that to take on a long ship you had to have plenty of warriors. Their disadvantage lay in their tubby design. They had more in common with a knarr than a drekar. We were long and lean and fast.

"Take us to steerboard and then prepare to come about. We will sail south and west. Let us make it a chase. The men can row for a little while longer and then rest while they chase us."

Erik Short Toe pointed to the west. "Out there is nothing, Jarl, save the edge of the world."

"We will turn before we fall from the edge. I just want the men rested and ready to fight." I turned to the crew. "One more hard row and then don your mail. We will teach these Saxons how to fight!"

"We cast the bones again eh Jarl. Furl the sail!"

When I judged it right I waved my arm.

"Come about!"

Chapter 9

We had a good supply of bows on the drekar including the two Saami bows. One was Snorri's and the other was mine. My plan was simple. When they closed with us we would use the bows to thin out their numbers. I hoped that we could fight them one at a time. We would be outnumbered but I doubted that, man for man, they would be the equal of my warriors. We would be in mail and they would not. It takes a brave man to fight in mail on a ship for if he falls overboard then he dies! I went to the chest and took out the bows and the arrows. I laid them out for my men to collect. I saw the strain on their faces for we were now sailing into the wind and towards the Saxons. We were closing rapidly. Timing was all. I looked at Erik and I nodded, "Back larboard. Come about! Let fly the sail! In oars!"

The oars made us almost spin and the ship's boys had been awaiting the order. The sail fluttered and flapped as Erik turned us. The oars were raised and dropped to the middle in a rapid succession. By the time the ship's boys had reached the deck we had spun and turned. The Saxons were less than a thousand paces from us. I saw the eager faces filling their bows as they saw their prey within their grasp. And then the '*Heart of the Drag*on' leapt like a greyhound. It was as though Erik had unleashed a wild beast.

I shouted, "Drink and then prepare for war. Take your bows!"

Each of my warriors had different rituals. Some smeared red on their eyes. Others took their swords and kissed them. Everyone made sure they had their wolf amulet secured. Gruffyd rose and I shook my head. "Take your shield and your sword. You are to protect Ylva and Erik Short Toe. I do not want to have to worry about Ylva while I fight. If anything happened to her then this whole voyage would have been a waste of time."

He nodded and donned his helmet. It was a newly made one. Bagsecg had made him one without a nasal. He was still growing and it needed to be light. I hoped he would not need to test its qualities but I feared he would. We would have to turn eventually. I looked astern and saw that one of the Saxon ships was heading to the north of us while the other went to the south. Raibeart saw my look and said, "Aye Jarl, they mean to cut us off. They know we must turn."

An idea began to form in my mind. I said nothing for I needed to see how the two Saxons sailed their vessels. They were not gaining and our lead was only increasing by the smallest of distances. We were fast but the extra sails on the Saxons made them faster than normal. With the wind, they had a chance of catching us. We could have extended our lead but that would have meant rowing and there was no guarantee that would help us to escape.

As the sun began to move further west I said, "In a moment, Erik, I want you to head south and west."

"Go with the wind?"

"That is it."

"But the Saxon to the south of us will catch us."

I pointed to their sails. "They have more canvas than we do and sail faster with the wind. What if we turned into the wind?"

Erik smiled, "They would be aback and would not be able to beat up wind and catch us."

"But that still leaves one Saxon, jarl."

"Aye Raibeart and I intend to hurt that Saxon. Ready on my command, Erik."

"Aye Jarl."

"Ulfheonar, you have sat on your backsides enough. Line up on the larboard side. I want us to rain death on that Saxon!"

Desperate to strike back they cheered and picked up their bows, choosing the best arrows that they could find.

"Now, Erik!"

As he put the steering board over I kept my eye on the northernmost Saxon. We took him by surprise. He did not change course immediately for the sails prevented him from seeing us well. When he did the turn was poorly executed and they lost way. The Saxon to the south was in even more disarray. He suddenly saw the wolf of the sea heading for him and he had to choose which way to turn. The delay meant that we were less than three hundred paces from him when he finally made up his mind and turned. He turned to cut us off from the west and that suited me.

I took my Saami bow and chose a black fletched arrow. As I pulled back the string I shouted, "Now!"

My men were expecting the turn and the ships' boys hauled on the sheets to make the turn as efficient as possible. We closed to within a hundred and fifty paces of the Saxon. Snorri and I loosed first. I aimed for their steering board. We managed to hit two of those standing there. We did not hit the steersman but shields were raised as they took cover. Human nature took over and the steersman, involuntarily perhaps, nudged the ship a little further south. When the rest of my men loosed their arrows, they fell in the well of the ship. There were many bodies there and their arrows found flesh. I loosed another and managed to hit the captain, who was standing next to the steersman, in the arm. He dropped to the deck and a warrior raised his shield. Snorri's arrow flew true. In protecting their captain the steersman was left exposed. Snorri's arrow pitched him overboard and the Saxon ship swung to larboard. The sails flapped helplessly.

"To the steerboard side!"

The second Saxon was a different prospect. He had more time to make his decision and our target would be the bow where I could see the shields being raised. They had seen our trick and were planning to avoid the same fate. The second Saxon would soon be following us. If they had been alone we might have escaped but we would have to deal with the northern Saxon first.

"Erik, make for his bow. Make him wonder which side we will pass. Let us see which one blinks first."

"Aye Jarl! Guthrum, get to the bow and direct me! I am relying on you!"

"I will not let you down, captain!" The eldest of the ship's boys ran quickly down the centre board.

The Saxon was travelling with the wind and was much faster. That also meant that the captain of the Saxon needed quicker reactions. It would be a waste of arrows to try to hit those at the steering board. The two sails and the masts would obscure our view and afford some protection. Instead I intended to kill as many of the Saxons on the deck as we could.

Snorri and I began releasing arrows as soon as we were in range. My first arrow fell short but the speed of the Saxon meant my second found flesh. Snorri was more accurate and shields were raised after he had struck two. The rest of my warriors, Ragnar included, began to send arrows towards the Saxon. Their shields protected the warriors but two sailors who were tightening sheets fell to the arrows. It meant their captain was unsighted. Guthrum waved to the steerboard. Suddenly I saw the bow of the Saxon. The Saxon captain, unsighted, had corrected his course by turning into us. Erik had quick reactions and he pushed the steering board over as fast as he could but a collision was inevitable.

Bolli had built a solid ship. The single trunk which formed the keel was a mighty oak from the Land of the Wolf. We struck the Saxon a glancing blow amidships. Our bowline snagged on the mast of the Saxon and we became entangled. Oleg Olegson, one of the ship's boys raced down the sheet to cut the bowline free but the Saxons saw their chance and warriors began to swarm over the side. My men had already dropped their bows and they drew their swords and hefted axes. None of us had time to grab our shields and so I drew my seax as I ran to the side.

I swung my sword at the knee of the Saxon who balanced on the thwarts with a raised spear. He fell screaming between the hulls. Although Oleg had finally freed us the Saxons had thrown grappling hooks and tied us together. I heard a cry from the stern and saw that a second party of Saxons had jumped aboard.

"Olaf! Free us! I go to the aid of Erik!" It was not just Erik Short Toe who needed my help. Ragnar and Gruffyd were there defending my granddaughter. Even as I watched Eystein Thorirson, one of Ragnar's hearth-weru was felled. I blocked the pike which was rammed at my head and I thrust my sword deep into the pikeman's body. I pushed it into the path of two Saxons who were trying to get at me. As they fell I brought Ragnar's Spirit overhand to split one skull in two and I gutted the second.

Ragnar and Gruffyd were fighting back to back. I guessed that they were standing over Ylva's body. A gaggle of Saxons had their backs to me. I threw myself at them. Both of my weapons found flesh and my charge, aided by the pitching drekar, knocked the others to the deck. They were all enemies and I twisted and slashed with my weapons as we writhed around on the deck. I felt weapons striking me but I wore mail and none penetrated it. A bearded face appeared before me. I pulled back my head and butted hard. Wriggling my seax free I began to raise it. The Saxon, his face bloody, saw my blade approaching but, like me, his arms were trapped beneath his dying comrades. I moved the seax closer. A sudden roll of the ship freed my arm and I rammed the seax under his chin and into his skull. His eyes closed.

"Jarl we are free!"

"Then let us send these as a sacrifice to the goddess, Ran! Ulfheonar!"

With a savage flurry of flashing blades, we hacked and stabbed until the deck ran red with Saxon blood. The Saxon ship lay thirty paces from us; the captain was trying to rig new lines to replace those cut by Oleg Olegson. The second Saxon ship was too far away to reach us. I saw the sun dipping to the west. Erik Short Toe was too good a sailor to be caught again. We had won. As I looked at the deck I saw that we had paid a price. Alf Jansson lay dead and a second hearth-weru, Leif the Silent, slept in a pool of his own blood.

My men cheered and chanted, "Dragonheart! Dragonheart! Dragonheart!"

We headed north into the darkening sky. I saw Ragnar and Einar the Tall standing over the bodies of the dead two hearth-weru. "They died well, lord. What better end for a warrior than to die protecting his lord. They are with your father now."

I put my arm around Ragnar, "And you and Gruffyd won great honour today. It takes great courage for a warrior to stand his ground. You have saved Ylva's life."

Gruffyd was bloody with Saxon blood. His eyes were wild and he could not speak. He just nodded. I lowered him to the ground and laid him next to Ylva. "Sleep son. Let your mind return to Cyninges-tūn."

I took off my wolf cloak and placed it over the two of them. My men were stripping the mail from the enemy dead and throwing their bodies over the side. We were not travelling quickly but already the Saxon ships lay too far behind us for them to be a threat.

Haaken walked up to me with Olaf at his side. Olaf was stroking the edge of his notched axe with his whetstone. "The Norns again, jarl? Is this punishment?"

I shook my head, "It is the Norns but this was put in place when we pulled into the bay for shelter. I do not doubt that the Norns will inflict some terror upon us for what Haaken and I did in the cave but this is not it. I fear that will be visited upon our land."

Haaken nodded, "Then the land must help us to fight them."

Cnut Cnutson came over to us. In his hand, he clutched a chain with a medallion hanging from it. "We took this from a leader. What does this signify jarl?"

I examined the medallion. It was a larger version of a coin. The head of King Egbert adorned it. I had seen one before worn by one of his thegns. "This confirms what we knew before. This Saxon ship came from Wessex. These were Egbert's men. I think that the day is drawing close when we will have to face our foe."

It was a slow journey north as Erik and Raibeart tacked back and forth. The crew were too tired to row. Many nursed minor wounds and our slow speed was safer. We reached the island of the puffins at dawn. The priests of the White Christ had a monastery there but we did not bother them. These were the poor ones. They had no treasures and no richly decorated holy books. They lived a simple life and we left them alone. We hove to and killed a few birds for a hot meal. We took our three dead ashore with us and buried them close by the beach where their spirits could watch over us as we sailed through these treacherous seas.

Gruffyd would not leave Ylva, "I have watched over her since Syllingar. When I dreamed last night, it was as when we were children swimming in the tarns near the Hows. She laughed. I will stay with her until we reach out home. It is my appointed duty."

I nodded, "I will have food sent to you."

Ragnar asked, "Why was I not appointed to this task, grandfather? I am the elder."

"You were not chosen." I shrugged, "I know not why save that Ylva and Gruffyd grew up together. Until you and your mother came to live with us they were inseparable. She was as an older sister. We choose not our own paths. They are chosen for us. There is a bond between them. Perhaps it is the water and their grandmother; I know not. Do not let it bother you, Ragnar. A path has been chosen for you. Let us see where it leads."

As the fires burned I watched the smoke. It was now blowing more from the east than the north. It would make our journey faster. I took the food back for Gruffyd and my two captains. "The wind should aid us."

"Aye, we should be there by dawn if we sail at night."

"You would risk Mona at night?"

"With the wind from the east it means that it would only push us to Dyflin. There is no danger there and the coast is kinder than Mona. I am anxious to examine the hull. She is a strong vessel but the blow we struck the Saxon has made us make water. The boys have bailed it but it will only get worse."

"Then I will have the men hurry. They can row for they have all slept."

After a hot meal and feet on the land the crew were happy to row. They knew it would bring us home quicker and they sang well. The song they sang also celebrated when we had defeated the Saxons. Until they built better ships then we would beat them every time.

Through the stormy Saxon Seas
The Ulfheonar they sailed
Fresh from killing faithless Danes
Their glory was assured
Heart of Dragon
Gift of a king
Two fine drekar
Flying o'er foreign seas
Then Saxons came out of the night
An ambush by their Isle of Wight
Vikings fight they do not run
The Jarl turned away from the rising sun
Heart of Dragon
Gift of a king
Two fine drekar
Flying o'er foreign seas
The galdramenn burned Dragon Fire
And the seas they burned bright red
Aboard 'The Gift' Asbjorn the Strong
And the rock Eystein
Rallied their men to board their foes

And face them beard to beard
Heart of Dragon
Gift of a king
Two fine drekar
Flying o'er foreign seas
Against great odds and back to back
The heroes fought as one
Their swords were red with Saxon blood
And the decks with bodies slain
Surrounded on all sides was he
But Eystein faltered not
He slew first one and then another
But the last one did for him
Even though he fought as a walking dead
He killed right to the end
Heart of Dragon
Gift of a king
Two fine drekar
Flying o'er foreign seas

It was sunset when we saw Mona to the east and Erik was able to use the wind and take us towards Hibernia and give the men a rest. Their arms would be needed when we had passed Man. Then we would be sailing almost directly into the wind.

The smell of smoke drifting from the land told us that we were near. The men were tiring for we had rowed since turning east just north of Man. I had sat with Gruffyd and Ylva. "She has not stirred, father."

"But she sleeps and she looks at peace. You have kept her lips moistened and made sure she is warm. You are a healer, my son."

"But she is not better!"

"Healing is often about preventing harm. That you have done. Soon we will be able to put her in the hands of those who can heal her. I fear it is not her body but her mind which has suffered."

Pasgen gave us the welcome news that our land had been safe in the short time we had been away. A few days' absence often invited disaster but there had been no news in Úlfarrston. As it was dawn we were able to leave the drekar beached and under the watchful eye of the shipwrights and we borrowed horses and a wagon to take Ylva back to her family.

As we prepared to leave we met Wighlek and Vibeke. They saw Ylva in the cart, "Jarl! What has happened to the little princess?"

Vibeke knew Kara for she often brought them herbs which Kara could not get. She was fond of Ylva, calling her the little princess. "She has fallen under a spell. I cannot tarry for I need to get her to her parents."

Vibeke handed me a carved bone. It was in the shape of a wolf. "This might help, Jarl."

"Thank you, you are kind,"

We hurried north to our home. News travels quickly and both Aiden and Kara rode to meet us half way along the water. Their faces showed their fear and the trepidation. We did not stop and they rode next to the cart. They were healers and did not need me to tell them that she lived. Gruffyd said, "She has not stirred since Haaken brought her from the cave. She has drunk but her eyes remained closed."

Kara smiled, "You have done well Gruffyd. I sense some of the healer in you." She looked at Haaken. "Were you in the cave too Haaken?"

He smiled, "Aye and I have a permanent reminder of it. Snorri only went partially grey. I am Haaken the White!"

She reached over and touched his arm, "Thank you for my daughter's life. We are in your debt."

He nodded, "I have known you since you were a babe in arms. You are as dear to me as my own family."

"And you father... you were right not to take us. I am not certain we could have faced her; even for our child. How did you defeat her?"

"Defeat is too strong a word. I used Ragnar's Spirit and it protected me from her power. She is there yet and I fear she has not finished with us."

"Since you have been gone we have spent many hours in the dream hut. The spirits have spoken to us. We have collected herbs and roots. We will make a spell to protect us."

I saw the welcoming walls of my stad ahead, "The Norns are the Norns. We can do little about them but there is a greater danger to us."

Aiden nodded, "The Skull Taker Clan."

"I have thought about this as we sailed north. They have two choices. Take their losses and forget us or make one almighty push and wrest this land from us." I pointed to Ylva. "They want her. They know not what has happened to her but that does not matter. If they come again, and I believe they will, then they will come for her. You need to heal her."

"More than that, father, we need to bring her back. Her body and her mind can be healed. The Norn has changed her. She has become a woman. Her powers are there in her body but they have been locked. Aiden and I will have to work to bring back the girl who has now become a woman. I fear we will not be of much use to you for a while." She gave a wan smile, "She is now a Viking witch. She has great powers but it needs us two to bring her back to the clan."

"And that is as it should be. Your child is your priority. Let me and my warriors prepare for war."

Chapter 10

I watched as Ylva was carried into the house of healing and then I went, with Ragnar and Gruffyd, to my hall. Already news of my battle beneath the earth had spread. I saw my people looking at me in fear. I had battled with those who had magical powers. I had not only survived, I had won. I saw that some of my people, especially the women, had fear in their eyes. Many liked the order that the Norns represented. I had upset that order. I knew that I would have to do something to put their minds at rest but first I had to see my wife and family.

My daughter, Erika, ran to meet me. She was a quiet shy child but since the birth of her little sister she had come out of her shell a little. She hugged me and then grabbed Gruffyd, "I have missed you both! Mother has been irritable since you left."

I picked her up and held her. She was getting too big for this. "Your mother worries. We are back and your big brother has done well. He has been caring for Ylva."

Her face became serious, "She is returned and she is well?"

Gruffyd answered, "She is and father battled a Norn beneath the earth! Haaken's hair has turned white!"

Her mouth opened. I saw that Brigid had emerged with Myfanwy and heard the last part. "A Norn? I thought it was a witch."

I embraced her and said, quietly in her ear, "I am safe as are all of our family. Do not become upset and fret over what might have happened. Besides you do not believe in Norns!"

She leaned back, "They are evil and I believe in the devil and evil. These Norns of which you speak sound to me like the devil!"

I laughed, "Devil or Norn it matters not, I survived! I am hungry. Let us eat."

The next morning, I went to see how Ylva was faring. She was still unresponsive. Kara had managed to feed her; I know not how and they were busy trying spells and potions to return her to our world.

I did not want to interfere but I was her grandfather and I offered a suggestion. "Kara, I think you need to seek the help of your mother." I pointed to the barrow across the Water. "I would take her there. She responded to Erika when I was in the cave."

Aiden nodded, "We will try that. Thank you, Jarl, and thank you for bringing her back. You did something that we feared to do."

"That is because you use magic yourselves and are too close. When I have an enemy, I use my sword."

"What will you do about the Danes?"

"When they come it will be as a horde. I need more warriors. I have to turn farmers, boys and fishermen into warriors and I have to do it quickly. I am afraid I will be of little help to Ylva."

"You have done all that you could."

My Ulfheonar made their way to my hall. On the voyage back we had spoken, not of Wessex, that problem was far in the future, but of the Skull Takers. Like me they were all worried about numbers. We had lost an Ulfheonar and two hearth-weru. It did not seem many but the ones we had lost were irreplaceable. I had Asbjorn and Ketil's men. I had Ulf's men at Stad on the Eden but it was still not enough. I needed my walls filling with armed men who could fight the Danes that I knew would come. That was not something which would happen overnight.

Olaf Leather Neck came up with the best idea. "The followers of the White Christ have one day a week when they worship him. We do not have that ritual. We do not need it but we could ask that every male comes on that day and we teach them to become warriors."

Cnut Cnutson asked, "Will one day in seven be enough?"

"It is better than no day at all. And we must make sure that it is enough. We pass on our skills. We see what skills they have and use those."

Everyone seemed happy and Haaken said, "If we had something to throw stones then we could hold them back. A machine such as we saw in Miklagård would be good then those who have little skills could use that."

We all knew of those who had no skills with any sort of weapon. They were not those who were Norse born but we had others who had joined our clan and they were the ones to whom Haaken referred.

"Let us make it so. I will see Scanlan and Bagsecg. You need to organise weapons, helmets and shields."

Olaf said, "We will show them how to make a shield. That will make them warriors faster than anything else."

I left them to divide the tasks amongst themselves. I noticed that Ragnar and Gruffyd had kept apart and were with the four hearth-weru by the Water. I smiled. They were practising. The sea battle had shown them their limitations. They were learning and they were growing. A slave was carrying water for the forge. "When you have taken that to Bagsecg find Scanlan and bring him too me."

"Aye jarl."

We did not have as many slaves as most other clans. If a slave proved his worth, then we gave him his freedom. Most only served as slaves for less than a year. I had been a slave and I had not forgotten the joy of being free once more.

Bagsecg stopped work when I entered. He poured us a horn of ale each. "It was good that you found Ylva. Men are talking of you as a hero once more."

"I did what most men would do for their family."

He laughed, "Face a witch in her cave? Some perhaps might talk of it but I cannot think of another who would do it." He raised his horn, "Here's to a hero and the sword." We both drank deeply, "I have never made a sword as good again, you know Jarl." I took it out and handed it to him. "I know it was touched by the gods but even without that it is still a well-balanced weapon." He held it by two fingers and a thumb. "See how few marks there are upon it. I have tried to make another which was as good and failed. I think that my hand was guided when I hammered and quenched. The steel was perfect, the tempering judged to an instant. Why cannot I make another?"

"It maybe you were only meant to make one." I took it and held it up to the light. "When I was in the cave it acted as a light for me. The cave was pitch black and yet I saw a light. It frightened away the witch. It is a remarkable weapon."

"They say a good sword chooses its owner. That is true of you." He smiled as I stroked the hilt. "But you did not come here for praise did you, Jarl?"

"I have sent for Scanlan. He needs to hear this too." While we waited, I said, "And I would have you make a gold wolf for my new Ulfheonar."

"He is a good warrior. It will be an honour but it may take time."

"Whenever it is ready will be good enough. I need Kara to put a spell upon it. My warriors need protection."

Scanlan appeared. He had been running and was out of breath. There had been a time when he could have run up the Old Man. Much of his work now involved organising. That would have to change. He too would have to become a warrior.

"The Danes will return. We all know that and next time it will not be a warband of a hundred warriors. It will be the whole clan and other clans who wish to pick over the body of the wolf for they wish to take over our land."

Although it was no surprise I saw that the words had an effect. They were used to warriors trying to kill me but this was different. They wanted what we had. I had their attention.

"Every male will have to defend the stad."

"They do that anyway, Jarl. What is different?"

"They have stood on my wall and made up the numbers. I need them to fight in a shield wall if necessary. I think we may have to face the Danes in open battle. I want every man to spend one day in every seven with the Ulfheonar. They will be trained by the best. When they come again I want these walls to be filled with armed warriors who know how to fight. I want warriors who will not need an Ulfheonar to stand beside them and give them orders. If there are slaves that we can free then do so, Scanlan. Give them land or give them a home but most importantly, give them a weapon. We can get more slaves."

"Give slaves weapons?"

I smiled, "As I recall, Scanlan, I took you as a slave on the Maeresea. You became free and I gave you a weapon."

He shook his head, "I am sorry. I have forgotten. I have been a free man for so long...."

"That you feel that this is your land. Make those slaves who show they have the right attitude free." We had, largely, taken slaves from so far away that they could not return home. We treated them well and once you became used to a place then it became home.

"You will need weapons."

"Aye Bagsecg but we have enough helmets. My men will show them how to make shields."

"Most should know! They were brought up Norse!"

"That is my fault. I have allowed the Ulfheonar to do most of the fighting. They have forgotten that which was in their blood. We will see if we can put it back in them. The Ulfheonar will assess their skills and allocate them a role. Olaf Leather Neck will make a list of weapons they will need."

"I will make a start and have my sons melt down the poorer weapons. Our iron is of a much higher standard and produces better swords but the poor iron makes fair arrows and shot."

I left Scanlan to tell every male the new arrangements while Bagsecg busied himself instructing his sons. I returned to the Ulfheonar. I waved over my three scouts. "When you are not training the bondi I have a task for you."

Snorri nodded, "Find the Danes."

"I wish the three of you to choose the best six horses that we have. Six days in seven I want you searching for signs of Danish scouts. I have learned that this Baggi Skull Splitter is a careful man. He does not rush into things. He can be patient. He will send scouts. They will be good but you will be better. You need to find his scouts and get rid of them. When they are eliminated then you can find his camps. He will have to gather his forces and he will not reach us in a day from the land around Loidis."

Aðils asked, "What if he comes on the day we are here?"

Beorn the Scout shook his head, "Did you not hear the Jarl? It will take more than two days for them to reach here. I would estimate three at the very least. His men will not be mounted and he will have the witches and women with them. It will be nearer to five or six days. We will find them."

Brigid had not been happy that I had chosen the day of the worship of the White Christ as our day of war. "But we will not interfere with your rituals. We will be far down the Water where the land is flat."

"I am just uncomfortable with the thought of war on that day."

"We will not be at war. Think of it as making arms stronger. No one will be hurt."

Although mollified she was never entirely happy. Nor had I been exactly truthful. We did have injuries. There were cuts and broken limbs. Even farmers, who were naturally strong, had to learn to use their arms and legs in different ways. The first time Olaf Leather Neck tried to teach a shield wall they fell in an untidy heap. Three of them suffered cuts and sprains while one broke his left hand. It was not an auspicious start.

Haaken stepped forward. Now that his hair was completely white he looked more like a wizard than a warrior. His one eye flashed angrily as he said to Olaf, "You are teaching them as though they have fought in a shield wall every day of their life. You are not trying to make them better. You are starting from the beginning."

"Then you teach them!"

"I will!" He turned to them. "Stand in your lines." He turned to Olaf. "You got that part right! Lay down your shields!" They obeyed. "Those in the front row put your left hand on the shoulder of the warrior to the left. Those in the second and third rank on the shoulder of the man who is before you." When that was done, he said. "I will teach you a simple chant such as we use when we row. We will all sing together and march on the spot. Begin with your sword leg." I knew what he intended. It was clever.

Viking enemy, taking heads
Viking warriors fighting back
Viking enemy, taking heads
Viking warriors fighting back

It did not take them long to learn it. He had chosen the most recent and the easiest of our rowing chants.

"Stop!" He bellowed. Almost all obeyed save Erik the Shepherd. He was still marching when all stopped. He looked in embarrassment at his feet when he realised that he was still marching. Haaken shook his head, "You must listen to your leader when you fight. We are not wild Hibernians who scream and shout when we fight. We are the warriors of the wolf and we either chant or remain silent. Even when we sing we listen for that voice which commands."

Njǫrðr Njǫrðrson asked, reasonably, "And who will that be, Haaken One Eye?"

Haaken looked at me. I smiled, "We do not know yet Njǫrðr. It may be an Ulfheonar but it is more likely to be one of you. Some men have the seeds of a warrior in them even if they are a fisherman or a shepherd or even, Njǫrðr, a baker of bread. I will watch and I will choose the one who will lead this shield wall." I pointed to the others who were training. There were archers and there were slingers. "Each part must be led. That is our way. Listen to Haaken. He and Olaf will watch you and they will choose a leader. That will not be yet for you need to learn how to walk."

Erik the Shepherd was paying more attention now, "Learn to walk? Are we bairns, jarl?"

I pointed to Finni the Unlucky who was having his broken hand tended. "It would seem so!"

Viking enemy, taking heads
Viking warriors fighting back
Viking enemy, taking heads
Viking warriors fighting back

Haaken had them march back and forth chanting. This time they marched closer together but they marched in perfect time. "Keep your eyes to the front! That is where the enemy will be! Your feet obey you!" He had them stop and he had them turn. When he was satisfied then he allowed them their shields. After they had managed to march to the Water, turn, and walk back he waved to Olaf to take over.

We had hoped to teach them to use spears and to interlock shields but that first day showed us how much work we had to do. As Haaken and I walked to the archers I said, "We have allowed them to lose the skills with which they were born. I have let the Ulfheonar fight too many of their battles."

"It is not your fault, Jarl. Many of the warriors who had skills were slain when we went to war. The ones who remain are the ones we could not take. The bakers, fishermen and shepherds are not farmers who can leave crops to grow themselves. They have to work each day. They are still part of the clan." He nodded to the archers, being trained by my scouts, "The archers are doing well.

All that Snorri needs to teach them is how to release together and how to use their war bows to full effect."

We had had war bows made for our would-be archers. They were longer than their hunting bows. The difference lay in the pull. I knew that the backs of my men would ache for a while but once they had mastered the stronger bow then their arrows would fly further.

The rest of my Ulfheonar were teaching our second shield wall how to use their swords. This shield wall was one made up of those who had fought in a shield wall before. They would still need Olaf Leather Neck to rid them of their rough edges but they knew how to march without tripping up. Bagsecg and his sons were still making swords as fast as they could but a good sword took time. The twenty with my men used the best of those we had captured and the new ones made by Bagsecg. I had thought of having them use wooden ones. Aiden had told me that the Romans had done that. We had no time to waste making them. This way the men would have to learn how to use the real thing and to sharpen them when they became blunt.

Einar Hammer Arm and Cnut Cnutson taught them while my other warriors identified weaknesses. Einar was holding his own sword up. It was longer than most for he was a strong man and could wield it. Cnut had the shorter one most of the men used. "This is an iron bar with an edge to it. That is all! Even if you do not hit an enemy with an edge it will hurt. You seek the place where it will hurt." He tapped his own head. "Even a helmet cannot totally protect from a sword blow." He pointed to his shield. "A shield protects most of the body. All that you do when you strike the shield is blunt your sword. True, you may make his arm numb but you will not end the battle." He pointed to Cnut's leg. It was not protected by his byrnie. "His leg can be hurt. Strike his leg and he cannot move. If he cannot move, then you can use your speed to get around him. When you fight be balanced and shift your weight from leg to leg. It confuses an enemy." They nodded.

Cnut shouted, "In pairs!" They faced each other. "Use the flat of your sword. I want no cuts! Make sure you are balanced. Look at your opponent's eyes. They will tell you where he will strike. You all have a choice of targets. Fight!"

I saw that some were better than others. They naturally shifted and feinted. Shouts and curses told who had made a blow which connected. Some had the skill to move a shield and strike at the same time. They would be the ones to place in the front rank.

I invited my Ulfheonar to my hall at the end of the day to discuss what they had done. Their charges were having wounds tended to and aching muscles eased with salves and balms.

"They are like rough ore from the mines, Jarl. We know that it can be turned into weapons but it is still lumpen at the moment."

Rolf Horse Killer shook his head, "If we had faced the Danes yesterday then that might have been true but I saw improvement. Einar's lessons made the ones we trained think about the blows that they struck. It takes many battles to do that normally." He smiled. He was still one of the younger Ulfheonar. "It was not until I slew that horse that I realised that you could choose your target and end a battle quicker. If the Danes came they would not panic. They would choose where to strike."

"And the men you trained Olaf, they can now march and raise their shields in time. They can present a wall of spears. They could not do that this morning. They have made their mistakes and they have learned from them. This horn is half full! It is not half empty!"

Olaf smiled, "Then let us fill it up!" Uhtric hurried over and added more foaming ale to Olaf Leather Neck's horn.

I stood, "We have all done well. For the next six days, they will be back at work. I want all of you to travel around the stad. When they are not working talk to them of the knowledge you have in your head and the battles you have fought. We all know that when we fight we use every part of our mail and our body. They do not." They nodded. "Snorri, tomorrow you and your scouts must begin your search for the enemy."

"We thought to head to Carr's Waite. He and his son have sharp eyes. We can then head over the high passes to the valley of the Dunum. Eggle Skulltaker had a stronghold there. They may have returned. If we find no one then when we next scout, we take the southern route. We start at Sigtrygg's stad."

I could see his plan. "You are leaving the central route until last?"

He shrugged, "It is like fighting a warrior you have fought before. Is that a blow coming to your head or does he feint so that he can hit your leg? You said they are cunning. They may choose where they have struck before. They may think we would rule that out as a threat. Besides the central route has the high ground and then the forests and the boggy lands which lie to the south of Elfridaby. Many Danes have used that route before. We have to start somewhere."

"I was not criticising, Snorri. I needed to know where you were going. I am going to take Ragnar and Gruffyd to Ketil's stad. I would speak with Prince Athelstan."

Chapter 11

Before we left I visited Ylva. There was still no sign of a recovery although she was no longer thin and emaciated. Both Kara and Aiden were more hopeful. "She does improve, father. We have spoken with her in her dreams."

Aiden nodded, "The witch still has her mind and she lies trapped in the cave. We have yet to break the hold but each day we learn more. Ylva now wishes to return." He smiled. "That was you. She said that you risked all to save her. She now knows what she must do."

I mounted my horse and headed north and east in a more optimistic frame of mind. We had Ragnar's hearth-weru with us and as we passed through Ulla's Water he asked me, "Should I have more hearth-weru, grandfather. I have but four."

"And I have none. Einar the Tall and the others came to you for they were your father's hearth-weru. The choice is yours to make but you would need coin to pay them."

"You do not pay the Ulfheonar?"

"No, they choose to follow me but I buy them gifts and give them weapons. If men follow you that is one thing but if you pay men, then you have to ask do you pay their hearts or their purses? I have never paid for warriors. I am not one to judge. You are a man now. You make your own decisions."

We rode in silence beneath Úlfarrberg's peak. The dark empty valley was a sombre place these days. Gruffyd broke the silence. "How do you get warriors to follow you?"

"You be yourself. If it is *wyrd* that men see you as someone who can lead them then so be it and if not… I followed Prince Butar until he was killed but others followed me." I shrugged. "Haaken thought I was lucky. Others chose me because I was Ulfheonar and they wished to be as I was. Some follow the sword. You have both done deeds which make men look at you and see warriors who are different but you are young and you are still learning." We rode in silence as the two of them took in my words.

I noticed that Ketil and his people had begun to change the land. They had cleared the valley bottoms and farms blossomed where once had been trees and scrubland. His people used the uplands for sheep but here, in the lower valley, were cows and grain. Running east to west his valley had more sun than Ulla's Valley. My decision to make him jarl had been a good one.

When I reached Ketil's stad it was to the news that Prince Athelstan had taken a war band south to take back the land from the Danes.

"Was that wise, Ketil?"

Shaking his head he said, "I tried to dissuade him. I even offered to take my warriors with me. He would have none of it. His father does not stir. I fear that the King is not a strong warrior. He is afraid of King Egbert. I think that the son goes to war to make a name so that men will follow his banner."

"He goes against his father? He would be king?"

"He will not fight his father but he feels he would be a better king who would be able to defend the land against the many enemies they have."

"It is a risk. If he is defeated by the Danes, he could lose everything."

Ketil nodded, "I tried to dissuade him. He heard how you defeated the bands sent against you. He has more warriors. I told him that yours were well trained and prepared but...."

"But he thinks it is easier than it is." I shook my head, "This does not hurt us yet but it may in the future. Watch your borders. Snorri is hunting to the east of you looking for Danes."

"Then Carr and his son will come to tell me. Since you met them they have become almost part of my people."

After three days in Ketil's valley we returned home. I spoke with Carr and I rode the greenways and Roman Roads. There was no sign of either Danes or Danish scouts. Ketil promised that he would be vigilant. We used the Grassy Mere for the route along Ulla's Water was a reminder of our failure. As we headed for the Rye Dale we were overtaken by a rider on a pony. It was Sihtric Thorkellson. He was one of the warriors from the stad on the Eden.

"Is there aught amiss, Sihtric?"

He grinned. When he did he reminded me of his father Thorkell the Tall. "No Jarl. The men of Hibernia raided." He laughed. "Our watch towers spied them coming and we were ready. As they tried to disembark we attacked them with arrows and then spears. Our slingers made many widows that day for they shun armour. The survivors barely escaped to their ships. It was a great slaughter. They had poor weapons and little treasure but we took them anyway. Ulf took a golden torc from their chief. We planted their heads by the Eden as a warning for others."

"Did you lose many?"

"None. We did not have to close with them. It was not glorious and there was little honour but what honour is there in killing a naked barbarian?" He patted his horse, "I am pleased that I have seen you. This is *wyrd*. I can now return to the Stad. The jarl holds a feast!"

"Good. Tell him I am pleased." I was pleased but disappointed at the same time. I had hoped to use some of Ketil's men and some of Ulf's to augment my warband. Both had experienced men in numbers. The prince's actions and the attack from Hibernia showed me that I could not. They would have to watch the borderlands. When the Danes came, we would have to use what we had.

Haaken asked me what worried me and I told him. "But surely if the prince attacks the Danes then they cannot attack here."

"You are right Haaken One Eye." I told the Ulfheonar the news when I returned. They all felt the same as Haaken. "And if the prince won then our troubles would be halved but do you think he can win? Can any Christian army succeed against Danes?" He shook his head. "Then if Baggi Skull Splitter wins he gains the arms of the Saxons. They have fine swords but even worse he becomes a rallying point for other Danes who will flock to his banner. This could increase the army of the Danes. More than that it would invite the Danes into the land of the Northumbrians and that would threaten Ketil. But you are right. We have more time. As we cannot use the men from the north then we must put even more effort into training the ones we have."

Snorri and his men arrived late at night. They were tired. "We scoured the lands to the east of Ketil and there were neither Danes nor Saxons. We discovered that the Saxons had headed south with an army. It made our task easier. We headed south and crossed the Dunum. There were Danes there but they were farmers and fishermen. As we had made good time we went to Stanwyck. Using that as a base we searched as far south as Eoforwic. I spoke with Agnete. She told us that the prince had taken most of the fyrd and thegns south to punish the Danes."

This was getting worse. "Did you see any sign of the Skull takers?"

"No. We returned here. When we head south next I will take us to Loidis. Perhaps the prince might win."

"When you spoke with Agnete did she talk of Saxon archers and many mailed men?"

"No Jarl. She spoke of Housecarls who were with the prince but the majority were the fyrd. A bow was a good weapon, she said and she wondered why the Saxons had so few."

"Then you have answered yourself. He will lose. I hope he shows wisdom and lessens his losses by fleeing when things go awry."

Snorri shook his head, "He has seen you fight, Jarl Dragonheart. He has seen the odds against you and yet you have prevailed."

"Perhaps you are right. I should have spent time telling him how we won." I nodded, "You have done well, Snorri. You have scouted more land than I thought possible."

"We now have a greater incentive to make sure we have many archers."

My scouts told the Ulfheonar of their discovery and the men were worked even harder than they had been the first week. At the end of the day I saw sweating exhausted men and I gathered them around me, "I know that you are tired. Your shoulders ache and your fingers bleed. You wonder at the madness of your jarl." I saw men shaking their heads. "We need to be ready for our enemies. We have lost Elfridaby and Ulla's Water. I would not add Cyninges-tūn to that list. What we do today and each of these war days makes us stronger."

As they wandered wearily back to their homes Bagsecg joined me. "I have ten swords ready. They are good swords. The iron had few impurities and the charcoal was the best that Ragi has ever produced."

"Good," turning to Cnut Cnutson I said, "we will award them to the best ten warriors the next time we practice. It will give them an incentive."

I spent the next six days in my stad. I spent many hours each day visiting my men as they worked and talking to them of their training. I needed to know them better. Everybody asked me the same thing; they all wanted to touch the sword, Ragnar's Spirit. There was a time I would have been reluctant to do so for I had feared it would lose its power. The cave had shown me that it was more powerful than ever. The blood of those it had slain and the spirits of the dead were now bonded into the blade. When I left the men, I saw fire in their eyes. The sword had that effect.

I was heading back through the gate when a voice called me. "Jarl!"

It was Siggi Olegson. He had been the brother of one of my Ulfheonar. Siggi had been wounded in a battle against the men of Strathclyde. He was lame and could not stand in a shield wall. He was still a powerful warrior. He was a bowman. He was also a tanner. He took the hides from the cattle we slaughtered and produced leather. It was an unpleasant job for the smell was pungent. For that reason, his workshop was outside the walls so that the smell was swept away from the houses by the prevailing winds.

"What is it Siggi?"

He lifted a hessian cloth. "I have been making armour for myself. I will not stand in a shield wall and I do not need mail. Nor do I need armour which stops my arms. This is a compromise and it works."

He handed me the leather tunic he had made. I saw that it did not cover the arms but the body would be protected. It would cover the waist up. The leather was supple but thick. The man had skill. However, what made it more impressive were the thin metal plates he has sewn over it. They did not completely cover it; that would have made it too heavy. It did, however, cover vital areas like the heart and the shoulders.

"This is fine armour."

"I could make it for some of the other archers."

"This is your livelihood. You trade the hides for that which you need."

"The clan needs it. I will survive."

"You have a wife and sons. I will buy them. I will see Scanlan and he will give you coins for them."

"Thank you, Jarl, but you have no need."

"You lost your brother and you were wounded fighting for the clan. This is the least we can do. I have spoken. You will be paid for the archer armour."

I felt better as I went in. My people were becoming stronger through adversity. I wondered if we had a chance to defeat the Danes.

When Snorri next returned, it was with dire news. He had seen the Saxon army and it was south of Eoforwic and moving towards Loidis. "It moves so slowly, Jarl Dragonheart, that the Danes will know exactly where they are."

"But they have not come to battle yet?"

"Not yet but I fear that if we go again then it will be over."

"You will need to. We need to know the outcome for good or ill."

We were helpless in our Land of the Wolf. We had not the men to go to Athelstan's aid. It was now out of our hands. What would be would be. After Snorri had left I was summoned to Ylva's bedside. Kara was weeping and I thought it meant bad news. "Has she worsened?"

She shook her head unable to speak and Aiden said, "She opened her eyes and looked at us. She did not speak but her mouth opened. Then her eyes closed again but it is a sign that she is fighting hard. Tonight, we dream again."

I could not keep the emotion from my voice as I said, "That is good. It has been a long journey but perhaps the end is in sight."

"I am sorry we have not been of any help with the Danes."

"If they bring the witches then we may need your help but, for the present, Athelstan is occupying them. I do not think it bodes well for him but we, at least, have a respite."

Snorri and his scouts had not returned when we held our next practice. I was concerned but not worried. I decided to hold a mock battle. We would not use slingers and archers. I wanted our two shield walls to go against each other. It was one thing to march up and down raising and lowering shields but it was another to charge at an enemy who was armed in the same way. We used ash staves with neither metal nor point. They would not need their swords.

The two bands were of a similar number. There were fifty in each one. My Ulfheonar stood with me to assess the strengths and weaknesses. We had appointed one warrior in each warband to shout out the commands and to keep the pace. Sven Bjornsson led one and Leif of the Woods led the other. I was impressed with their movements. They did not move as smoothly as the Ulfheonar but they were in step. Both bands used the same chant. It sounded strange. The problem came when they charged. They both moved too quickly and their formation faltered. They came together piecemeal and Leif's band managed to break into the centre of Sven's. Had they been fighting Danes it would have been a disaster.

We allowed them to spar with their spears for a while and then I nodded to Olaf Leather Neck.

"Hold!"

Olaf could not keep the look of disappointment from his face but I was less unhappy. "You have all come a long way. That was far from perfect but that is my fault. I did not tell my men to show you how to charge. Remember this, it is better to approach slowly and keep your formation than run and lose it. Form your shield walls again!"

"You heard the jarl! Move!"

I waved Olaf to my side. "Olaf, they are trying."

"And I do not want them to die in their first battle."

I shouted, "Hold firm. The Ulfheonar will attack you!" I gestured for my men to come towards me. "Let us try to jump on to the shield wall. It will show them what may happen on the field of battle."

They all grinned. This would be a game. Haaken and I stood to the side as my warriors leapt into the air and landed on the shields. They used the flat of their swords to bang on the shield wall. It took a few blows but, eventually both were broken.

"Good. You held for longer than I thought. If an enemy does that then you need to use your swords. A battle between shield walls is even. You push together and move the enemy gradually. A clever enemy will have men try to climb on top of the shields." I pointed to the archers. "They are our secret weapon. When the enemy attempt that then the archers and slingers can slay them. Now go back to your practice."

With Snorri, Aðils Shape Shifter and Beorn scouting I took the archers to train with them. Siggi had made four new suits of leather armour and I allowed him to choose the men who would wear them. "With this armour you can fight with a bow and, if needs be, with a sword. Our enemies will receive a shock. When you fight, you will be standing behind the rear rank of the shield wall. Each of you will have a small shield around your back. If you are threatened, then you can join the rear of the shield wall. You slingers, you will climb under the shields. You protect the shield wall and it will protect you!"

Snorri arrived late the next day. Their horses were lathered and his face told me the worst. "Jarl the Saxons had been routed. They fought south of Eoforwic. They were drawn into an attack on a small warband of Skull Takers. Then Baggi Skull Splitter launched an attack on their flanks with two huge warbands. The fyrd broke and Prince Athelstan and his housecarls were slaughtered." He shook his head, "They died well and took many Danes with them but they died and Baggi now wears the prince's skull."

"What happened to the fyrd?"

"Some escaped. Those that reached the Dunum swam and reached the village of Stocc. Others were caught and butchered. Eoforwic holds out still. The Danes have made no attempt to attack it. They are too busy pillaging and plundering."

"Then they will come."

"They will."

"Tomorrow send Aðils to Ketil and let him know the extent of the disaster. I am guessing he will know that the prince has lost if not the extent of the disaster. I will go to Asbjorn. He may be in as much danger as we are."

I held a council of war with Aiden, Haaken and Olaf Leather Neck. "They will come soon. I believe we have a month at the most. The men we have trained are better now than they were but I do not believe that they can face a Danish army in the field. We will have to weaken it."

"We?"

"The Ulfheonar. We leave in four days. We will terrorise them in their own land. While we are gone Finni can continue to train the men. I know that the farmers will be gathering in their crops and that must continue. I would not starve in the winter but we needed the women and the girls to do more. Aiden, I want more animal pens built to the west of the stad. I want every animal taken there when we get word of the Danes."

"Ylva…"

"You said she is getting better. Divide your time between her and the work on the defences. If the stad falls then she dies along with the rest of us." It was a stark comment but this was no time to mince words.

I saw Brigid and Elfrida and told them what I had said to Aiden. "I need you two to organize the women. I know that Kara would normally do that but…"

"But she has her daughter to care for." Elfrida nodded. "We will carry the burden, Jarl. This is our time."

As I went to organize what I would need I saw Ragnar and Gruffyd approach. They had a purposeful walk and I knew why they came. "Before you speak know that you cannot come with me. This is work for Ulfheonar. This is knife work in black of night. You have to stay here."

Gruffyd looked disappointed but Ragnar nodded, "I know but we would be of more help than waiting here behind the wooden walls. I know that we have no skills for what you do but we have eyes and we can ride. We would ride the borderlands. We would hunt their scouts."

I looked at Ragnar anew. He had changed. It was not only the burgeoning beard nor was it his broadening shoulders it was something else. His eyes showed a steely detonation which was echoed by the confidence of his words. I remembered young Hrolf who had gone off to become a horseman in Frankia. He had been younger than Ragnar when he had led men. I too had been younger when I had taken responsibility. It was his time.

"Aye, it is a good idea. Scouts may slip by us. There will be only seven of you."

Ragnar shook his head. "No, grandfather. There are four of the young warriors in the stad who wish to follow my banner."

"Are they oathsworn yet?"

He hesitated, "I was waiting to ask your permission. You may want them to swear an oath to you."

"That shows you are growing, Ragnar. Take their oath. But you must keep both Asbjorn and Finni informed. Do not let them worry about you. If you scout, then it is not for glory it is to keep the land safe."

"Aye, we will."

I rode with Haaken to visit Asbjorn. As I did I thought about my son and grandson. Ragnar now looked like his father. I hoped I had made the right decision. Arturus had begun to grow distant from me. I now believed that had been my fault. I would not make the same mistake.

Part Three

The Viking Witch

Chapter 12

We took four horses with us to carry our mail and our meagre supplies. I had told Finni that we would be away for a month at the most but that we would, in all likelihood, return in half a month. We headed south, towards the land which had been ruled by Sigtrygg. It mirrored the route the Danes had taken to reach us. I calculated that their eye would be fixed north and the Saxons. I hoped that an approach from the south and west might prove to be more secret. The first day took us to the high divide. Here the moors and fells were less exposed than those closer to home and we found a sheltered dell in which to camp. It was high summer and the nights were short. We kept a watch all night. The second day we meandered south and east. Snorri was leading us to where the battle had taken place. When we saw the fires of farms we deviated from our course. Aðils Shape Shifter rode at the head of our column. Even Snorri and Beorn now deferred to his unbelievable skills.

Snorri rode next to Haaken and me, "He is as I was when I was young." He stroked his grey flecked beard. "I thought age just brought white hairs. I did not expect to lose some of my skills."

"You are still more skilful than any other warrior I know, save Aðils."

"I know and it was *wyrd* that he chose to come down the mountain and seek to be Ulfheonar." He turned and gave me a wry smile. "Has it escaped your attention Jarl Dragonheart, that he came to us after I had returned from the cave and after I had slain the witch? The Allfather sent him. I fear my time is almost done. But at least I now have a son."

"I am pleased for you. What have you named him?"

"Bjorn, after my oldest friend. I hope that he will be as good a warrior as his namesake."

"His father is one of the finest I have ever fought alongside and that is a good name: Bjorn Snorrison."

118

"It is what we all hope." He nodded to my son and grandson. "Gruffyd is growing, jarl."

I nodded. The thought had crossed my mind. "And I have noticed a change in Ragnar too. Perhaps the Allfather has decided that we have led the clan for long enough."

"When Prince Butar died we were already warriors with reputations, Jarl. I do not think our time is yet."

"No Haaken One Eye, but that day is coming."

We had left before dawn. I was still acutely aware that there were spies in my land. I did not want to let them know my whereabouts. My three scouts left us after we passed the ruins of Elfridaby. They were seeking the Danish army. The Danes had destroyed the Saxons and would have pursued them. I guessed they would stop at the Dunum. With Eoforwic under siege they could afford to pillage the land. We were seeking the bands which would be enjoying the fruits of victory. We could, hopefully, pick off the smaller bands. It would weaken our foes and make them look over their shoulders for the wolves who hunted them.

The land through which we travelled was wild. There were sudden steep sided valleys and some precipitous drops. Within a few thousand paces the land could change to high pasture and forest. We went carefully. We found a well-worn path which headed towards Eoforwic. We joined it and the going became easier. Beorn rode back not long before noon. We had just watered the horses at a stream which cascaded through the trees. We were safe from observation although the greenway ran through the small wood. I guessed that we were, perhaps, twenty or thirty miles from Eoforwic. Certainly, I knew that the wide vale would begin soon.

"Jarl, there is a band of Danes ahead."

"How many?"

"Thirty, perhaps, forty. They have six captives with them. They look like Northumbrians."

"Warriors?"

"Aye they have their hands bound. They are heading in this direction."

"Are they Skull Takers?"

"No Jarl. They have different clan markings. Snorri and Aðils are shadowing them. They are travelling slowly." He looked up at the sun and pointed to the right of it. "We have until the sun reaches there."

I looked around. We were on a well-used greenway. They would be coming this way. "We will ambush them here. They must be on their way home. Take the horses into the woods and hobble them. Bring bows."

While my men did as I had commanded I walked down the path. I wanted to see the trap I was planning from the point of view of the Danes. Their better warriors would be at the front and the prisoners would be at the rear. If we could I would save the Saxons but we needed surprise if we were to remain a secret. I found the edge of the wood and I peered down the valley. I could not see them. That meant we had time. Snorri and Aðils would be behind the Danes. They could slam the door shut when I sprung my trap. I wanted none of the Danes to escape. I headed up the trail. It turned sharply after it entered the wood. There was a huge ancient oak. I guessed that when the tree had been young then the path had been straighter but the branches had spread and small saplings sprouted around its base. It had made men make a turn in the path over the years. The tree was mighty and I saw that the branches would support warriors. I wondered if the ancient people had ambushed Romans here.

By the time I reach the clearing my men had returned. I gathered them around and explained my plan. "Rolf and Rollo, you are young and you are agile. Take your bows and climb the mighty oak. You can use the height to rain death on the Danes. Beorn, take Karl Karlsson. Hide at the entrance to the wood and when the last warrior has passed then begin the slaughter. Rolf and Rollo can release arrows when you attack. Olaf Leather Neck take half of the rest of the men and go to the west side of the path. Haaken take the rest to the east. Spread yourselves out."

"And you, Jarl?"

I grinned, "I well get their attention."

I watched my men get into position. I saw them disappear as only Ulfheonar can. One moment they were there and when I blinked they were gone. I rammed three arrows into the ground and held another ready. I might be seen before Beorn and Karl could close the trap but I expected them to try to get at me. With their attention on me they would not expect the attacks which would begin on both sides. There were only five men on each side of the path but they were the best of warriors. They all had their bows. They would use an arrow first. That way the enemy would not know where they were. When they erupted from the tress, dressed in wolf skins, it would add to the terror. I had to hold them. We could not afford any to escape. If Baggi Skull Splitter knew that I was on the loose he would use every warrior to seek me out. I wanted them to wonder who was killing their men. With luck they would think it was some of Prince Athelstan's men who had escaped the battle.

I heard them before I saw them. They were not trying to hide. I heard their laughter and their shouts. They had no scouts out. Why should they, this was their land? I readied my bow and arrow. I aimed at the trail some forty paces from me. The path turned again around a second oak which had spread out. It was a ridiculously close range and I could not miss. I would have to be fast. I saw one warrior begin to emerge and I resisted the temptation to release. He was not looking ahead in any case. I waited until three of them had turned. As one looked ahead and saw me I released.

He wore mail but that was no hindrance to the Saami bow. The arrow tore into his chest and I had another ready before his comrades saw the black fletched arrow sticking from his chest. My second hit the next Dane so hard that he was pitched backwards; an arrow in his face. The third drew his weapon and ran at me. Behind him I saw other Danes as they ran to get at me. I was vaguely aware of screams and shouts from further down the column but I did not lose concentration. My third arrow hit the Dane when he was twenty paces from me. It was buried in his chest to its fletch. My last arrow was hurriedly released and it smacked into the shoulder of another Dane.

I dropped my bow, drew my sword and, pulling my shield around ran at them shouting, "Ulfheonar!"

There were four warriors running towards me. They were handicapped by the bodies of the three dead Danes lying before them and the fact that Olaf Leather Neck and Haaken were leading my warriors to assault the warriors behind them. Two had spears while the other two were trying to draw swords at the same time as they swung their shields around. I fended off the two spears which obligingly came at my left side. I brought my sword across at head height. It bit into the neck of one of them. His blood spurted across the face of the second. I twisted my sword as I whipped it sideways so that its point rammed into his face. The two spearmen had pulled back their weapons to strike at me again. This time they divided their attack. I stepped closer to them and punched with my shield while I stabbed with my sword. I found flesh with my sword and the boss of my shield hit the other Dane in the face. Too close to me for it to be of any use he dropped his spear and tried to reach my neck with two mighty hams of fists. I brought the hilt of my sword around and, hitting him hard in the side of the head, it knocked him to the ground. He lay stunned and I gave him a warrior's death.

As I withdrew my sword a Dane with a war axe saw his chance and swung it as I was standing upright. Rolf's arrow appeared out of his mouth as though it was a magic trick. He, too fell to the floor. Haaken was being beset by three warriors. His hands whirled as he fought them off. I ran at them with my sword held before me. One sensed my movement and turned. He had no mail and my sword tore into his side. I used my shield to push him from my blade and then blocked the axe which had threatened to take Haaken's head. I swung my shield around so that the metal edge cracked into the chin of the other warrior and Haaken gutted him.

"Thank you, Jarl Dragonheart!"

The ambush was almost at an end. None had passed me and my men were despatching the wounded. I saw that at least half of the dead had arrows in them. My archers had reaped a fine harvest. As the last Dane sighed his way to the Otherworld I sheathed my sword and headed down to the end of the column. I was anxious to speak with the Saxons. It was ironic that a couple of years ago I would have slain them too but now they were allies.

It was only as I walked among the corpses that I realised I should have left one alive, to interrogate. It was too late now. My three scouts were tending to the Saxons. My men had captured two Danish horses. One Saxon stood. He held out his hand, "Thank you Jarl Dragonheart. I am Thegn Tostig of Beadnell. I am indebted to you. They planned to give us the blood eagle at their camp."

"Do you know where their home is?"

"They boasted that by nightfall we would be in their homes and our lungs would flap like an eagle."

That gave me a rough idea of where their village would be. We needed to backtrack down the trail. "Our horses are there. We will take you there and decide what it so to be done."

"We will join you! We will have vengeance on these butchers. They take heads!"

I shook my head, "Your king will need brave warriors like you. When I said what is to be done I wondered if it might be safer to head west and pass through my land."

I could see he was disappointed but, as we headed up the trail I saw him examining my men. Our mail and our weapons marked us as different to ordinary warriors but they also carried themselves differently. After we had given them food Thegn Tostig said, "You may be right. There were few of us who survived the battle. We fought well but they outwitted us. I think we will travel due north. We will be travelling through land we know and reach home quicker. If you give us weapons, then we will make sure we are not captured a second time. Better to die with a sword in the hand than have your backbone laid bare."

"Take the two horses and any of the weapons and arms you wish from the dead. Take their mail. We will not need it. When you rise, we will be gone. We have work to do."

While he and his men searched the dead I gathered my men around me. "We did not pass a settlement and so it must be to the south of us. We back track down the trail and seek it. Tomorrow we find it and in the night, we will sow the seeds of terror."

Erik Ulfsson nodded, "We have already profited by the death of these Danes. They had taken much treasure from the Saxons." He held up a golden torc. It was not large but it was the type some Saxons wore.

Haaken said, "It is not treasure we need. We need to slay as many Danes as we can and make them think twice about attacking the Land of the Wolf."

Snorri said, "We found the signs of more trails heading south, Jarl. I think the Danes are finished harrying the ones who fled the battle."

"Then we have come at the perfect time. They will drink and they will celebrate. There will be other prisoners to torture. The last thing they will expect is an attack in their own homes. They will feel safe there."

We left so quietly, the next morning, that the Saxons did not even stir. We were Ulfheonar and no one heard us unless we intended it. Snorri went with Aðils to find this Danish camp. We had examined the bodies and from the clan markings on their helmets we discovered that this was the clan of serpent. One of the dead had a fresh skull attached to his belt. However, he was serpent clan. It showed that the cult of the skulls was growing.

In the end, any of us could have found the settlement. We could smell their wood fires. Snorri and Aðils rode back to tell us that there was just a ditch and a palisade around the Danish village to keep out animals. "It has a large warrior hall and the hall of a jarl. The warriors we slew were not the only ones for there are twenty, at least, in the stad. There may have been others in the warrior hall."

"How far away is it?"

"Not far. We have found somewhere we can hobble the horses."

I looked at the sky. It was just after noon. "Then we will camp and rest. This will be a busy night."

After finding the clearing we prepared for war as we always did. I used a whetstone to put an edge on my sword and seax. I then applied the red cochineal around my eyes. I slung my shield over my back and finally donned my wolf cloak. While the others went through their rituals I hung my bow and quiver from the saddle of my horse. Night was not the time for arrows. I had taken a seax from one of the Danes I had killed and I put that in my boot.

When all were ready we followed Aðils through the dark. The night favoured us for it hid the moon. We went in single file. I was in the middle. We had the younger ears and eyes at the fore. I saw the glow of a huge fire in the heart of the settlement. It would spoil the night vision of the sentries. I smelled those who lived here. The Danes were not as clean as we and the smell of their night soil and water hung in the air. We heard their animals as they waited to be milked and we heard the sound of laughter. The laughter would soon turn to tears.

I waved Olaf and Haaken to the left and right. They led the men who had followed them in the ambush. I had my three scouts and Rolf and Rollo with me. Rolf's axe hung from his back and he held a short sword and seax in his hand. I just held a seax. There would be time for Ragnar's Spirit later on.

We moved slowly towards the gate. It was open. I wondered if they expected the band we had slain. There were two sentries there. I saw their shadows and we heard their words as they talked. We crept closer and I heard them speaking of the great victory. I discovered the name of their thegn. His name was Peder Poulson. It sounded as though he had managed to gain some honour by killing Prince Athelstan's standard bearer. It explained the celebration.

Snorri and I crept forward. Aðils and Beorn had been happy to do this but I was still jarl and I needed to show my men that I was not yet ready to watch others do my fighting for me. I moved stealthily. I just moved one limb at a time and my eyes never left the shadow I was stalking. I could smell them. It was the smell of stale sweat and unwashed blood mixed with pig fat. When I was just two paces from the Danish sentry I began to rise. I did not need to look at Snorri. We had done this before. I took one more step as I reached out with my left hand. I pulled his head towards me as I ripped my seax across his throat. He gave a sigh of death and then I caught his body before it hit the ground. Snorri's sentry was dead too.

I waved my hand and the other four joined us. As we stepped through the gate I saw the huge fire. The smoke drifted towards us. I kept low as I led my men inside the wooden wall. There would be at least two other gates and Haaken and Olaf would be using those. I changed hands with my seax and drew Ragnar's Spirit. I immediately felt the power surge through my body. I felt invincible. The others spread out. Our aim was to kill as many of the Danes as we could. I headed for the jarl's hall. I knew that Rolf and Rollo would follow me and guard my back. It gave me the confidence to move swiftly.

There was a sudden cry from my left. Someone had died noisily. I saw the two warriors at the door of the thegn's hall stand and draw their swords. They were hearth-weru. I hurried towards them. The hearth-weru were looking to their right and the origin of the cry. There were just three steps leading up to the hall and I leapt up them. I had not swung my shield around. I had my seax in my hand. Neither of the hearth-weru had a shield but they both grabbed their axes when they sensed my approach. Holding my seax up I swung my sword in a wide arc. I saw the axe sweeping down and I jabbed the seax at the Dane's hands. It was sharp and I severed two fingers with my seax as my sword bit into his side.

Rolf's axe head was buried in the side of the second hearth-weru. I pushed the body from my sword and ran into the hall.

The jarl was drinking with four of his hearth-weru. He looked up in surprise as the three of us burst into the hall. Speed was vital and I ran across to the five of them even as they were trying to get to weapons. The jarl threw his horn at me. I ducked and then swung my sword into the back and side of a hearth-weru who was trying to draw his weapon. He had been drinking and was slow. He paid for that with his life.

His death, however, afforded the jarl the chance to grab his shield and his sword. He rushed at me swinging his sword wildly. I think he expected me to flinch but I did not. I blocked his sword at the hilt with my seax. His shield covered his body and so I stabbed down at his exposed boot with my sword. I pinned his foot to the wooden floor. He screamed with pain and I ripped my seax across the back of his hand. He reeled and before he could regain his balance I brought my sword overhand and split his head in two.

One of the hearth-weru threw a chair at me. I was not expecting it and it knocked me to the side. His companion saw his chance and he pulled back his sword to stab me. As I tumbled over I struck out with Ragnar's Spirit. I caught the edge of the blade which swung to end my life and then Rollo Thin Skin used his own sword to take the head of the hearth-weru.

"Thank you Rollo!"

The jarl's hall was now filled with the dead. I grabbed the seal from around the jarls' neck and stuffed it in my pouch. We moved out of the door. The hall had been relatively quiet. Outside was a cacophony of screams and cries. The warrior hall was on fire. As I glanced to my left I saw women and children fleeing. It could not be helped. I would not worry about the fact that the Danes would know I was abroad; there was nothing I could do now. This was *wyrd*. By the time they discovered the news we would have moved. I had decided to be the will o'the wisp. We had horses and we would vanish into the night.

The fight was still not over. We had caught them unawares but a man will fight hard for his family even if he knows he is doomed to die. And die they did. The women and children fled, leaving us with the stad to ourselves.

"Aðils, take Rollo and fetch the horses. Karl Karlsson go with Olvir and search the bodies. Beorn, see if there are any horses here."

Olaf came over with a large hunk of venison. "There is food, jarl! We eat hot food and drink ale tonight."

"Before you do take four men and make sure that all of the Danes are dead. Are there any injuries?" I saw Leif the Banner tying a bandage around Einar Hammer Arm's arm.

"Einar forgot that he has no mail on his arms!"

"The Dane had a hidden knife. Besides, it is just a scratch!"

It was almost dawn by the time we had devoured the food, gathered the treasure and found four horses. We packed our treasure in the spare horses and headed south. I had spent the night contemplating what we might do. South would seem the strangest of choices for it led us towards Loidis and the heartland of the Danes. I hoped they would think we had fled west or north. It would take the refugees some time to reach friends and by the time riders had been sent to the stad we would be long gone.

Snorri led us up over a high ridge which was rock covered. It would make tracking difficult. It would still be possible to follow us but we would increase our lead and make it hard for them to find us. I had Beorn trailing us by a thousand paces. He removed any sign we left and watched for any Danish scouts who were seeking us. Snorri knew the land well and he found little used shepherd's paths. Eventually we came to a heavily wooded area. He stopped and turned, "We are five Roman miles from Loidis here, Jarl. Eoforwic is just twenty miles north and east of us. If we had to flee quickly then we could find the Roman Road."

"You have done well, Snorri."

We entered the woods and travelled until we came to a clearing with a stream. We had plenty of cold meat taken from the Serpent clan's feast. After we had unsaddled, fed and watered our horses we set guards. Each of us would take a watch. I lay in my furs and examined the seal. There was no serpent upon it. When I examined it, I recognised the writing. It was the writing of the Romans. I could read a little Latin and I recognised the double XX. It was Roman for twenty. There was an eagle too. I remembered that Aiden had told me this was the symbol of the Roman legions. The jarl had been given this but by whom? I fell asleep speculating.

The next morning, we split up into three groups. We would seek out Danes. I led my scouts, Rollo and Rolf. I felt safe with my skilled scouts. Their noses were worth gold. Aðils followed a path from the woods. I would have chosen the broader greenway which Haaken took but he seemed confident. The path twisted and turned through the trees. Eventually it came out above a small Roman Road. Signalling for us to wait he went down to the road and put his ear to it.

He hurried back. "Men are coming from the east."

We disappeared into the bracken, gorse and shrubs. We were invisible. We heard the approach of the Danes. It was a large warband. I did not move my head but peered through the leaves. It was the Skull Takers. We saw skulls, some bleached white, hanging from their belts and spears. I had no idea how many there were. We would have to watch them pass. We would not harm them. We needed to find out where their homes were. The night was made for the Ulfheonar. It disguised our numbers and made us more terrifying. We used the day to find our enemies. After they had passed I pointed towards them. With Aðils leading we followed, always keeping to the cover which Aðils seemed to find as easily as a fisherman might find a shoal of plump fish.

After we had followed them for a couple of Roman miles I was able to estimate numbers. There looked to be thirty. Only Aðils was close enough to hear their words. I saw the tendril of smoke in the distance. The ground was descending. We were heading into a valley. I was close enough to Aðils to see him signal for us to take cover. We dropped and disappeared in an instant. I heard voices from ahead. There were more Danes. I had to know more. I snaked my way past the others until I lay next to Aðils. He held his finger to his lips. I nodded.

We listened. At first it was hard to discern their words for they had a strong accent but gradually I did. There was a second band of Danes and they were coming from the west. They spoke of a summons from one they called the chief. I guessed they meant Baggi Skull Splitter. They spoke of his great victory over the Saxons. There was a disagreement about their next action. One of those we could hear wished the clan to attack and conquer the rest of the land of the Saxons but the other said that was not the chief's plan. After they had rested they moved off. When they had gone I raised my head and saw that there was a spring where they had stopped. This was a halt only. They had yet to reach their final destination.

I waved Snorri forward, "Is Loidis close?"

"Can you not smell the smoke from their fires? It is less than three Roman miles away."

"Then we can return to our camp."

We were the first ones back and we spoke of what we had seen. "We have a problem. If we attack again and they discover we are here, then it may prompt them to attack our land."

Rolf Horse Killer said, "But this is a perfect chance for us to kill Danes. We could have slain many of those we saw today. We could have disappeared after."

"Perhaps. We need a prisoner who can tell us what they are saying in Loidis."

Haaken was right, "Then tomorrow we will return to the same place and capture one who is heading away from Loidis."

Haaken had discovered a village five miles south of us. Olaf Leather Neck had been bolder. He had found a small band of Danes and he had attacked them and killed them. "There were only twelve of them. Our arrows killed seven and the rest were no match for us."

"What clan?"

"The clan of the otter."

We had met those before. I explained what I intended. Tomorrow, Olaf and Haaken, you keep your men here. Be ready to raid the village Haaken One Eye found. We will go to the greenway and try to take a prisoner."

We had to wait until late afternoon but we heard hooves as four horsemen rode down the road. It was child's play to use our bows to kill three and for Rolf to live up to his name and slay the fourth horse. The rider fell heavily and cracked his head. We took the three horses and the weapons. Rollo cut a couple of hunks of horsemeat. I hoped they would think we were Saxons, fled from the battle, who were starving. It would confuse the Danes at the very least.

The Dane awoke to find his arms pinned to the ground and an axe head close enough to shave him. "You are a warrior of the Skull Taker clan."

I spoke the words quietly and with confidence. We had seen the skull hanging from his belt and spied the crude metal skull amulet he wore around his neck. He nodded sullenly.

"Before you die what is your name; taker of babies' heads?"

He struggled in vain. My men held all four limbs tightly, "I am Næwe Nefison and I kill no babies."

We had cut the skull from his waist and I held it up. "This was no warrior! Do you fight dwarves?"

"Just give me my sword and kill me! I will wait for you in the Otherworld."

I smiled and took out my seax. "It is not as simple as that. My men do not like Skull Takers. You have slain too many of our people for that. If I am to give you your sword, then I need something in return." I had begun to make him speak to me. Had he remained silent then I would have learned nothing. Once a warrior started to talk it was easier to extract information. Belligerent silence was the worst thing. "Just answer one or two questions and you shall have your sword." I allowed my seax to hover close to his eye.

"I will not betray Prince Baggi Skull Splitter."

"I would not dream of asking a warrior such as you to betray your leader. I wish to find your prince. I would fight him."

I saw his eyes and head turn as he looked at how few of us there were. "You would be slain. There are but a handful of you."

"We are Ulfheonar and besides, the result of such a fight is in the hands of the Norns."

"Prince Baggi is a mighty warrior. He has never lost a combat."

"Then you would be sending me to my death and we would meet in the Otherworld sooner."

I saw him considering. If he told us where his leader was then I would die. That much was clear. He gave a smile, "Prince Baggi has twenty oathsworn warriors. They have never lost a warrior in battle and never tasted defeat."

"Perhaps when we get there then they shall. We beat you four."

"You caught us unawares and used arrows! Warriors do not use arrows! You are all nithings!" He spat.

I nodded, "Then where is he? Loidis?"

I saw him decide to speak. He had weighed all up in his mind and saw neither dishonour nor disloyalty in sending me to meet his prince and his death. "He has escorted the four witches to the magical cave on the Nidd. When they have spoken with the spirits of the stone witches he will return! The holy women have promised that we will have victory in the Land of the Wolf! Soon every Dane will descend upon your land and it will be ours! Now give me my sword!"

I stood and nodded to Aðils. He gave him his sword. As soon as he held it he swung it at me. It was a treacherous act. He was close enough to me so that he could have connected with my leg. Rolf's axe took his head before the sword had moved a hand span.

"Treacherous Dane!" He spat at the dead body.

Aðils asked, "Where is this cave? Should we go there and end the life of this prince and his witches?"

Snorri shook his head and clutched his wolf amulet. "I know this cave. We went there once and found stone bodies within. They were trolls. The place is sacred to witches. We would die; even the Dragonheart."

His voice was laden with doom and I saw my younger warriors taken aback. "Snorri is right. I risked the isle of Syllingar to rescue Ylva for I had no choice. Now I have a choice. Besides I think it is *wyrd* that we met this warrior. The Nidd is half a day north of here. We have the opportunity to hurt this Baggi Skull Splitter in his own home. We can attack Loidis!"

Chapter 13

"Attack Loidis? That is madness, Jarl!" The reaction of my warriors when I told them was mixed. Olaf Leather Neck's words reflected the view of most of them.

Haaken smiled, "Olaf Leather Neck, you will never be a jarl for your vision does not extend beyond the end of your axe. The jarl does not intend for us to assault their walls but to get within them and create terror."

"Is that true jarl?"

I nodded, "We know that the witches and the best of his warriors are away. We gain entry to the town and strike in the night."

"How do we gain entry?"

"Three of us will take skulls from the dead we killed today and pretend to be Danes returned from hunting Saxons. The three of us slay the guards on the gates and let us in. If we ride the three horses we captured today and wear their mail then they will not be suspicious."

Snorri said, "You cannot go Jarl."

"Why not?"

"Because you are known. Your sword is known. You have spoken without your helmet and your wolf cloak. We have not. When we have taken off our cloaks and changed armour then we are unrecognisable. We three scouts will go. It is *wyrd*."

"Snorri is right Jarl and," Haaken pointed to the sun which was beginning to dip, "we should leave now before the men you slew are discovered."

They were right and I acquiesced. We rode back and stripped the bodies. We put our men's cloaks, bows and mail on their horses and the three of them headed back down the road to Loidis. I clasped Snorri's arm, "May the Allfather be with you."

He nodded, "If you see our heads on the walls then know that I died happy serving you and the clan jarl."

"You will not die."

"We all die and each time we fight it brings our death just a little bit closer."

He was right. We were no longer as young as we had been. Our experience and skills could only keep us alive so long. We gave them a start and then took to the woods to follow the road which led to the old capital of Elmet. The town nestled on the side of a valley with a bubbling river running close by. From our vantage point a thousand paces away we could see that there were a number of large halls. It was a busy place and reminded me of my own stad. I could hear the ringing of hammers on metal. Smoke rose from fires and the smell of smoking fish drifted up to us. I peered anxiously at the gate. Our men were not there. If they had been apprehended, then there would be some sign of commotion within. There appeared to be none. We hobbled our horses and prepared to descend when darkness fell.

We were to the east of the walls and when the sun began to dip we started our approach. We would be hidden in the dark. Once again I held my sharpened seax. I had two additional ones now. One in each boot. Every man knew what to do. Once we gained entry we would slay the sentries who remained on the walls. My plan was to set fire to their warrior halls and to escape in the confusion. Our victories so far had been small. We had slain Danes but they were like the grains of sand on a beach. If we could fire their warrior halls, then we had the chance to hurt the Skull Takers.

We crept to within forty paces of the walls and lay in the undergrowth watching the walls. We saw the shadows of the sentries above the gate. They had no towers but we could see other sentries walking the walls. There looked to be eight in total. We were in the hands of Snorri and the others. When the gates opened then we could enter. Until then we waited and we watched.

It was a low whistle which alerted us. I rose and hurried to the walls. The gates were not yet open but the whistle was Snorri's. We crossed the bridge over the ditch and waited. I heard the sound of a bar being removed and then the gates opened just wide enough to admit us. We slipped through. I pointed to the walls and Rolf and Rollo went one way while Olvir Grey Eye and Cnut Cnutson went the other. They would slay the sentries on the walls.

These were short nights and we would have to work quickly. Luckily the people were all asleep and the only ones awake were the sentries. Even as we headed towards the halls they were dying. The fire in the middle of the settlement was still burning; it would warm the sentries no more. As we approached I saw that there were two men seated with their backs to us. I waved and Aðils and Snorri were on them in an instant. Their knives tore through the Danes' throats. We each grabbed a burning brand. There were three halls. One looked larger and more imposing than the others. I took that to be the jarl's. They were built much as were ours with one door only. It made defence easier.

I ran with Aðils and Snorri. We threw our brands at the door and then stood with our swords ready. The overhanging roof meant that the door was bone dry and I saw the flames flicker and climb up the oaken door. Those sleeping within would be unaware of their danger until the door was aflame. I saw the four warriors who had slain the sentries descending. Their task was to secure horses for us. That would enable us to escape quickly while also denying our enemies the means to pursue us.

As they descended they must have made a noise. The door of the bakery opened and a flour covered baker spied us. Before we could react, he had shouted. "Alarm!"

Snorri hurled a spear and impaled him. It was too late, however, for the alarm had been sounded. The doors of the three halls were already burning but there were other dwellings close by and those within came out. They were not warriors but the men ran at us with whatever weapon they had. I saw Haaken One Eye and his men lay about them with their swords and axes. Those who attacked them fell. Then the door of the hall they had fired burst open. Warriors erupted. Two of them were on fire and they ran out screaming. Others came out like angry wasps from a nest which had been disturbed. Without mail, half asleep and with streaming eyes my men were able to hold them off. The door to our hall stayed ominously shut. The flames had leapt to the roof and the whole building was an inferno. It must have had more materials inside which would catch fire.

It was Olaf Leather Neck and his men who were in danger. Their fire looked to be slower to catch. The door and the front was on fire but not the roof. Even as we watched men hacked an opening in the side of a wall.

"At them!" Aðils, Snorri and Beorn followed me with raised weapons as we hurried to stem the breach. I hurled one of my seaxes at the leading warrior. An awkward weapon to throw I was lucky. The Dane had no helmet and the seax struck him in the eye. He raised his hand to remove it and my sword sliced though his middle. As I bent down to pull a second seax from my boot an axe swung where my head had just been. The warrior was to my left and as I pulled out the seax I lunged upwards. The wickedly sharp seax ripped him open from his crotch to his chest. His wriggling, writhing body spoke of a painful death. Although the four of us had stopped some of the warriors, others had emerged from the far side. Even as we slew the ones before us I heard a shout as Olaf and his men were surrounded.

The sound of horses' hooves told me that Cnut and the others had horses. We had to extricate ourselves. Already there was a light appearing in the east. "Haaken! Olaf needs help!"

Olaf and his men were desperately fighting against overwhelming odds. I picked up a shield and ran at the five Danes who were left before us. They had the light behind them and we had the dark. They misjudged their blows and we did not. I ducked beneath the swinging sword as I blocked a blow from a sword.

My own sword swung below the Danish shield and hacked his left leg in two. He fell screaming, his life blood pumping away. The Dane behind was so shocked that he stared. There is no time for hesitation in a battle. I pulled back my arm and my sword rammed through his neck. The five Danes were dead.

"Let us help Olaf!" As we ran I saw that we were too late for Olvir Grey Eye. He lay dead with four dead Danes around him. The sight of our dead comrade enraged my men and the Danish warriors who remained were slaughtered. "Mount and bring Olvir with us! They shall not have his skull!" I picked up a brand from the fire.

Most of the warriors were now dead, dying or lay in the halls burning. As Olvir was draped over a horse I mounted. "Set fire to as many buildings as you can." I spied a round building. I had not seen it before for it was hidden by the halls. I saw the skulls which adorned the outside. I know not how but I knew that this was the lair of the witches. I rode between the burning buildings. The heat was intense. When I reached the round building, I rode into the door. I hurled the burning brand inside. There must have been something inside which burned easily for a wall of flame rose before me making my horse rear. I was lucky I was a good rider. I leant forward and, as he landed whipped his head around and galloped out. The fires were now out of control. The wind had spread them to nearby buildings and the Danes ignored us as they tried to douse the fires. We galloped through the gates and headed into the rising sun.

I allowed my scouts to ride ahead and I followed at the rear with Haaken One Eye. I turned around to see the inferno we had created. I saw a column of smoke rising to the skies. Haaken said, "Olvir has a good journey to Valhalla, Jarl. He is taken there by the very fires we lit. It was a good death!"

By the time we reached our horses dawn had broken. We took Olvir the Grey and buried him by the stream. With his sword in his hands and his wolf cloak covering his body we placed him in the grave we had dug and then laid stones upon it before finally adding turf. When the winter snow melted and the stream flooded his body would be washed away and reach the sea. There it would join with the other warriors who had died fighting for the Land of the Wolf.

We led the Danish horses and rode our own which were rested. I had a plan in my mind and it was now being put into action. We would head for Eoforwic. There were Danes who served Baggi Skull Splitter. They were laying siege to the Saxons. We could not raise the siege but we could inspire terror in those who lay outside the gates.

We rode in sombre mood. We had done what I intended but an invaluable warrior now lay dead. Each time an Ulfheonar died it brought us closer to our own death. When I had been young it had not bothered me but now it did. Every death seemed to lessen me. There was just Haaken One Eye left from those warriors who had first served with me. Snorri had been a young boy on Man when he had joined us. He was even younger than Aðils was. Men had become Ulfheonar and fought alongside me and now they were dead. It just made me more determined than ever to make my land safe. Even if all of my Ulfheonar died it would be worth it if the clan lived on.

We passed some small settlements but they were all burned out. I was heading for Fulford and Stamford. It was a vain hope but I thought one of Athelstan's thegns might live yet. We took the secret, hidden ways away from prying eyes. We were nowhere near the Nidd; that lay to the north of us but I worried about riders heading north to tell the Skull Takers that we were loose in their land. It was late afternoon when we reached Fulford. It too was burned out. The corpses we found had no heads. It was a sure sign that the clan of the Skull Takers had been here. Eoforwic was to the north of us and so we pushed on the eight miles or so to Stamford.

It was becoming dark when we reached it and it had all the signs of having been burned out. It had been a vain hope. However, as Snorri and Beorn examined the ground they saw that there were no bodies.

"Here is a mystery. Were they slain and then buried or did the Danes come here and find that there was no one here?" Even Aðils was confused.

"It is as good a place to camp as anywhere else. If the Danes have burned it then they will not return."

Haaken was right, "Get that horsemeat on a fire. We will have hot food tonight." My men all went about their tasks with efficiency. This was what we did. The horses were unsaddled, watered and hobbled. They would graze beneath the trees. Others lit the fires while four of them stood watch. I suddenly noticed that one was missing. "Where is Aðils Shape Shifter?"

Beorn looked around, "He was here with me and now..."

Aðils' skills were such that I did not worry about him but I wondered what he had found. There was a shout from the woods. Our hands went to our weapons and we were alert instantly. Two figures emerged from the woods. One was Aðils and he had his sword in the back of a young Saxon. "I thought I heard something. He was watching us."

"This is my master's hall and he asked me to watch for Danes like you! I am not afraid of you!"

I laughed, "Then learn to recognise the difference. We are not Danes and we know your master, Alfred."

He looked sullenly at me. "You are Vikings! The Danes are Vikings! You are lying to me!"

The humour left my face. "I never lie, Saxon. Where are the people who lived here?" He was silent. "Cnut, hold him. Snorri, take your men and find them. They will be close."

The boy struggled but he was no match for an Ulfheonar. Cnut smiled, "There is little point in struggling. If you annoy me I will cuff you. You will not be harmed, Jarl Dragonheart has spoken."

The Saxon recognised my name and he stopped struggling. He seemed to be appraising me. "You are the warrior who fought the Danes." I nodded. "I have heard that you are the only man who has beaten the Skull Takers but you are of their race."

I shook my head, "No we are not!"

I heard voices approaching. I saw that Beorn and Aðils supported Alfred of Stamford; he was wounded. There were twenty people following. Only four looked to be warriors. The rest were women and children.

"Alfred, what happened?"

My men laid him by the fire. He had a bad cut to his leg. "I was with Prince Athelstan when we met the Danes. You were right, jarl. We should not have fought them. Asser died protecting the prince. I had been wounded already and the priests were tending to my wounds when the banner fell." He pointed to the four warriors. "My oathsworn brought me here. I would have died defending the standard otherwise."

"Then they did well. A banner is of no use if its master lies dead."

"Aye you are right. We came back here. We had a message that the Danes were burning halls and we fled into the woods. They found the hall and burned it. They took our animals but my family survived."

"And they are better off than Asser's family for all of those lie dead. You cannot stay here."

"It is my land."

"The Danes will come again. You have women and children."

"Then they will fight too."

I pointed to the horses. "We have taken some Danish horses. Take them. Twelve of you can be mounted."

"We stay here."

I could see that he was adamant. "Very well. We will try to help you."

"What is it that you do, Jarl Dragonheart?"

"We have been raiding the Danish homes weakening them. We intend to attack those who lay siege to Eoforwic. Perhaps we can help Prince Athelstan's people who took shelter there. He was our ally and I feel I owe it to him."

He brightened. "Then my men can help you. Cedric and Oswald know the land well. They would like the opportunity to get back at these savages."

It was a good idea. "They follow my orders though, thegn."

"Of course."

We shared our food with them and I told Alfred what we had done. I saw the young Saxon boy, Ethelred, taking in every word. "But how do you survive when you are so few. Prince Athelstan had a mighty army. I saw them march to war and they were slaughtered."

"They did not fight them the right way. You need more than courage to defeat a Dane. You need a mind as cunning as theirs."

Olaf Leather Neck added, "You need good armour and you need skill. Courage alone will not win you the battle. Your prince was brave but he was ill equipped to fight such an enemy."

Ethelred looked at Olaf, "But you are?"

Olaf Leather Neck laughed. He held out his arm. It was festooned with warrior bracelets. "These came from the enemies I killed. We are killers, Ethelred the Saxon. If you fight us, then you had better make sure we are dead for we will fight on even though the odds are stacked against us."

The next morning Ethelred wished to accompany us. I refused, "We need warriors and not boys. Stay here and learn to be a killer."

Cedric led us to the eastern gate. It was the closest to Stamford. He said that there was a camp of Danes there. They guarded a bridge into the city. The Fosse river was a natural defence. "I think, lord, that they are there to stop the city being reinforced or those within escaping. They do not have ditches and they seem content to sit and drink."

"How many are there?"

"Perhaps forty; some slept and one or two kept watch. Most were seated around the fire."

An idea came into my mind. It was suicide for Alfred and his people to remain in the woods. They would either be found or they would starve to death. If we could eliminate these Danes, then they could enter the city. Five more warriors and the boy might make a difference. Cedric took us to a low rise overlooking the position. The Saxon was right.

"Cedric, I want you and Oswald to take our horses and return to your master. Fetch them here."

"Here, lord?"

"Tonight we rid the land of this band of Danes and then you can take shelter in the city. You will be safe there."

He nodded and left.

I turned to my men. "We have the afternoon to devise a way to get close to these Danes and, as soon as it is night, kill them!"

Snorri took his scouts and returned some hours later. "The trees and the bushes go to within thirty paces of them. We could have slit a few throats even now, in daylight. They are drinking."

"Take your men and head west. See where the next band is. I am guessing by the next bridge. I need to know if they can aid this band or not."

They returned shortly before Alfred and his people arrived, "It will be close, Jarl. There are fifty men there and they look as though they know their business. They are using arrows to harass the defenders and their leaders are vigilant."

It did not change my plans but it gave me added problems. When Alfred arrived, he frowned, "Can this be done and is it wise?"

"It is wiser than risking a winter in the woods with Danes all around you. You can take some of the Danish horses in with you. They will augment the food."

He nodded, "Many of Prince Athelstan's advisers did not trust you, jarl. They thought that you lied to the prince to inveigle yourself to his confidence. He always believed you would keep your word. I know not what will happen now but I will be your advocate. You have come to aid us here even though it appears a hopeless cause."

"Do not think too well of me, Thegn, I came here to kill Danes and to weaken them. They wish to take my land from me."

"I do not think they will succeed."

"If they do then you will find our bleached bones where we fought to the last man. That is our way."

We mounted all of the thegn's people. His warriors took children with them and the older women doubled up with a man on each horse. We left them, as night fell, and slipped down close to the Danes. Those within the walls had not attempted to discourage the Danes and they were in a festive mood. We waited until they began to roast their food on the open fire and drink heavily. We moved into position. With just twenty paces to cover we were confident that we could manage it in the dark. It seemed to take an age for the sun to dip behind the castle walls. Once again I left my shield around my back. We would hit the Danes like a whirlwind. Aðils, Snorri and Beorn slipped in first. They were fast and they were silent. The four sentries who were talking closest to us died with barely a murmur. The fourth to die watched as his three companions grew another mouth and then he too fell.

The others saw nothing. With the city walls quiet it was another night to pleasure themselves. We burst in on them silently with flashing blades. I hacked across a Dane's back as I gutted a second. A third warrior looked around in disbelief as his two friends died. My sword took his head. It was barely a heartbeat into the attack and six of the forty had died. I saw Olaf's axe as it took two Danes in one blow. Then the noise and the cries began. The first eight had died silently. Now men shouted, first in alarm and then in pain as swords, axes and seaxes ripped and tore through flesh. Two men fled west, towards the next Danish camp. Aðils had brought his bow. He had the fastest hands I had ever seen. The two arrows pitched them into the Fosse.

"Now Thegn! Ride!"

Already Cnut and some of our men were racing into the woods to fetch our horses. We stood back as the Saxons galloped over the bridge. We heard the challenge from the walls and then Thegn Alfred's voice rang out, "Open the gate! We are friends!"

Cedric and the other warriors, along with Ethelred dismounted before the bridge and handed their reins to us. Ethelred said, "I will remember you Jarl."

Cedric just said, "Jarl you are a true warrior. You are like Beowulf. I would follow you into any battle!" I nodded and clasped his arm.

Even as we mounted our horses I heard the clamour from our left. I threw my leg over the horse and, with Haaken and Snorri, rode towards the advancing Danes. They were a noisy shadow to the west. I heard a cry from the walls of Eoforwic, "We are safe, Jarl!" They were within Eoforwic's walls and we could make our own escape.

I whipped my horse's head around, "Ride! Ride!"

I saw the wall of metal and wood as the Danes raced along the Fosse in an attempt to get to us. We were mounted and we knew how to ride. I kicked my horse in the flanks and he took off east. We would ride back to Stamford where we would spend the night and the morning. I had already decided where we would head next. We would go north. We had one more raid to make and then I would head for the Land of the Wolf. We had risked too much already. I had to get home and then plan how to defeat these Danes.

Chapter 14

I awoke stiff. I was getting too old to spend nights sleeping rough. The constant fighting made my muscles and joints ache. I did not feel it when I fought but when I stopped and I slept then I knew. We left our camp in the late afternoon and headed north and east. I wanted the Danes to think we were heading for Hwitebi. That would make sense. I could have a drekar waiting. As we approached the small village of Mal's Tun we headed north and west. The land was clear of Danes. They had scoured the land and slaughtered those Saxons who had not taken refuge in Eoforwic. I planned an attack on the north gate. The Danes would have a strong presence there. If the garrison fled for safety it would be north. We would have to use all of our skills to get close and to terrify our foes. Then we would head home.

We headed for the gate known as Gillygate. We rode cautiously for I knew that we would not catch the Danes unawares this time. They knew we were hunting. They would be expecting us to attack and they would have guards watching every direction. This would be a true test of the Ulfheonar.

We found a marshy area close to a wood and it was perfect. We could tether our horses in the woods and use the boggy ground as a defence for our camp. We rested there for half a day. This would be our last raid before we headed home. We had already done all that I had hoped and we had weakened the Danes. I wondered if it would be enough to make them think twice about attacking us. If we had done this much damage with a handful of men, then how much could we do with the whole clan? Even as the hope flickered through my mind I dismissed it. Baggi Skull Splitter and his witches would want revenge. Their warriors were expendable.

As dusk approached I sent my three scouts to inspect the Danish siege works. I prepared for battle. As I sharpened my blade I realised how weary I felt. There had been a time when I could have campaigned for months and felt fresh but my joints ached when I rose each morning. My body took longer to obey my commands. Had he still been alive I would have considered handing power to Wolf Killer but that hope had been snatched away by the Norns and my enemies. Now that hope lay with Ragnar and Gruffyd.

Karl Karlsson came to me, "Jarl we are running out of food. The salted meat and fish we brought have been almost exhausted. We shared the horsemeat with the Saxons. Had we not we might have had enough for a few more days. We run out tomorrow."

"Then we will have to tighten our belts, Karl. Have the men pick the early blackberries and crab apples."

The scouts returned. Snorri shook his head ruefully. "This will not be as easy, Jarl Dragonheart. They are like an ant's nest which has been disturbed. They scurry and prepare for an attack. They are looking outward, jarl as well as in."

"How many are there?"

"There is a band of sixty."

"And the ground?"

"It is flat and cleared. Even as we watched they were hacking down the elder and the blackberries which would have hidden us. The only cover now is a few deserted huts a hundred paces from their lines and they are astride the road to the north."

"What lies north of the huts?"

"There is a cleared area that they farmed. It is grazing land and then the woods begin. If we travelled a thousand paces, then we would reach them. This is the same wood."

I looked at the wood for the first time. The bog to the west gave us protection there. We had the road to the east for escape. I said, "Gather round, I have decided how we will attack these Danes."

None had their helmets on but each of my warriors held a weapon in his hand. So long as we were in the land of our enemies they would be prepared for an attack. Others might be caught unawares but not my men. I saw that Aðils Shape Shifter stood to one side where he could both hear and smell an enemy.

"We will attack them." None showed any surprise. "Snorri has told us that there are huts within bow range of the Danes. We use them before it is dark. Then we draw them into these woods after the sun has set. We make them risk the night and the Ulfheonar. We lead them in the woods to confuse them. If we are beset, then we disappear." I pointed to the west. "The boggy ground there will catch them unawares. The trees here are our allies. When dawn comes, we meet back at the horses and then we go home. This will be our last night here in the land which is now the land of the Danes. Each warrior we slay this night is one less for our people to fight when they come."

Haaken nodded, "And they will still come, jarl. We have hurt this Baggi Skull Splitter. He will be like a wild bear roused from a sleep."

Olaf Leather Neck nodded as he stroked the edge of his axe, "And like a wild bear, while its attack might be furious and terrifying, it is wild. The wolves which hunt the wild bear use cunning and guile. They are cold and work together. I am happy, Haaken One Eye, for the bear to be wild and angry. I would not relish a cold and calculating foe. These Danes have already shown us that when they plan they can be dangerous. Sigtrygg found that to his cost. This is a good plan."

"We work in pairs. Let us go now and be ready towards day's last light."

I took my Saami bow. I had ten arrows left. They would be enough. Haaken naturally came with me. We had fought side by side since we were young and he had two eyes. We filtered through the woods in our pairs. We were like afternoon shadows flitting through the dappled ground. The huts hid us from the Danes although those on the walls might have seen shadows emerge from the woods and scurry to the shelter of the four huts. With our wolf cloaks we would have been taken for animals. I saw, by the design of the huts, that they were Saxon. They were now deserted. Although there was no sign of those who had occupied them I guessed that they had either fled within the walls of Eoforwic or had been slain.

All of us knew our own range with our bows. Snorri had told us that the Danes were a hundred paces from us. I had risked a glance around the end of the last house and seen that the Danes had erected a crude barricade of stakes intertwined with brambles which would both deter and slow down an enemy in the night. They were close together guarding the road and the approach to the gate. These walls and this gate had been built by the Romans and the Danes would not be able to take them without loss. After returning to the others I nodded and pulled back my bow. The others copied me. As I released so did they. I had another in the air even as the first plunged down. I heard the cries and shouts. The arrows coming from the sky would disorientate and confuse the enemy. I sent a third arrow. They would now be taking cover.

I went to the end of the last hut and peered around. By the light of their braziers and the last rays of the sun I could see that the Danes had their shields up. I held up my hand to stop the shower of arrows. It would be a waste of valuable arrows to continue. I had no idea how many we had slain but I knew, from the cries, that we had hurt them. I was close enough to hear their voices although I could not make out what they were saying. I saw a pair of Danes detach themselves from the shield wall and clamber over the barrier. I dropped my hand and my men sent arrows into the air. I dropped my hand as the arrows struck. Three arrows struck one Dane who fell across the barrier. As the other hurried back he was hit in the leg.

I glanced to the west. The sun was beginning to set. An orange glow lit up the walls of Eoforwic as though they were on fire. I heard more orders being shouted and a head appeared out of the shield wall. When the Danish sentry gave a shout,

I knew that I had been spotted. I had my bow ready and I sent an arrow towards the sharp-eyed Dane. My arrow smacked into his nose and he fell back. They knew where we were. I raised my arm again. They would have to move their own barrier to get at me. I heard more orders and then the shield wall began to break up as they started to move the stakes and brambles. I dropped my arm and arrows showered them. My men were releasing blindly but they had the area well covered. The Danes were forced to work one handed with their shields held above them. It would tire them. I saw men struck. Some were slight wounds but I saw others crawling away. They would not follow us.

The light was fading fast as they cleared the last of their defences. I turned and hurried back to my men, "Enough. They come!" We moved back toward the woods. Behind me I heard a roar as the barricade was dismantled and the angry Danes hurried after us. We reached the eaves of the woods. Here the trees were open and there was space. Deeper within was darker and treacherous underfoot. We turned with bows at the ready. There was still enough light to see the enemy. When the Danes emerged from behind the huts we took aim and sent our arrows at the Danes. Our first arrows caught them unawares and six fell. Then they raised their shields. At a range of fifty paces I could not miss. I lowered my aim and sent an arrow at the knee of the leading warrior. The arrow head smashed the kneecap and the warrior crumpled to the ground. A second arrow ended his life.

"Shield wall!"

They formed a shield wall. I circled my arm and we headed back into the woods. It was now becoming too dark for our arrows to be effective and I slung my bow as we hurried back into the darkness of the trees. Haaken and I could have been alone for the others disappeared as though they had been swallowed by the night. With black armour, black wolf cloaks and faces smeared with cochineal we were invisible. We stopped and drew our swords. The noise we heard was the noise of angry Danes as they entered the woods. Their shield wall had to break up. We were still and they were not. The fading light showed them up while, in the darkness, we remained hidden. They came with their shields up for they were expecting arrows. I heard cries as they tripped on tree roots. The woods were our ally. The Danes spread out.

Haaken and I were sheltering behind a rowan tree. We peered out from either side. Our black helmets and the cochineal on our faces hid us. The Danes had to keep lowering their shields to see where they were going. We saw their white faces beneath their helmets. I held my sword at shoulder level and watched the Dane approach me. To my right I heard a cry as one of my men slew a Dane. The one approaching me glanced to the side and pulled his shield closer to him. Just his eyes appeared over the rim of his shield. He thought he was safe. I could smell him and I heard his panting breath. I lunged forward. He could only have seen the tip of my sword at the last moment as it entered his eye and then his brain. The only sound of death was his body falling to the ground.

A warrior to his right said, "Sweyn!" It was followed by a cry as Haaken ended his life. I tapped Haaken and we moved further back into the woods. We headed toward the boggy ground. It was away from our horses and the ground was uneven. We knew where the banks were and had walked the paths. The Danes would be unfamiliar.

We halted behind a pair of saplings and waited. We could hear the Danes as they moved through the woods. They clattered into branches and stumbled over roots. We also heard the sound of Danes being slain by the invisible Ulfheonar.

"Come out and fight like men you shape shifters! We are not afraid of you! We are protected by the magic of Asta!"

They were shouting to make us answer and then they would know where we hid. We remained silent. It forced them to move. I saw a leaf move and a flash of white showed me a Dane. I swung Ragnar's Spirit at neck height. The Dane's shield covered most of his body but my sword found flesh. The first his comrades knew was when they were spattered with blood. Haaken's sword darted out and there was a scream. I heard movements from behind as more Danes ran to the aid of their comrades. I stepped out from behind the tree and brought the seax up under the metal byrnie of the third Dane. He hit me with the hilt of his sword. It made my helmet ring.

As he fell from my blade I stepped back and Haaken followed me. We walked gingerly down the slope. Years of falling leaves had made it soft and slippery. Our boots tore through the brambles and ivy which twined together. We had to move slowly to avoid falling. Behind us we heard a yell of joy as one of the Danes saw our movement. We did not speed up but kept moving steadily, hunched over, until we were on flatter ground and then we stood. I put my seax in my belt and pulled my shield around.

"We have two of them!" In the distance, I heard the other Danes as they died. The white faces beneath the helmets showed us that there were six Danes. They did not want us to escape and they ran down the bank. It was a mistake. The first three slipped and tripped on the slippery ground and became entangled in the undergrowth. The last three fell over the bodies of the comrades and tumbled down the slope. We stepped forward and in four savage strokes the three lay dead. We wasted no time in stabbing them in the neck. They bled to death. The other three disentangled themselves and ran at us. They were angry. Once again one fell over a dead comrade.

The one who came at me swung his axe with all the force he could muster. I stepped back away from the swing and then, as the head passed before me, darted in with my sword. Its tip was sharp and it pierced the mail, his shirt and his side. I twisted and turned it as I pulled it out. It grated on his ribs and pulled out a tangle of intestines. The third Dane stood and Haaken and I ended his life together.

I pointed to our left and we made our way around the slope. I could hear little in the woods now. By the time we reached our camp most of the Ulfheonar had arrived. They began to clean their weapons. Most were covered in blood but from their movements it was not their own. The last to arrive was Aðils. "The ones who survived have returned to the walls of Eoforwic. They are talking of demons and shape shifters." He laughed, "One was begging for the help of the witches." Fighting in the night was always frightening. Especially when you are used to fighting in a shield wall. The isolation of the wood made the terror of sudden death greater.

"Then let us put distance between us. We have done all that we intended and more."

We headed north, riding through the night. We made better time once we reached the Roman Road. I intended to cross the Dunum at the Roman fort. We would break our journey by the waterfall on the Dunum. We did not spy any pursuers but that was not to say we were not vigilant. With our spare horses, we were able to change them often. It meant we could ride with armour and make much better time.

Haaken rode next to me, "What is on your mind, jarl?"

"My mind?"

"I have not fought alongside you these many years without recognising the signs when you are worried."

"We have a Danish army coming for us. Surely I have reason to be worried."

"You knew that before we left. What has changed?"

"I had thought we had to defeat one clan. I hoped to damage the Skull Takers. Now I see that the witches of the clan have attracted other clans. How do we deal with those? One clan cannot have many warriors but a confederation?"

"It is just numbers you are worried about?"

"If they have large numbers then there is little point in sitting behind our walls. They will make my land a wasteland and then pick off our settlements one by one. It will matter little if we sit behind our walls." I gestured behind me with my thumb, "They were happy just to sit around Eoforwic and wait for it to fall. Cyninges-tūn has no well. We would not last a month. We have to beat them."

"Then we need to meet them on the field of battle."

144

I turned and looked at him, "How many men do we have?"

"Not enough. I know that. But we would never have enough." I saw him look northwards. "You will not want to hear this but we would have to take Ulf's, Ketil's and Asbjorn's men, not to mention Raibeart's. If we had all of those and our bondi then we would stand a fighting chance. Those three jarls have warriors who are better than any Danish warrior. You must have had this in the back of your mind, Jarl Dragonheart, for our men are prepared to stand in a shield wall. If they were only intended to stand on a wall then they would be trained already."

"But I did not know that our enemies would have to be met on the field of battle."

"And yet you have prepared for one. This is *wyrd*."

That night, as we camped by the roaring waterfall I told the others what Haaken and I had discussed. Surprisingly none were surprised. "I would rather meet them on the field of battle, Jarl. When I swing my axe, I need room. I like not fighting from a wall." Olaf Leather Neck was afraid of no one.

"And a Danish army cannot hide like a warband, Jarl. When they attacked Sigtrygg they came in small warbands. An army leaves a mark. It is like a giant snake crawling across the land. Aðils, Beorn and I can find a warband. How much easier to find an army." Snorri might have changed since he killed the witch but he knew his own skills and they were undiminished.

"But what of the stad on the Eden and Ketil's stad? If we take men from there who will defend them?"

"The question is who will attack them? The Saxons? I think they will fear the Danes and King Eanred will hide behind the walls of Bebbanburgh. The Scots? Hibernians? Ulf sent their ships back filled with corpses. They will not attack. The old men and the boys can defend their walls. Haaken is right, we need every warrior we have."

"You are right, Olaf Leather Neck, but I am gambling with my whole land. I am not a gambler."

Haaken laughed, "I have never known such a gambler! You run when common sense says walk. You go into the dark places when you know danger lies there and you take on great odds each time you fight. You are a gambler, Jarl. The difference is this time you are gambling with your people. We speak for the clan. We are happy to stake all alongside you."

By the time we rolled into our furs I was persuaded. Their arguments had won me over. As we crossed the high divide I sent Beorn to Ketil and Asbjorn to ask them to visit and Aðils to Ulf to do the same.

We all looked at our land differently as we travelled the last forty miles west. This would be the land over which the Danes would travel. We would need to find somewhere that we could fight and hold them. We had a small army but it was an army which would fight together. The weakness of the Danes lay in the fact that they were made up of many clans and they were reliant on the witches. I knew the danger that lay in that faith. I had put too much in Kara and Aiden before now. Perhaps faith in the Danish witch and her sisters might prove to be the downfall of the Danes. I began to see a little light.

As we dropped through the dale of Mungo I noticed how beautiful was my land. The rolling hills to the north were like a giant rampart. To the south the land was jagged and steep. Yet even that had a beauty. The sheep dotted about the green fells was a sign of our prosperity. When first we had come that would have been impossible. Raiders would have taken them. Now families farmed. Children were raised and I would not allow a barbarian like Baggi destroy that. Brigid's face came to me as we turned to head south. She was a patient woman and put up with my many faults. I knew that I was lucky to have her. When I reached home, I would show her just what she meant to me. We crossed the gap into the start of my land. I was coming home.

When we neared Ulla's Water I looked up at Úlfarrberg. It was a symbol of our land. The wolves had terrorised us when first we came but now they were a memory here at the mountain named after them. The Danes were a potential terror. If we could draw the Danes here, then we stood a chance. The valley was narrow and the Water deep. With our mountain on one side and the Water on the other we could face them with our best. This was a narrow piece of land on which to fight. I would happily match our best warriors with those we had seen. I now needed to work out how to make Baggi Skull Splitter come the way I wanted.

Chapter 15

It was dusk by the time we reached my home. I had barely passed through the gates when Elfrida ran to me, "Jarl Dragonheart! Great news! Ylva has woken!"

"Those are great tidings; thanks to the Allfather. He has answered my prayers. When did this happen?"

"A few days ago! Kara and Aiden both wept tears of joy!"

I cast my mind back and realised that had been when we had sacked the Skull Taker's home. I wondered if the witch's power had lessened. When I had burned their hut had I destroyed some token which gave them power? Had I forced them to seek me in their own land? If so it was an effect I had not expected but I was grateful, nonetheless. I went directly to their hall. I stepped through the door and I heard Ylva's voice, "It is The Dragonheart! Let me see him!"

She ran to me. She looked like a wraith but her eyes were bright and her arms wide. I picked her up and hugged her. I could not speak. Had I done so I would have unmanned myself. Her voice came in my ear, "Grandfather, you faced a Norn to save me. I have never known such courage. You fought the spirits and you won! Forgive me for ever thinking less of you."

I pulled her away. I had my voice again. "You are of my blood. I would give my life for you. I would give all for any of my family. I am just grateful that you are returned to us."

She nodded, tears streaming down her face. "My place is here with the clan. I am determined that I will help you fight this evil which comes this way."

"You have dreamed?"

"We have dreamt together. There are four witches and they are powerful. They are aided by the Norns for you have angered them."

I nodded, "But are they close?"

She shook her head, "You have hurt them more than you can know. When you burned their shrine…"

"You know of that?"

"We dreamed it. You destroyed some of their power. Just as we harness the power of the Water and the spirits so they harness the power of their bones and they were burned and destroyed. It will take time for them to regain their power."

I nodded and Kara came towards me, "Thank you, father. I feel so foolish. My arrogance almost cost me my daughter and the clan their land. I had begun to believe that the safety of the clan lay with the dreamers. It does not. It lies with the warriors. It is you and the Ulfheonar who should be honoured."

I shook my head, "Honour is nothing! We will have need of you. I believe that the Danes will come and come in such numbers as we have never seen before. I intend to meet them on the field of battle but I would choose the place."

The three of them looked at me. Aiden asked the question, "But how can you make Baggi Skull Splitter do what you wish?"

"I would trick him. I will need your help but I believe we have time to prepare. We have hurt their plans. We have destroyed Loidis. They still have their best warriors but they will need to build. The witches will come for Ylva and to hurt me. My scouts will watch for our foes. But I need you three to make a fog so that the witches cannot discover what we are doing."

They looked at each other. Kara said, "We are stronger now for we know what we face. We will do as you ask but..."

"But they will send spies into our land!"

She looked shocked, "Have you become galdramenn too?"

"You forget that you get your power through your mother and through me. My mother was of the old people. They have had spies in my land for some time. They have known things which they should not know. I know not yet who they are but I am getting closer. I am counting on their spies for I intend to use them."

"But how will you know who they are?"

I took my sword from its scabbard, "This will tell me. I have not used the power that Odin gave me when he struck this sword." I put my arm around Ylva. "It was Ylva that made me begin to harness that power. It defeated a Norn for the gods are greater than the Weird Sisters and their witches." I smiled apologetically, "I am sorry but it is true."

Kara nodded, "A year ago I would have said you were wrong but I believe you are right. We will do all that we can."

"Good."

Ylva took my hand, "And grandfather."

"Yes?"

"I am now a woman. I have attained my true power. I entered the cave a girl and you rescued a woman. I am now a witch and will grow as powerful as my mother."

There was hope in my granddaughter's words.

I hurried to Brigid. I had missed her. I saw that Wighlek and Vibeke were just leaving my hall. Vibeke beamed, "It is good news is it not jarl? The little princess is healed. Perhaps my charm helped."

"Perhaps it did, Vibeke." I did not like to say that other forces were at work. The old woman was kind.

She had a twinkle in her eye as she said, "You will want to be with your wife. We have taken up enough of her time. Farewell!"

As Brigid waved to the pair I whisked her in my arms, taking her by surprise. "What has happened?"

I smiled, "Nothing save that I missed you."

She laughed, "Then you must show me how much!"

We headed to my chamber. I needed to show my wife what she meant to me. Who knew how many more nights we would have together?

When I rose the next morning I felt refreshed and invigorated. I had had good news and that was rare. My mind looked for solutions rather than just seeing the problem. I had an idea how to draw the Danes to Ulla's Water but it would take time. Much of it depended upon my belief that the Danes would send spies; indeed I knew they had spies. I would need to deceive not only my enemies but my people too. It did not sit well with me but it was necessary. I first met with Karl One Leg.

"How goes the training?"

"They have improved beyond all recognition. However, they are all desperate for the Ulfheonar to train them again. It seems a crippled old warrior does not do."

"You are still as good a warrior as ever you were. You are just slower. I am these days."

"By the end of the year they will be able to stand on the walls and defend this stad."

"I am afraid I need them to do more. We must beat the Danes on the field of battle. If we sit behind our walls they will kill us with famine. I have seen how they fight. Our farmers and boys, our bakers and smiths; all must be able to stand in a shield wall and stand firm."

"You are asking much, jarl."

"If we do not then we die. The Danes do not take prisoners. I have seen the burned-out farms and bleached bones of the dead. This is not about one battle, Karl. This is about survival." He nodded. "And when we go to war then you must defend the stad with women, children and old men. We will take all who can wield a weapon. If we go to war and lose then none will return."

"Then they will be ready."

My jarls arrived the next day. I met with Haaken and Olaf as well as my son and grandson. The eight of us sat around my table. "The Danes are coming and I will need every warrior the three of you have. You will have to leave the defence of your stad to old men, women, children and slaves."

The three of them nodded. I rarely gave commands. Ketil asked, "When?"

"That is a good question. We have hurt them and hurt them badly. They will need to recruit more warriors. These are not farmers. These are plunderers. They may come in winter."

"In winter? No one fights in winter."

"We have done but you are right and that is why I think they will come in winter. It is the time we least expect it. This Baggi does the unexpected. However, I aim to fight them in the valley of Ulla's Water, beneath the Úlfarrberg. No matter when they come we will try to fight them there."

"How can you manage that, Jarl Dragonheart? Will Aiden and Kara use magic?"

"No Asbjorn for we fight witches this time. I hope to trick them."

"And if you do not trick them?"

"Then, Ulf, we shall fight them wherever they come. They will outnumber us and we need somewhere that gives us an advantage."

"You will use Snorri and the scouts?"

"Aye and Kara, Aiden and Ylva."

"Ylva is well?"

"Aye Ketil. She has come back from the brink. Ylva may be the salvation of our people. She is now a woman and a witch. Let us match our witches against theirs. I know that our warriors are better."

Ketil said, "I believe my lands are safe. King Eanred sent a messenger. He hoped that our alliance still held. He would not have done so if he thought we were a threat."

Ulf Olafsson nodded his agreement, "We have had embassies from the men of Strathclyde and Hibernia suing for peace. They sent hostages in lieu of were geld."

"Then we can begin to plan. I want every warrior to have a bow, shield, spear, sword and helmet. Every boy who can use a sling should be so armed and armed with a seax too. What we lack in numbers we make up for in equipment."

When I told them of the place I would draw the Danes they all nodded their approval. I outlined the bare bones of my plan. They were all clever and knew what I meant.

"The dead of Ulla's Water, who were slain by those mercenaries hired by the Franks and King Egbert, will watch over us as we fight. The Danes will have an army of the dead to fight as well as the wolves of the north."

"Aye. They died bravely."

"This must be kept secret. I tell you for you are my jarls but keep the place we battle a secret. There are spies abroad in our land. If the Danes discover what I plan, then it is we who will be trapped."

"We understand, Jarl. We know of Danish treachery and cunning."

"I need as many of the men you bring to be mounted. Speed is vital. Ulf, you have the furthest to travel when we fight you may not arrive in time for the start of the battle. You were Ulfheonar and you are a wise leader. You will need to use your own judgement."

"I have not forgotten the lessons you taught. I have also learned from the men I have fought. We will do all that we can."

"We fight Danes. These are neither Saxons nor Hibernians. Do not underestimate them. They can use the shield wall as well as we. Remember Sigtrygg. When they attacked Cyninges-tūn things might have gone ill for us if Aiden had not had the foresight to use fire. Return to your people. Lay in food and prepare weapons. Be vigilant and await my riders. I hope that my scouts will give us warning of the Danish advance."

After they had left me I summoned Ragnar and Gruffyd. Ragnar now had six other warriors to follow his standard in addition to Einar the Tall and his hearth-weru. "I have a task for you. I need you to go to Ulla's Water. I wish you to climb up to the tarn there and build a home with a ditch and palisade around it."

Gruffyd said, "But no one lives there. No one has ever lived on the mountain. The stad that was there lay close to the Water."

Ragnar smiled, "Have you not learned, Gruffyd, that your father never does the most obvious thing. How many people will live there, grandfather?"

"No more than ten and the garrison who will protect the stronghold. I wish you to do this in secret. It needs to be completed by the end of Haustmánuður. I will visit you while you are there but I will come in secret. I tell no one of this. You will tell your mothers that you go on a hunt. Take boar spears with you."

"We should lie to our mothers?"

"No for you will hunt will you not? You will need food. If necessary, then I will tell your mothers what you do but I do not think that they will be overly worried." I leaned closer to them. "The Danes have spies and they are hidden. There may even be spies here in Cyninges-tūn now. It is careless tongues which might end our way of life. Do not be chattering magpies." I looked at Gruffyd,

"You are young. If this task is beyond you then say so and there will be neither shame nor dishonour."

"I am one of this clan and I will serve. When you fight the Danes, you will need every sword. Even one wielded by a cub! The Danes will learn that this cub can bite!"

"Good. Then begin to talk loudly of your planned hunt. People will expect you to be excited. When you leave if you head for Lang's Dale first then that will aid your disappearance. You are right, Gruffyd, no one has ever built at the tarn before. It is open and it is deserted but although there are no people there is a barrow there where we buried Ulla and his people. It is close to the tarn and their spirits will protect you. Be careful not to disturb the dead. If you can build the ditch around the barrow, then that will make it stronger."

"Who is to live there, grandfather?"

I paused and spoke slowly, "When the Danes come they will bring witches. We have our own but I would not risk my family again. The walls will protect Kara, Aiden, Ylva and," I looked at Ragnar, "And your mother. So build well."

He stood, "Thank you for entrusting us with this task. I am honoured and we will make the walls strong enough to withstand all that the Danes can throw at it."

Brigid frowned when she heard what Gruffyd and Ragnar had planned but she saw nothing ill in it. I would tell her the truth but it suited my plans to keep her in the dark as well. After they had gone Snorri took my scouts east. They would live off the land and wait in the woods and forests to the north of the land of the Skull Takers. Snorri was confident that they would know when the Danes were gathering. He and Aðils Shape Shifter and Beorn the Scout were looking forward to a month of hunting and foraging.

Of course, those in Cyninges-tūn noticed the absence of the two groups of warriors and there was much speculation. Rather than explain it I remained silent and remote. Haaken and I took to climbing the Old Man or riding around my Water. It would add to the air of mystery. I wanted my people to speculate. The spies would hear conflicting stories and the Danes would be equally confused. I was relying on the Danes trying to be cleverer than I was. I knew not if the Danish spies were close yet but if they were I wanted them to wonder at my actions. I spent my nights in my hall with my wife and daughters. Brigid enjoyed my attention and it made up for Gruffyd's absence.

In the middle of Haustmánuður I took Elfrida to the house of women. The four of them were the only ones in the hall. The women who served Kara were busy with the many tasks which Haustmánuður brought. I explained my plan to them. I told them all of it. Ragnar and Gruffyd knew a part but until I told them only

Haaken and the Ulfheonar knew the full extent of it. Even Ketil and my jarls knew but a part. None of the four showed any fear at my idea nor any surprise at my deception. Ylva smiled, "You have done well, grandfather. I did not dream this. If I did not, then the Skull Takers and their witches will also be in the dark."

"Then I hope we can keep them there. What I need to know from you is if there are any spies in my land?"

"There are no strangers who have joined us. All those who are here have lived in the stad since before the last snows. We have not sensed danger."

"That does not mean that we are secure. They could have arrived before. Remember that your thoughts were on Ylva for so long even before she was taken by the witch. They could be here already. It does not change my plan. If they are not here yet, then they will be soon."

Elfrida said, "And Brigid, will you tell her?"

I shook my head, "Brigid is without guile. She would not be able to maintain the deception. I will suffer the wrath of her tongue after this is over. If she can make my life a misery, then it will be because we have won and the Danes are defeated. I will take that as a punishment."

Everything was in place and I took Haaken to Úlfarrston where I wished to speak with Raibeart and his brother. Haaken and I spoke of my family. "It is good that you have given Gruffyd and Ragnar responsibility, jarl."

"I should have done so with Wolf Killer but I have learned my lesson." When I left they knew that I would need their warriors too.

We were riding through the forest north of Úlfarrston and Haaken pointed east. "What if they choose to come this way? Ketil and Ulf will take too long to reach us and even Asbjorn would struggle."

"I will draw them to one thing they want above all others."

"And what is that? The sword?"

"They do not desire the sword. It is Ylva they want. They will come for Ylva."

"And that is why Ragnar and Gruffyd are building a stronghold. They are making somewhere where Ylva can be protected."

"Úlfarrberg is wolf mountain. What better protection can she have. The tarn will give Kara and Aiden more power to fight the witches of the skull."

"You just need our enemies to discover this."

"They are clever, Haaken. I cannot be too obvious about it. They must believe that I am making somewhere which is secret. Today we add to that illusion. I will sow seeds here too."

Pasgen ap Coen insisted on us staying the night. It suited me to do so. Úlfarrston was now a busy trading centre. Our friends in Dyflin sent many goods there and our knarr traded as far north as Orkneyjar and as far south as the Sabrina. We ate and drank well. After we had eaten Raibeart and Pasgen looked at me expectantly.

"The Danes are coming. Our raid merely delayed it so that we could get our harvest in. They will be coming to have vengeance on me and to take our land but the greatest prize is Ylva, my granddaughter."

"But why Jarl Dragonheart?"

"Because she is a powerful witch and they need her to use the power of the other witches. We will have to guard her."

"And that is why you have improved the defences of your land..."

"It is but we cannot defeat the Danes with the men I lead. I need others. I need your men Raibeart and as many men as you can supply, Pasgen ap Coen."

"Of course but we leave ourselves weak if we do so."

"I think not for King Egbert is the only enemy who could cause harm to you and he is busy fighting in Corn Walum."

"Then you can have the men but when will you need them?"

"I am rebuilding the watch towers along the southern arm of Windar's Mere and the Water of Cyninges-tūn. We will have ample warning."

"And if they come from the north and east?"

"Then Ketil will give us warning."

"Do not fear, jarl, we will be ready."

"Will you seek help from Dyflin or the isle of the Raven Wing Clan?"

"The Raven Wing Clan is too far away and Jarl Gunnstein Berserk Killer has too many enemies of his own. Have you had word from him of late?"

"One of his knarr is in port. He buys iron, slate and timber from us. It is a good trade for he pays in gold and silver."

Before we left, the next day, Haaken and I went to the quay where ships were loading and unloading. I sought the knarr from Dyflin. I noticed that there were four other knarr in port. The captain recognised me, "Jarl Dragonheart, this is an honour. How can I help you?"

"I would have you take a message to your jarl for me. I need news of the Danes who follow Baggi Skull Splitter. I fear that they mean to come to my home and try to wrest it from me. Worse I believe they intend to take my granddaughter. I would have the Jarl send me any news which comes his way. It matters not how trivial."

The captain shook his head, "It is one thing to make war on men but to take children..."

"Aye we will keep her safe and keep her secret. They shall not have her."

"I will pass the word to other captains. Some trade with Lundenwic and Eoforwic. Someone will hear news."

Our last visit was to Erik Short Toe. We warned him that we might need his crew to fight on the walls of Cyninges-tūn. He was happy to do so. He had grown up there. His brothers still farmed the land his father had bequeathed them. "We will fight, jarl."

Heading back to my home I was more than happy. Word would get back to the Danes that we expected them. They would know that we had towers watching for them. They would also know that I planned on hiding her. The witches had already shown how clever and cunning they were. They would try to find out where I was hiding her. I had no doubt that word would get out about the task I had given my son and grandson. They would say nothing but there would be questions when they returned and no matter how cleverly they answered then people would discover where they had been.

Our training now had more urgency. Karl One Leg and the Ulfheonar knew that our warriors would have to face our enemies not from behind a protective wooden wall but on a battlefield. The bondi would need more skills than they had at present. Time was not on our side.

More of our archers now wore the leather mail with the metal plates. Snorri organised them so that those with the armour stood in the front rank. "If you are attacked then you will have more protection. But eventually all of you will have such armour."

The archers were pleased for their armour marked them out as different. Snorri smiled when they began to release their arrows for they flew further than they had done. He nodded his approval, "They are getting better, jarl."

The shield wall with the new swords also showed greater improvement. The ones who had the least training, however, did not. I went to Bagsecg. He was training with the first shield wall. "We will need something for the other shield wall, Bagsecg. What can be made quickly?"

"Something which is made quickly is rarely of any use in a battle. What we could do is give them a wolf emblem for their helmets. It would make them all look the same and make them feel as one. We have enough made for them by the next training day. I was going to make them for all your warriors. It is the mark of the clan. It will make the helmets stronger in any case."

And so, we gradually improved the morale of our men. I knew that when the day came to fight it would be down to that morale and the clan identity which would see us through. We had to fight as one people. We had made a start.

I travelled, with Haaken, up to Ulla's Water. I knew that we would not see the walls from the Water. The tarn was high up. There was a twisting path which led to it. It passed alongside a bubbling mountain stream. The barrow where we had buried our dead was five hundred paces from the tarn on a piece of high ground above the stream. Once there had been trees covering this land but now most were gone. Isolated copses stood. The building of the walls had taken half of one such copse. Einar the Tall had chosen the saplings rather than the thicker, more mature trees. It meant that, as we approached, I could see that they had finished the ditch and mound and had half of the stakes buried in the soil. They had used many of the stones which littered the mountain side to make supports for both the ditch and the palisade. It was cleverly done. An enemy could not hack through the wooden walls.

"You have done well." We had brought a barrel of ale and they stopped work so that we could talk with them and enjoy the freshly brewed beer.

Ragnar was keen to show us their plans and, with horn in hand, he led me through what would be the gate, eventually. "We are building a gate which doubles as a bridge. Once inside we have made a second ditch and a mound." He pointed to the pile of earth which looked just like Ulla's barrow which lay alongside. "The door to the hall will be half way up the hall and will need a ladder to reach it. You want Kara and her family to be safe, do you not?"

I flashed him a searching look, "Who has spoken?"

"No one. I said to Gruffyd that you are a thinker who plans far ahead. You would bring Ylva and her family here. That way the Danes would attack Cyninges-tūn and they would be safe here. It is a good plan."

I did not like deceiving my grandson. He had only seen half of the plan. "Keep this to yourself or it could go ill with your cousin."

"I have not even told Gruffyd although I suspect he will work it out when he has time." He frowned, "The worry I have, grandfather, is that this is far from any help. What if the Danes discover their presence here? They could be captured. We have made it as strong as we could but..."

I pointed down to the Water. "Here you have a good view of the Water and the path which climbs here. They could spy an enemy. If the numbers were too great, then they would have time to climb Úlfarrberg and head for either the Grassy Mere or the Rye Dale."

"It is still a risk."

"Life is a risk." I patted his back, "You are doing well and it is better than I might have hoped. What do you name it?"

"I would have thought Ylva's Stad but that would give away its purpose. We have been calling it Eagle's Nest for it is like an eagle's eyrie."

"And that is a good name. Let it be so."

We spent the night with them in their lonely camp. They had organised it well. They had fish from the Water and a squirrel stew. It was pleasant sheltering behind the first of their wooden walls even though the nights were drawing in and there was a chill to the air. Gruffyd had changed in the short time he had been working on the stronghold. His hands had hardened up and I saw that he had become more muscular. The hard work suited him. He was also excited about his work. "I would like to build my own stronghold when I am Jarl."

Haaken smiled, "So you would replace your father already eh?" He waggled a finger at me, "I told you, Jarl, that those grey hairs would make these youngsters think you are past it!"

"I did not say that Haaken One Eye!" Poor Gruffyd was appalled at Haaken's words.

"He is teasing, cousin. Do not listen to him."

Haaken ruffled Gruffyd's hair, "It is what warriors do, Gruffyd, they banter."

Gruffyd nodded and then said, "I would have a name like yours Haaken One Eye if I am to be a warrior."

"You do not just choose a name. It must choose you. Mine was obvious and your father's because he had the heart of a dragon. Ragnar's father slew a wolf. We know not yet what you will do. Perhaps Gruffyd the Cub until then, eh?"

"I am more than a cub!"

Haaken shrugged as he lay down, "Then we will have to wait until the Norns have spun and they have shown us what you will become."

As we rode down to the Water, the next day, I examined the land. If things went wrong, then the Danes would ascend the path. It was steep and it twisted. A shield wall could not advance quickly. "We need to make our own avalanche, Haaken. If we piled stones behind a wooden wall, we could release them. They would sweep away any who climbed."

Haaken pointed to the bottom of the slope and the ruined building which were the only remains of Ulla's Stad. "If your plan succeeds then the Danes will all die there."

"The Norns play games with us. Let us plan for every eventuality. I will have Gruffyd, Ragnar, and his warriors behind the walls along with Snorri and his scouts."

"You put all of your family in one nest."

"It is the Eagle's Nest and it is on Úlfarrberg. I pray the land and the Allfather will aid me against this clan of witches."

I sent Snorri and his scouts east when I returned. I had had no news from Dyflin but I believed that the Danes were still in the east. I would only see my scouts when the arrival of the Danes was imminent. By then I needed all of my plans to be ready.

Chapter 16

Raibeart himself brought the news from Úlfarrston, "We have had a message from Dyflin, Jarl. Danes are flocking to join the Skull Takers. The power of the witches is what is attracting them. Many have tried to defeat you before, Jarl but Jarl Gunnstein said that the witches have promised that they can defeat you and your sword and the Land of the Wolf will be theirs."

I nodded, "Thank you, Raibeart. Was there any other news?"

"I am afraid, Jarl, that the fact that your Ulfheonar wear golden wolves and the lands seems so rich means that many believe that the land of wolf has a hidden gold mine. The stories of you being buried beneath a mountain and emerging alive have been take to suggest that the cave is the secret lair of a dragon and you are harvesting the gold."

I shook my head, "That is not true!"

"We know that for we know you trade to get gold but it is what people believe. The rumour has been spread beyond your borders. It draws Danes like moths to a flame. They are not farmers nor are they true warriors. They are treasure hunters. Those who live along the Sabrina and in Orkneyjar confirm this."

"Did your captains know when they might be coming?"

He shook his head, "Our ships just visit the western coasts. You need someone who travels east for better news. What of Wighlek and his wife? They must visit Eoforwic and the land of the Danes."

"Why do you say that?"

"They trade jet and that comes from Hwitebi. It is worked only in Eoforwic. It takes great skill."

"Thank you Raibeart."

I berated myself for not thinking of our traders myself. I would interrogate them when next they visited. They would have heard of a gathering of Danish warriors. I found my eye drawn to the jet necklace my wife wore. I asked, "May I see the necklace, my love?"

"Of course, but why?"

"I did not know how intricate the work was. Raibeart mentioned it. I would see it close up." She untied it and gave it to me. I saw that the necklace was a dragon and was a bone stained dark red; it was probably cochineal. The scales were made up mainly of jet but the eyes were amber. It was beautiful work and the skill to make it was impressive.

"This must have cost a great deal to buy." I handed it back to her.

She shook her head as she tied it, "Not particularly." She smiled, "I pay less than most for I am the wife of the jarl. Wighlek and his wife like the patronage and when the other women in the stad saw me wearing it they asked for similar ones. It is why they return here so often. They make profits."

I confess I did not know how many times they had come but it made sense. I was hopeful now that they would return again soon and I would be able to gather more information.

They had not returned seven days later nor had my scouts returned but Ragnar, Gruffyd and their men did. They looked happy and entered the stad with a swagger I had not noticed before. They did as I had asked and refused to answer questions about what they had been doing. Olaf Leather Neck and the Ulfheonar were there to greet them and make sure that no news slipped out. They took Einar and the hearth-weru to the warrior hall to celebrate the successful completion of their task and I led my son and grandson into the hall.

Brigid wrinkled her nose, "You two! Get to the Water and bathe! The smell offends me!"

I laughed, "Come, I will join you and you can tell me all."

Once we entered the icily cold Water I found my thoughts clarified. As they used the soap Brigid had thrust into their hands I asked my questions. "I take it that it is finished?"

"It is. The hall is simply made. We have a ladder next to the door and the gate bridge works. If you wanted it more secure then you would have to ask Bagsecg to make a pair of chains."

"But we did not think it necessary." Gruffyd grinned, "I know why you have built this hall! It is there to protect Ylva and her family. It is their last refuge."

My eyes flickered to Ragnar, "I said nothing, grandfather. He worked it out."

"I can remain silent!"

"Good. For the lives of our family depend upon your silence. But you have not finished. In two days' time, we will return with the Ulfheonar. I have thought of another device which might help." I explained what I needed.

"Who will defend it grandfather?"

"You will be there with your men."

Gruffyd looked disappointed, "But I thought we would be fighting Danes!"

"You might be but is not protecting your family more important? Ragnar's mother will be there too. Would you leave her unprotected?"

He looked deflated, "Of course not but…"

"None of us know what the Weird Sisters have planned. I can plan and I can plot but I do not know the outcome. I want my family protected by the best."

"Then you use the Ulfheonar."

"Ragnar, the Ulfheonar are good but they are like the wolves we slew to wear the skin. We do not fight well behind walls. We are better in the open and when we are attacking. You two have grown much but I would not have you face a Skull Taker yet. Your Eagle's Nest is both well named and well made. An enemy will be tired when he reaches the top. Archers can find gaps when warriors are tired. You could well face Danes but you would have your own walls for protection."

Ragnar nodded, "There is no dishonour in this, Gruffyd."

Brigid questioned the two of them throughout our meal. Elfrida did not but she kept watching me. Elfrida could read men's thoughts. I did not think she divined mine but she was suspicious. Eventually Brigid shook her head and snapped, "I asked a simple question! My son has been missing for almost a month! Why the secrecy?"

I smiled enigmatically, "It would spoil the surprise." I left it at that knowing that she would take it to mean a Yule present.

When Snorri did not return, I took the Ulfheonar to Eagle's Nest. They were impressed with the work of Ragnar and Gruffyd. Olaf Leather Neck tapped the stones around the base of the wooden palisade. "A clever idea! Well done!"

We then stripped to the waist and toiled to make two cradles to hold stones. We took some old ship's rope to make a net and then filled the cradle with stones. They were not put in haphazardly. I wanted the stones to create an avalanche. We needed two such devices. The Danes could try to divide the arrows of the defenders. The stones would be released when the ropes which tethered them was cut by an axe. It was dark when we finished and we stayed the night in the new hall. It was cosy although we were a little cramped. When we left, the next day, we were filled with optimism. My plans were coming to fruition.

The day of training was a cold, sharp one. The air was dry but the ground was hard. There had been a frost. When we trained our bondi I allowed Ragnar and Gruffyd to work with the second shield wall. I did it for a number of reasons: firstly, it allowed my son and grandson to give them their newly refurbished helmets with the symbol of the wolf but, more importantly, it gave the two of them a connection to the warriors they might be leading. The second shield wall had many young warriors. If they survived this battle, then they might become the warriors who followed Ragnar and Gruffyd as my men had.

One warrior was late. If was Erik Finnison. We watched him as he rowed across the Water. Olaf Leather Neck strode up to him and stood, his hand resting on his axe, towering over the young warrior who lived on the eastern shore of the Water.

"You have kept your shield brothers waiting! I hope you have a good excuse!"

"I am sorry, I found tracks. There are Danes in the forest below the How."

Olaf Leather Neck turned to look at me and the Ulfheonar, close enough to hear, all stopped too. Snorri and his scouts had not sent word back and so I did not think this was the Danish army. It would be scouts and they had got close. "Ulfheonar to horse." I turned to Karl One Leg. "You keep training the men. Ragnar and Gruffyd you and Einar take charge of the second shield wall. Train them well for I feel the day is coming when we will need them."

The days when Gruffyd would have argued were gone and they nodded. Rolf Horse Killer had my horse ready for me by the time I reached the gates. I said to him, as I mounted, "Where does Erik Finnison live exactly?"

"Just south of Fir Island. His house nestles beneath Crow Brow. He is a hunter."

"Then he knows how to track?" I waved my men north around the Water.

"If he said they are Danes then they are. There are few people there now. Erik's family were slain at the same time as Wolf Killer. He stayed there. He is like Aðils Shape Shifter. He is solitary but he likes his life. Snorri has hopes for him as an archer."

"Then when we return I will give him my Saami bow. He has done us great service already."

The ride up the hill on the far side of the Water was taxing. The journey across the Water was shorter but we would not have been able to transport our horses. As soon as we crested the hill which lay above the ruins of my former home we halted. "Cnut Cnutson, take Rolf and Rollo. Cover our left side."

My three riders would keep a thousand paces to the east of us. If these Danish scouts were any good they would use the shelter to the forests rather than the greenway we used. My three riders would see them if they hurried away from us. We rode slowly now. If Erik had seen them and they were heading north, then they could be within sight soon. On the other hand, if they had been moving south there was less urgency. I missed Aðils' nose. I was forced to use my own. I sniffed the air. There were few smells. It was winter and it was cold. The little wind there was blew in my face. I was seeking the smell of men. There was nothing; not even the smell of fox piss. I waved my men left and right and we moved south.

We had dropped to the clearing made by charcoal burners many years earlier when my nose caught the faint aroma of unwashed bodies. It was not our smell. I looked to my left and saw Leif the Banner nod. He had smelled it too. I drew my sword, silently. Others did the same. We kept the same pace but I peered into the trees. These were pine trees and did not shed their leaves but they were so close together that there were few branches lower down. It also meant that a warrior could not climb them to hide. I moved my head slowly watching for something which was not natural.

To my left, forty paces from me a conifer branch moved and I saw something which was not the white of frost but was lighter than the tree behind which it sheltered. It was a hand. Once I recognised the hand then I saw the sword which rested on the ground. There was a Dane and he was lying behind a tree. I halted. Was he the lead scout or had we walked into a trap? The Ulfheonar stopped too. They were all doing as I did. Having found one the second was slightly easier to spot. He lay on the ground with his cloak over him. I might have taken it for a shadow save that it was too even for ground which was littered with pine cones and branches dropped there in the last storm. I kicked my heels into the flanks of my horse and started him forward.

When a deer is hunted, it moves as soon as it senses a hunter. With a man, he waits until he thinks he is discovered. My movement towards the two Danes I had seen was enough to make them, and the other five scouts, move. The two I had seen were the ones at the front. As they rose and ran south and east their five fellows jumped up and joined them. I was already moving and I kicked harder. My horse leapt forward. I leaned slightly forward for using a weapon from the back of a horse was hazardous. The only one I had seen do so easily was Hrolf the Horseman. I did not have his skill.

Using my hands and knees I guided my horse after the first Dane I had seen. He had a cloak on his back made from the skin of a wild boar. I saw no shield and I guessed that would be under his cloak. The sword I had seen was in his right hand. He twisted and turned as he sought to evade me. My horse was nimble footed. He avoided the tree roots and stones which could have sent us both skittering to the floor. The Dane's helmet, while it gave him protection also impaired his hearing. He could feel the hooves of my thundering horse but he could not know where I was. He was an experienced scout. He did not turn his head. Such a move invited disaster. Instead he ran an erratic course. He did not always turn the same way. I would be patient.

The ground was falling away and that caused his downfall; quite literally. He ran down a slight slope which still had thick frost upon it. Running on packed frost had left a slippery sole to his boot. When he struck the fresh, hard frost he lost his footing. He was on his feet in an instant and turned but I was ready. I brought my sword in an arc to hack through his arm close to his shoulder. The movement meant I was not knocked form my horse. Even as I reined in I saw the other six turn east to run through the forest away from us. I saw, coming through the forest, Cnut and my other two Ulfheonar. Their appearance was enough to cause the Danes to hesitate. It was enough. Olaf, Haaken and the rest galloped towards them. The six stood, like brothers in arms in a circle but they were slain. They had no mail and they had spent nights out in the open. One lasted long enough for Olaf to question him before he sent him to the Otherworld.

We took their bodies back to Cyninges-tūn. I wished to examine them. Were these the Skull Takers? Haaken rode next to me, "We were lucky that Erik has such sharp eyes, jarl."

"We are indeed. I cannot see how we can guard our land against such intrusions."

"If they need to scout does that not mean they do not have spies in our land?"

I shook my head, "I am more convinced than ever that there are spies in our land. It was not just that Sigtrygg said they knew his passwords it was the familiarity with our stad. They chose to attack from the side which afforded the greatest chance of success. No, Haaken, we have spies. I have my own thoughts on that but it does not change our plans. We have to wait now until Snorri tells us that the Danish worm is slithering towards us and then we can put my plans into place."

The bondi all stood as we rode into the training ground and deposited the bodies on the earth. Ragnar asked, "Is this all of them grandfather?"

"I know not. Take your hearth-weru and ride to Asbjorn. Warn him that there may be scouts about."

Olaf dismounted and said, "Tell him they are of the clan of the snake and that their jarl is Ragnar Halfdansson." I looked at Olaf. "The one who was wounded asked to be sent to Valhalla. This was the price."

Ragnar nodded and led his men towards the stables. I pointed to the bodies and said, "Second shield wall take what you wish from their bodies and then burn them."

Gruffyd wandered over, "Does this mean they are coming?"

Haaken and Olaf were by my side and I saw them listening for my comments. "I think this is like the attack on Sigtrygg. They send small bands in before the main attack. They strike where we do not expect it. Remember the band we found?" They nodded. "I would have the Ulfheonar ride the Grize Dale and over the Hawk's Head each day looking for sign."

"The ground is frozen."

"We can still see signs."

"Aye jarl."

"And Gruffyd, fetch my Saami bow."

164

He did not question me but went. Karl One Leg joined me. "They will be ready Jarl. When Erik brought the news, it made them realise that this practice has a purpose." He pointed to the corpses being piled on to a pyre of kindling and driftwood. "They have seen their enemy."

I nodded. The Danes were obviously experienced warriors. They all wore warrior bands on their arms. Their weapons were those of men who valued arms. These were the men they would be facing across a shield wall.

Karl turned to them. "You have your weapons! Back to training!"

I wandered over to the archers. I waved Erik Finnison over. "That was a timely warning. We are in your debt."

"My parents were slain by Danes. I would do anything to have my vengeance upon them."

Gruffyd appeared and handed me my bow. "They say you are a good archer. Take this and you will be a better one."

He held it and shook his head. "Jarl this is a gift worthy of a king. I cannot take it!"

"I am your jarl and you will do more good with this than I. Besides you will be fighting for the clan. I can always get another."

He nodded and did as I would have done. He took an arrow and, pulling back his arm as far as it would go, he sent the missile high into the air. Every eye was upon it as it soared. Everyone, it seemed, held their breath as it continued to rise and then, reaching its apex, plunged to earth. One of them, Leif the Red said, in awe, "That is over three hundred paces! It is a wondrous weapon!"

Erik turned to me, "Thank you, Jarl. I will put this to good use."

"Aye. Make longer arrows. You will gain ever more distance. It is a worthy weapon. Make sure your arrows and their fletch matches it."

We were now on a war footing and it was none too soon for the weather changed the next morning. The air warmed a little and that was always a bad sign. The skies filled with thick black and threatening clouds. Kara came to me. She knew weather better than any. "It is good that we have the animals from the fells, father, for winter will begin soon."

"And the Danes? Is there any sign of them?"

She hung her head a little. "I fear we are blind. These are four powerful witches and they have used a spell to hide their intentions from us."

"Then my plan must remain the best chance we have."

"We are prepared. Some of my women who also have powers have offered to come with us."

"How do they know? This was supposed to be secret."

"They know not where we go. They just know that we will seek shelter. Aiden said we would go to Myrddyn's cave."

I did not like it but I hoped it would do no harm. I nodded, "That may put them off the scent."

"And we have fresh herbs. Wighlek and his wife brought us a fresh quantity of millefoil, yew and yarrow when they came two days ago. We have a good supply."

I allowed a smile to play across my lips. Kara frowned. "You are hiding thoughts from me father."

"I am Jarl, Kara, and I have many things on my mind. You need to make sure that your family is safe and I will ensure that the clan is too."

The Ulfheonar split into two parties and crisscrossed the high ground to the south and west. Asbjorn and his men did the same as far as Ulla's Water. Two days after they had begun they found signs of more Danes. This time the Danes fled east before Asbjorn could find them. As Yule approached I wondered if I had misjudged the Danes. Were they keeping us on a war footing to weaken us? The answer came at the end of Gormánuður. Audun Thin hair had had his sons collecting in the last of the sheep from the Lough Rigg. They saw signs of Danes around the cave of Myrddyn. I sent Olaf and the Ulfheonar. They brought back five corpses. It was the Snake Clan again. The Danes had not given up and now I knew where the spies gathered their information. More than that I knew who they were. I would bide my time for it served my purpose.

I was watching my fire and wondering if I had done all that I could. Brigid was putting Myfanwy to bed while Gruffyd and Ragnar were at Bagsecg's forge putting a fresh edge on their weapons. Uhtric came in. he hesitated and that was not his way. "Come, Uhtric, approach and tell me what is in your mind for I can see concern written all over it."

"Jarl, I am a good servant. I know how to keep secrets."

"I know. You are as faithful a freeman as I have ever met."

"I know of Eagle's Nest and the plans to keep Ylva there."

A shiver went down my spine. How did he know? "As you say you can keep a secret. I trust you. There is not a problem."

He hesitated again and when I frowned he spread his arms, "Jarl, your wife knows the secret you share with Gruffyd and Ragnar or she knows of Eagle's Nest. She knows not that Ylva will use it but she has spoken of it. She believes it is to be a home for Ragnar and his mother."

My wife was a chatterbox. She was without guile. If I had sworn her to secrecy, then she would not have uttered a word but she would have fretted and worried about my plan. This was *wyrd*. I had hoped that the Danes would discover what I intended but not through my wife. I smiled at Uhtric, "There is no harm, Uhtric and I thank you for keeping the secret. Do not mention this to my wife. It will avail her nothing."

"But the Danes will come for Ylva! It is common knowledge that the Danish witches want her."

"And know this, Uhtric. They shall not have her, not so long as I draw breath."

Two days later Beorn the Scout galloped in. "Jarl Dragonheart. The Danes are coming!"

Olaf Leather Neck snorted, "In this weather?" There was a blizzard blowing.

"It is not as bad in the east but they are coming." Snorri and Aðils shadow them. They are on the far side of the high ground. We have four days and they will be here. There are five hundred of them, jarl."

"Then it begins. Olaf send the riders to Ketil, Ulf, Raibeart and Asbjorn. We need the clan! They know where to meet!" I turned to Beorn, "Find Snorri."

Chapter 17

My men took Kara and her family north two days before the horde was due to descend upon us. Macha and Deidra were unhappy to be left behind but they were mollified when I explained that we had to deceive the enemy into thinking that the house of women was still full. With Ragnar and his men, along with Gruffyd, Leif the Banner and Karl Karlsson they left with horses laden with supplies. Ragnar now commanded his four hearth-weru and fifteen others. I hoped that the twenty three of them would be enough. They headed north, towards the Lough Rigg.

I had summoned all those who lived in the outlying farms. They would be safer inside my walls than without. Beorn returned with the news that the Danes had camped east of Windar's Mere. Had we planned on stopping them at Elfridaby then we would have missed them. Now they had two routes they could take. If they continued west, then they would attack Windar's Mere. If they headed north, then they would be making for Ulla's Water. I knew now that their spies had let them know that it would be Eagle's Nest where Ylva would be hiding. They had thought they had uncovered my plot. Instead, they had done just what I wanted them to. When this was over the two spies would pay with their lives. I now knew who they were.

I summoned the Ulfheonar, Scanlan, Bagsecg and Karl One Leg. "Tomorrow we ride to Windar's Mere. Unless they travel the length of the Mere they cannot reach here. I leave you three to hold my home. I know that you would fight with me if I asked but we have enough now to do what I need."

"Aye, jarl. The walls will still be standing when you return. Those with wounds, the women and the young, all will be standing a post."

Raibeart and his crew marched with us. He also brought archers and slingers. Raibeart had but thirty men in his shield wall but they were hardened in battle both on land and sea. I would be happy to have him guarding my flank. The other three war bands were now to the north of us. They were preparing the ground for the trap I hoped to spring.

We marched at the speed of the bondi. Our horses were there to be led. It would take some hours to reach Windar's Mere. Beorn told me that there was little chance of the Danes reaching the Mere before the next day. We had time.

The walls of Asbjorn's stronghold were lined with old men, crippled warriors and boys. I saw the relief on their faces as we approached. My spears did not enter the stronghold. I arrayed the two shield walls before it, facing the fells which rolled eastwards. My archers and slingers trooped inside and added their numbers to those who stood on the walls. Behind us was the ruined old Roman fort. It had been fortified by the old people in the time of the Warlord but it had been destroyed so many times that Windar had moved his settlement east on to a higher piece of ground. If we were forced back, then we had the ruins to use for defence. I knew it well. The snow might make the walls look like driven snow but they would make a barrier against advancing Danes. Ulla's Water was where I wanted to fight my battle but I had a plan to hold them here if they managed to discover my trap.

It was a cold, biting wind which hurtled from the north. The Danes had counted on my people assuming that war would not come when it was winter. They were in for a shock. We had supplies and our animals were all protected.

The women of the stad brought us hot food and fresh oat bread. I knew that could make all the difference. The Danes would have marched in the midst of winter and would be on short rations. We had our horses taken into the stad by the women. We would not need them again. We waited. In the late afternoon Snorri and Aðils rode in from the south. Snorri pointed to the eastern fells, "Jarl, the Danes are there massing on the ground above High Street." High Street was the old name for the Roman Road which ran north to the old Roman Wall. It eventually climbed high above the eastern shore of Ulla's Water.

I nodded, "You have done well. Take your horses in the stad and have some food. This is just the beginning. When you have eaten take charge of the archers and the slingers on the walls!" I handed him my banner. "My son is not here to wield this. Take it to the fighting platform. Let the Danes know who they fight!"

"Aye jarl."

I joined Haaken and my Ulfheonar. Raibeart and his men were to our right. The two shield walls were drawn up behind us. There were two blocks of warriors. They were twenty men wide and three men deep. I would have preferred them to be deeper but I had to use what we had. The Danes would see a little over a hundred men. They would guess that Asbjorn and his men were within the walls of his stad. We would look like an easy target for them.

Rolf Horse Killer spotted the Danish scouts as they began to filter through the trees to the ground which had been cleared by both Windar and Asbjorn. There was an open area four hundred paces wide. The scouts halted. They were beyond bow range and we just stood. A late afternoon shaft of sunlight suddenly pierced the clouds. It flared briefly but while it shone it made a corona behind us. It was as though the Land of the Wolf was bathed in gold.

Behind me I heard the shield wall begin to bang their shields rhythmically as they chanted, "Dragonheart! Dragonheart! Dragonheart!" Over and over. It spread to the stad where the banging on the fighting platform and the walls seemed to echo down the valley. It rolled through the hills as though the land itself was chanting. Suddenly four Danes on horses made their way through the scouts and stood there. Behind them I saw the Danish shield wall appear. It stretched for a long way. It would easily overlap us.

I raised my sword and the chanting stopped instantly. I stepped forward and shouted, "Baggi Skull Splitter of the Skulltaker clan, this land is not for you! Our women are not for you! The sword has defeated the witch! It will defeat you if you try to wrest this land from us. Leave now and I will forget the insult you do me by bringing men to my land. If we fight, then the crows will feast as your army drags itself back to Loidis! We will slaughter every Dane who remains in the Land of the Wolf; this I swear!"

I stepped back and my men all cheered.

The cheering stopped when three witches, their hair bedecked with the skulls of what looked like babies, moved closer to us. I could not hear their words but I knew that they were chanting. They threw something in my direction. I sensed the fear in my men but I said nothing. Then the three parted and a hideously bloated woman stepped forward. Even from a distance of four hundred paces I could see that she had neither teeth nor hair and her skin was covered in pustules and warts or perhaps she had painted her face that way. Either way she had a face made to terrorise. Her voice, when she spoke, was high pitched and piercing, "Dragonheart, you have killed a sister and you will die! You and your men have despoiled the shrine of the mother on Loidis and they will die! You have dared to take from the Norns and for that your people will perish!"

In answer, I raised my sword and Haaken began to sing.

"The Dragonheart sailed with warriors brave
To find the child he was meant to save
With Haaken and Ragnar's Spirit
They dared to delve with true warrior's grit
With Aðils Shape Shifter with scout skills honed
They found the island close by the rocky stones
The Jarl and Haaken will bravely roar
The Jarl and Haaken and the Ulfheonar
Beneath the earth the two they went
With the sword by Odin sent
In the dark the witch grew strong

170

Even though her deeds were wrong
A dragon's form she took to kill
Dragonheart faced her still
He drew the sword touched by the god
Made by Odin and staunched in blood
The Jarl and Haaken will bravely roar
The Jarl and Haaken and the Ulfheonar
With a mighty blow, he struck the beast
On Dragonheart's flesh he would not feast
The blade struck true and the witch she fled
Ylva lay as though she were dead
The witch's power could not match the blade
The Ulfheonar are not afraid
The Jarl and Haaken will bravely roar
The Jarl and Haaken and the Ulfheonar
And now the sword will strike once more
Using all the Allfather's power
Fear the wrath you Danish lost
You fight the wolf you pay the cost
The Jarl and Haaken will bravely roar
The Jarl and Haaken and the Ulfheonar"

When he had finished, there was a moment of silence and then the whole of our army roared as though we had won the battle already! The witches' curses seemed to disappear in the air. The shaft of light which had briefly appeared before suddenly flashed for an instant and lit my sword. It sent a shaft of light towards the witches and Baggi Skull Splitter. I saw them shade their eyes. Then the light disappeared but the damage had been done. The Danes had expected us to quake before the curses of the witches. Haaken's song had been prepared a month since and we had waited until just the right moment for him to sing it. The Ulfheonar sang the last refrain over and over. The shield walls joined in and the song sounded like a death knell for the Danes.

And now the sword will strike once more
Using all the Allfather's power
Fear the wrath you Danish lost
You fight the wolf and pay the cost
The Jarl and Haaken will bravely roar
The Jarl and Haaken and the Ulfheonar
And now the sword will strike once more
Using all the Allfather's power
Fear the wrath you Danish lost
You fight the wolf and pay the cost
The Jarl and Haaken will bravely roar
The Jarl and Haaken and the Ulfheonar

171

I saw a movement backwards from the Danes and then Baggi Skull Splitter roared, "Charge! Let us slaughter these wolfmen!" The lines of Danes rushed with reckless abandon towards us.

"Shield wall!"

Now would be a test of our training. We formed our shield wall and locked it next to that of Raibeart and his war band. My bondi, behind us, did the same. We had a solid block of shields. The Danes had not used arrows to weaken us and they had not advanced together. It was a mad rush of Danes who were eager to get to us. The rough, frozen ground was not the ground over which to run. Danes fell. Most did not get up. They were trampled by those behind.

Our rear rank was next to the wooden wall and above us were over a hundred and twenty archers and slingers. I heard Snorri yell, "Release!"

The air above us darkened as the deadly missiles flew. I peered over my shield. Two arrows flew beyond the others. They would be Erik Finnison's and Snorri's. One arrow pitched into the chest of the standard bearer and he fell backwards. The second was even more successful. It struck a witch and she fell dead. Immediately the others ran to safety while Baggi and his men lifted their own shields. Even the arrows of my ordinary archers had an effect. Danes were struck for they came as individuals. At least forty fell in the first wave of arrows. Urged on by Snorri they continued to release. They had remembered their training.

When the Danes were thirty paces from us I shouted, "Ulfheonar! Shields!"

Along with Raibeart and his men we brought up our shields and stepped back to be covered by the spears and shields of the front rank of our bondi shield walls. I had no spear. The rest did but I held Ragnar's Spirit out before me. My own promise and the song of Haaken had had an effect. I saw that the Danes were avoiding me. They spread out to the side. This was a sword which had defeated a witch and none wished to face me.

The Danes ran into our spears. Had they come in one line then they might have moved us. As it was we stood like a rock. We did not move. Two men struck at Haaken to my right. My sword darted out and I stabbed the Dane below his right ear. I twisted and he fell dead. Haaken slew the other. Above us the arrows still flew and I heard the clatter of lead balls against helmets and shields. The afternoon light was fading but that suited us. It was our land and we knew the ground. A Dane swung his axe towards me. It caught on Finni Svensson's shield and the metal edge of mine. Wielded two handed the Dane had no shield and I thrust forward with all the power I could muster. I tore through his mail and my blade scraped along his backbone.

172

The Danes had managed to force enough men into line to face us. We had the advantage of a wooden wall behind us and archers who, even in the fading light, could hit the smallest area of bare flesh. When a black fletched arrow suddenly sprouted from the eye of the Dane who was close enough for me to smell what he had last eaten then I knew that either Snorri or Erik were watching over me. As the Dane fell I took my chance and stabbed forward at the warrior in the second rank. We were not falling back and we were inflicting wounds and deaths on the Danes. I heard a horn sound three times and the Danes began to disengage. That was always a difficult thing to do and they paid a price. As they stepped back we walked forwards and stabbed, thrust and slashed at the warriors who were trying to escape the bloodbath. As they fell back stones and arrows continued to take a toll. As they ran my men all chanted one line as a final insult to the defeated Danes.

> *You fight the wolf you pay the cost*
> *You fight the wolf you pay the cost*
> *You fight the wolf you pay the cost*
> *You fight the wolf you pay the cost*

As the enemy disappeared into the safety of the fell I stepped beyond the front rank and turned. I held up my arms. "Have the wounded taken inside the stad. Reform the shield wall. This is not yet over!"

Returning to my place between Haaken and Olaf I saw that almost a hundred Danes lay dead or were crawling back to their lines. We had not won but we had hurt them. I knew now that they had intended to capture Windar's Mere and then take Eagle's Nest. Now that we had stopped that from happening what would they do?

"How many did we lose?"

"Not as many as we might have expected. Snorri and the archers broke up their attack." Haaken pointed behind us. The sun had almost set. "Will they come again this night?"

Olaf Leather Neck growled, "I hope they do. I saw nothing today to make me fear them and our bondi made me proud. They did not flinch."

As darkness fell we saw lights on the fell side. The cold ground began to get to us. I turned and shouted, "Aðils Shape Shifter; your jarl has need of you."

Almost immediately Aðils appeared, "Yes jarl?"

"I would have you disappear and see what they are up to."

He nodded as though I had asked him to fetch me a horn of ale, "Aye Jarl!"

He vanished before our eyes. "Erik Ulfsson, go and ask for hot food to be prepared."

I wore sealskin boots but, even so, the cold gradually began to climb up my legs. My hands started to grow numb. We could not stand outside all night. I almost jumped when Aðils appeared next to me, "They have made camp, Jarl. The witches are performing some sort of ceremony over the witch Snorri killed and they are preparing some magic. They have sentries out. They are vigilant and if we tried to get close we would lose men. I think they fear an attack by the Ulfheonar. They will not come again."

It was a confident statement but I believed him. "Everyone, back into the stad. We have frozen long enough. Tomorrow we fight again."

The army filtered back through the gates. I paused in the entrance, bathed in the fire from the two braziers which were next to the gates and I stared into the darkness. The Danes could see me even if I could not see them. I took out my sword and I raised it defiantly. We had not been beaten and I was letting them know it. I was the last through. The gates slammed behind me and the bar was lowered.

Inside there was a buzz of excitement. Most of the warriors who had fought that day and night had never experienced a battle before. To have escaped unscathed, as most of them had, and to have retained the field was a cause for celebration. The exception was the Ulfheonar. I joined them in Asbjorn's warrior hall with Raibeart's men. They were all subdued.

Olaf Leather Neck handed me a horn of ale, "It was well that you angered them, Jarl. Your actions and Haaken's words made them forget to be warriors. In the cold light of morning they will be less easy to defeat."

I nodded as I swallowed the dark brown ale. "You are right but it is like climbing a mountain. You measure each step as you go. This is not the way I planned it but it has gone better than we might have hoped. You are right about tomorrow. Dawn will bring us new problems but we have survived this day. Let us enjoy the night." I pointed to the pot of steaming stew. "How many times have we been able to eat hot food after killing Danes?"

Haaken had been the only one of my Ulfheonar who had been smiling when I had been speaking, "The jarl is right. It was a good day."

I saw Snorri standing alone and sharpening his seax. As I went to him Aðils approached me, "Jarl, he is fearful. It was his arrow which slew the witch. He murmured, '*I am cursed*' when he did so."

"He killed a witch last year and he had to atone in Syllingar. He cannot do that again. You did well today, you both did. Go, eat and I will speak with him." I reached into my leather pouch and took out the golden wolf which Bagsecg had made, "I should have given you this before we set off but..."

His eyes widened. He knew that all of my wolf warriors wore one but he had not asked for his. "Thank you, jarl. I need no reward to serve you."

"And it is not a reward. It is the token which binds us. Kara has put a spell of protection upon it."

"Thank you." He wandered off clutching the wolf.

Snorri had seen me, "That was well done, jarl. He is a fine warrior. I fear, however, that I will need more than Kara's spell to protect me."

"Snorri, you have served with me longer than any save Haaken One Eye. You were a young boy little older than Aðils when first you killed your wolf. Now you sprout white hairs. I know why you are despondent; you killed a witch."

"I killed another witch."

"Aye, another witch and tomorrow there are three more who must die. I hope that it is I who kill them but it may well be others." I took out Ragnar's Spirit. "This sword defeated the Norn in the cave. Until that moment I thought I was doomed to die in the cave. I did not flinch for it was Ylva for whom I fought but I believed death awaited me. It did not because the power of the witch is nothing compared with the power of the gods. Touch the hilt and let its power fill you with hope and not despair."

He took the hilt, gingerly as though it might burn. I saw his eyes widen as the power surged through him. "You feel this each time you fight?"

"Each time I hold it, aye. I wish you to sleep with it this night. Others can watch. I wish the sword to heal you within. Tomorrow I need Snorri the warrior to be at his best."

He clutched it, "Thank you, jarl. This is an honour for you have never let the sword be parted from you before."

I nodded, "And none of my warriors has needed its power before. This is *wyrd*."

He went to a corner of the hall and rolled himself in his fur. He held the sword in both hands and cradled it to his chest. As I turned I saw Olaf, Haaken and Beorn the Scout watching me. Haaken smiled his approval, "He needed that, Jarl Dragonheart. We are all worried for him. Beorn here told us that when they camped, watching the Danes by Loidis, he was melancholy. The witch he first killed preyed upon his mind. After your return from Syllingar he became worse."

"Aye Jarl, Aðils and I feared for him."

"I was not lying to him when I said that we had another three to kill. Baggi Skull Splitter is the figurehead. It is the witches who wield the power. No matter what happens on the morrow they have to die."

"And risk their curse?"

"Beorn, they cursed us before the battle did they not? We survived. I said to Snorri that we are warriors. In the war between the gods and the witches I put my faith in the Allfather and the right arms of my Ulfheonar. The witches have power but that power diminishes if you face up to them."

Haaken clapped me on the back, "There speaks the fellow who descended into a cave and fought the witch when she took the form of a dragon! The jarl is right. Whatever comes tomorrow we face it together. We are Ulfheonar!"

He said it loudly and everyone in the hall took up the chant.

"We are Ulfheonar, we are Ulfheonar, we are Ulfheonar."

After they had eaten I wrapped my wolf cloak around me and headed for the walls. Asbjorn's old men and cripples stood a watch and I joined Siggi One Hand as he stared at the eastern fells. He bowed as I approached, "Will they come again on the morrow, jarl?"

"I know not but we fight the same way. We meet them shield to shield. Your people did well."

He smiled, "It was strange to fight without the jarl." He glanced to the north to where our other men waited. "He will be less comfortable than we I fear."

"Aye but he and the others are vital to our plans."

"We only know that he is north of here."

"And that is how it should be. We have had spies in our land, Siggi One Hand. We kept this plan within the heads of my jarls. The men they led did not know where they were going until they arrived two days since. We fight a treacherous enemy. We have to use treachery ourselves. I do not like it but the clan comes first."

"We all trust you and the jarl. You have made this land safe for our people."

We watched the flickering fires of the enemy sentries. The Danes knew my men's skill. I guessed that at least a third stood watch as they waited for the wolf warriors to slip into their camps to slit some throats. They would be disappointed. My men slept. I had no time for sleep. My plans were only half come to fruition.

Haaken joined me as the thin grey line of dawn appeared above the sky line. "Any sign of them jarl?"

"We have heard nothing save the changing of their sentries. They are beyond the ridgeline so that we cannot hear them. I have been talking of the old days with Siggi One Hand. It was pleasant."

The old warrior smiled, "And now this old warrior will go and make water and then rouse the watch. Today will be a blood day. I can feel it in my bones."

He left. Haaken pointed towards the shadows of the dead still lying on the battlefield, "They paid a heavy price for their recklessness."

"Not heavy enough. Beorn told us that they have many men in this warband. There are other clans who fight alongside the Skull Takers. It is the witches who bind them together."

"How do you plan on killing witches? I am intrigued."

"I do not know yet. Snorri's arrows will make them keep at a distance. We will need some way to get close to them."

"We could have gone last night into their camp and slain them."

"They would have expected that. In fact, I suspect that even Baggi will wonder at their powers now for they will have said that I would come and I did not. Their curse failed, they lost a witch and I did not do as they expected. Those three things are as great a victory as the deaths we inflicted upon them." I stretched, "And I will now go to prepare for war."

By the time I had eaten, made water and donned my war face dawn had broken. Snorri joined me with my sword. He smiled, almost shyly. "Thank you, jarl. I dreamed. It was a good dream. I saw the prince and old Olaf, Bjorn and Cnut came to me. You were right, the sword does have power. They told me not to fear the witches' curse. Just before I woke I saw Wolf Killer. He said nothing but his smile was as it had always been. I am ready this day." He handed me my sword.

"Then let us go to war!"

My Ulfheonar led the warriors through the gates. I had the Danish bodies moved to form a barrier before us. I held a spear in my hand for I knew that this time the Danes would come at us in organised lines. They would use archers and they would fight as we had fought. This day would not be as easy. We would have more men to bury at the end of this day.

We waited.

It soon became obvious that they were not going to attack. I waved Snorri, Beorn and Aðils forward. The three of them ran towards the enemy camps. They dodged, twisted and turned but no arrows came their way. They disappeared into the undergrowth, the bushes and the trees. I waited for a cry which would be the signal to go to their aid with my warriors but none came. Eventually Aðils and Snorri returned.

Snorri stood before me. "Jarl, they have gone. They have buried their dead and abandoned their camp. Their tracks head north. I sent Beorn to follow them but I fear they have gone to Ulla's Water."

I nodded, "This is *wyrd*. They want Ylva more than they want me. We have killed another witch. They go now to replace her with Kara and Ylva! Fetch our archers and slingers. We march north and I pray that we are in time!"

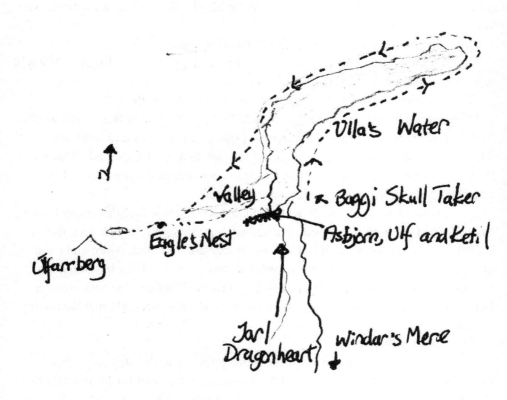

Chapter 18

They had been clever and left on the eastern side of the ridge. It was a slightly longer road but it was hidden from us. That gave us our only chance for the greenway there was exposed and rough. We travelled up the road. We would make better time. This would be a test of my plans. Up the road, just south of the valley and path which led to Eagle's Nest was a barrier of stakes and logs behind which stood my three jarls with their warriors. With over a hundred of the best warriors in the lands I hoped that they could hold up the Danish behemoth until we fell upon their rear. No matter the numerical superiority a warrior is never happy when he is assailed from the front and the rear. I sent Snorri ahead to join Beorn.

As we marched, as quickly as we could, I said quietly, "Aðils Shape Shifter, I would have you take charge of the archers today. It is normally Snorri's task but I fear his mind is not in the right place. I would have him fight in the shield wall. You are a good archer and you have a sharp mind."

"I will do so, jarl and it is an honour. Where would you like the archers and the slingers to come with us?"

"I would have them pressed as closely as they can to the rear rank of the shield wall. Those with mail and leather jerkins have swords and can aid the shield wall if their arrows run out or we are pressed too closely."

That was, indeed, my worry. If the Danes turned away from the barrier they had enough men to push us from the road. I wanted as solid a block of men as I could get. As we climbed the slope which would lead us to Ulla's Water I began to worry that I had omitted something in my planning. The Danes had done as I had planned and we were in the perfect position. Had they thought of something I had not?

We had passed the water at Hartsop when Snorri returned to us. "Jarl, they are forming up to attack our defences."

"How long do we have?"

"They will be ready before the sun has travelled to sit over Windar's Mere."

This was one time when we needed to arrive together. If we came piecemeal, then we would be defeated. I looked along the column which snaked along the old Roman Road. "Olaf go to the rear and see if you can hasten them."

"Aye, jarl! They shall hear the bite of my tongue."

Haaken said, "It is not their fault, jarl. Many feet have made this muddy and slippery. They are farmers and metal workers, shepherds and miners."

"I know, Haaken One Eye but much depends upon our reaching our men before they have fallen to our foes."

"Asbjorn is a rock and Ketil knows how to fight! They will hold." I turned to Snorri, "Give your bow to Aðils Shape Shifter, Snorri. I would have you fight in the shield wall today. Aðils is good but he is young and I need your experience."

"Aye jarl and he is a good archer. He will do the bow honour."

As we descended towards the beck we saw them. The barricade spanned the area between the Water and the rocky outcrops of the steep side of the valley. Beyond them lay the stream and path which led to the Eagle's Nest and the tarn. Ulf Olafsson had placed the archers on the knoll which marked the western end of their line. From their lofty position, they were able to rain arrows down on the Danes. This time, however, the Danes had their own bow men and even as we watched I saw one of our men fall to his death as they fought each other. The Danes had formed up their men and were approaching in a boar's snout formation. They had, however, weighted the left-hand snout. They were trying to force Ulf and his men from their position. That would allow them to break through to the Eagle's Nest. I was just grateful that they could not see it. I knew where it was but even I could not see it.

We were a Roman mile away from the Danes. I waited until we had halved the distance and then I shouted my orders. "Raibeart, take the first shield, make a wedge and attack by the Water."

"Aye jarl!"

"Second shield wall form up behind the Ulfheonar! Today you will gain great honour for you fight with the wolf warriors!"

Even though they knew that many would be going to their death they all cheered for this was a great honour and when they died, and went to Valhalla, they would be treated as heroes. I stood in front of Olaf and Haaken. The rest of the Ulfheonar formed the next two ranks. After that it was the better armed and mailed bondi. Behind the last rank Aðils Shape Shifter organized the archers.

We had been seen; it was inevitable and the rear two ranks of the Danes turned to make a shield wall to face us. I saw that the Danes were ten men deep. It was a mighty army. As I waited for all the men to position themselves I suddenly noticed that I could not see Baggi Skull Splitter. I had expected him to have a vantage point behind his men so that he could direct their attack. Perhaps he was in the front rank. Where he was, the witches would not be far away.

Olaf shouted, "Ready!"

Spears sprouted above me and shields made it darker for those behind me. Haaken began the chant and we stepped forward.

> *The Danes they came in dark of night*
> *They slew Harland without a fight*
> *Babies, children all were slain*
> *Mothers and daughters split in twain*
> *Viking enemy, taking heads*
> *Viking warriors fighting back*
> *Viking enemy, taking heads*
> *Viking warriors fighting back*
> *Viking enemy, taking heads*
> *Viking warriors fighting back*
> *Viking enemy, taking heads*
> *Viking warriors fighting back*

I stepped on to my right foot knowing that every warrior was in perfect time. The ash shaft of the spear was comforting and I held it loosely at waist height. There would be time enough to raise it. The chant helped the warriors not only to march but to feel not as an individual but part of a whole. It was as though we were one warrior and I was just the head. We took it steadily as we marched towards them. Already the effect of our movement had managed to distract some of those fighting my three war warbands. I saw that my archers on the knoll had won the battle of the bowmen and some of those facing us fell as arrows struck unprotected backs. Aðils and our archers would have no chance to send the arrows towards the Danes until we stopped. Then the Danes would see a powerful weapon unleashed.

I led the wedge obliquely towards Ulf Olafsson and his men. That was where the Danes were trying to break through. We had to destroy that wing or all of my plans would be wasted. When we were twenty paces from the Danes Haaken raised his spear and Olaf yelled, "At the bastards!"

It was not a run but we moved faster than we normally did. All of our training paid off and we moved in perfect time. I lifted my spear and held it above my shoulder. The Danish spears were held like a hedgehog. It seemed impossible that they would not hit all of us but that was an illusion. I was the target and the first spears would strike me. I had a good shield, the best mail and a superbly manufactured helmet. In addition, I had the wolf skin over my head and I would frighten the Danes.

When we were five paces from them I raised my shield so that only my eyes were showing above the metal rim and I pulled back my arm. A Dane in the second rank hurled his spear at me. I heard a curse from the leader of the shield wall. The spear was wasted. It stuck in my shield and the shaft rammed into the

Danish shields when I struck. The crack of the spear shaft on the shield distracted them a little and I thrust down at the Dane who faced me. One spear caught the rim of my shield while a second hit the top of my helmet but the wolf skin and my strap held it in place. My own spear found a gap between the shield and the top of the open helmet. My spear smashed through the Dane's face and his skull.

Our wedge now had a momentum of its own and my shield, still with the Danish spear stuck there, rammed into the second rank. The Dane who had thrown his spear at me was weaponless and the boss of my shield hit him squarely in the face. My Ulfheonar now had bodies to strike. The Danes had the same problem with my men as they had with me. We were too well armoured for them to make a telling blow. We broke through their front two ranks. It would have been easy to go wild and just charge recklessly at the others but that would have been a mistake.

Olaf shouted, "Reform!"

Dead men were replaced and the wounded dragged back to the archers, as we dressed our lines.

I heard Aðils shout, "Release!"

It was perfect timing. The Danes were also trying to reform for our next attack and there was not a solid line of shields. When the stones began to fall too it was as though there was a hailstorm.

I saw our opportunity, "Charge!"

With shields raised we stepped forward and I readied my spear. I was still the tip of the wedge and I was well protected by my men. I strode forward with confidence. This time Haaken and Olaf struck at exactly the same time as I did. Three men fell to our spears and two others were bowled over for they had not locked their shields.

Ahead of me I heard a Danish voice cry out, "Rear three ranks, turn!" The pressure on Ulf would be almost gone as the Danes faced our threat and I readied myself to face even more men.

An axe came from my side and smashed my spear in two. Snorri's spear killed the man. I pulled my shield up as I drew my sword. "Ragnar's Spirit! The sword that was touched by the gods! Witch killer!" The effect was instantaneous. The Danes before me did not want to face such a weapon and they took a step back. It allowed us to step into the void and more of my men's spears jabbed, stabbed and struck home. I took two steps, Haaken and Olaf could barely keep pace with me but I was anxious to exploit this opening. A Dane swung his sword at me and I easily deflected it with my shield. The edge caught on my boss. The Danish warrior's eyes flicked to it and I thrust into his neck. His left hand was slow to bring up his shield and he fell.

Some order was restored to the Danes when a chief brought his hearth-weru to fill the gap we had created. He was a Skull Taker. He had a skull on his helmet and he had a mighty war axe. The shields of his hearth-weru were held tightly before their leader allowing him to swing with impunity. The blow struck my shield and made my arm shiver. Even as I reeled Haaken and Olaf Leather Neck stabbed forward with their spears as did Rolf, Rollo and Snorri. I could not get past the shield and so I swung my sword in an arc below them. I was rewarded by flesh and two screams as the blade tore through thighs and knees.

"Men of Cyninges-tūn, push for your jarl!" Olaf's voice carried through the clamour, cries screams and curses.

It was as though a huge wave swept us all forward as my bondi used their weight to push against our backs. They might not be as skilled as the Danes but they had strength. The effect was to push us closer to the Danes. As we neared them I pulled back my head and butted a Danish warrior. His nose splattered like a ripe plum hitting the ground. He had his hand on his axe raised ready to strike another blow and, as he lost his balance, I pulled back my arm and stabbed forward. Ragnar's Spirit tore through the mail links and into his stomach. I twisted my sword out and punched at the next Dane with my shield. I saw that the warriors behind the Skull Takers had little mail. Now was the time for a decisive move.

"Ulfheonar! Now is your time!" I lifted my head and howled like a wolf. My men joined me. This was the signal for us to go wild. I threw myself through the gap I had made and swung my sword with all of my might. It smashed through the side of a Danish head. Olaf Leather Neck and Rolf Horse Killer had discarded their spears and were whirling their axes around their heads. Danish spears were rammed ineffectually against their mail and helmets. The two of them drove through the disheartened Danes.

Aðils' archers arrows continued to rain death upon the enemy and it was those which finally broke the Danes who faced us. They fled towards the Water. There was no time for congratulations as I saw that those at the front had finally broken through the barrier and they were falling upon Ulf Olafsson and his men. Two Danes faced me and tried to block my way. I took the sword blow from one on my shield and tried to take the head of the other. He had quick hands and his shield came up. I suddenly spun around so that they both slashed their swords at the space I had just occupied. My sword found an unprotected back and laid him open to his spine. His companion tried to turn and I punched him in the mouth with the boss of my shield. My sword was stuck in the spine of the first warrior and so I punched again. The body slid from my sword and I was able to bring it down with a crushing blow. It caved in the skull of the Dane.

My men slew the last of those who had climbed the barrier and we rushed through to see who needed help. Ulf Olafsson lay dead. He was surrounded by ten dead Danes and four of his hearth-weru. Unlike Sigtrygg he had not been able to hang on to speak with me but he and his people had done their duty.

I hung my head. Haaken One Eye said, "Jarl Dragonheart, victory is within touching distance. Come, let us aid Raibeart and drive these Danes into the Water."

"Reform!"

We had no time to grieve or mourn our friend. The battle was not yet over. We wheeled to our right. "Aðils, put your archers on the knoll. They can release over our heads!"

"Aye Jarl Dragonheart." He led his men up the slope towards the knoll which afforded a view up the valley to the north of Ulla's Water.

"Shield wall this time. Ulfheonar will be the front rank!" I wanted to inflict the maximum casualties on the Danes. I knew they would be tiring. We were. It was now after noon. We had been fighting for hours. Assailed and assaulted on two sides had weakened our foes but if we did not attack now then they might escape and I wanted them to remember this day with fear.

Haaken began the chant. We were aided by the slope down to the Water but the dead bodies which littered the field were a hazard.

Viking enemy, taking heads
Viking warriors fighting back
Viking enemy, taking heads
Viking warriors fighting back
Viking enemy, taking heads
Viking warriors fighting back
Viking enemy, taking heads
Viking warriors fighting back

A Danish chief, not a Skull Taker, shouted to his men, "Clan of the tree bear, turn and face these wolves. We will have the honour of slaying them. Then this will be our land. Tree Bear!" They all cheered and began to chant.

He hurriedly tried to form them into a line. I saw that Raibeart and the other shield wall were struggling against their enemies. They had not made the inroads we had. We had to finish off these Danes and relieve the pressure on them. I had lost too many old friends to lose my young captain. To my left I heard Asbjorn and Ketil extoling their men to even greater deeds. We were all fighting to our limits.

Few warriors had spears left. Some were even using the broken shafts as weapons. Aðils ordered the archers to release and the slingers to hurl. It was like a flock of birds over our heads. The Danes held up their shields. It stopped some

184

of the arrows and stones but what it did do was make them shelter behind their shields.

We were twenty paces from them and it was time. I raised my sword, "Now! Attack!"

We launched ourselves over the last few paces. It was reckless but the arrows and lead balls had weakened them. I saw Olaf Leather Neck race ahead of us all and swing his axe at the Danish chief. The Dane was no coward and he stepped from the shield wall swinging his own axe. Both weapons were heading for the head of their enemy. It seemed to me that I was about to lose another Ulfheonar. What saved Olaf and ended the life of the Dane was the height difference. Olaf was on a higher piece of ground and his axe struck first. Even so the dying arms of the Dane carried the head to strike the shoulder of Olaf Leather Neck. He was hurt but he had succeeded in breaking their line.

I leapt through the gap stabbing first left and then right with hands as quick as ever. My shield seemed to have a mind of its own and I blocked blows I did not even see. It is sometimes that way when you fight. Your body ignores your head and just does what it needs to. I suddenly saw Raibeart. There were less than thirty warriors between us. It was then that some of the Danes went berserk. I had not seen it for some time but four of the tree bear clan suddenly hurled their shields at us and threw their helmets away. The threw themselves at my warriors. It was not the Ulfheonar who were in their path but my bondi. Six died in as many blows. I could not let this happen.

I ran straight at the four of them. Their axes whirled above their heads. They had scythed down my six men who had no defence against their axes. I saw that they had arrows sticking from their bodies but they fought on. Such was the power of a berserker. Olaf Leather Neck lay on the ground, his wounds were being tended to and I had just Haaken, Rolf and Rollo behind me. They would have to do.

I put my shield at an angle and held my sword behind me. As the two Danish axes splintered my shield I swung my sword at their knees. A berserker can fight with arrows in their body but they cannot fight on one leg. I hacked through the knee of one and then flicked my sword to tear the tendons of a second. Rolf's axe smashed into the skull of a third one. Rollo had his shield destroyed by the axe of the third but his long arms meant he was able to decapitate the Dane. Haaken One Eye used a trick he had seen me use before now. He rolled forward below the swinging axe and drove his sword up through the Danes' groin and deep not his body. He pulled it out, tearing open the Dane's rib cage. I turned and brought Ragnar's Spirit down across the neck of the last berserker who was still trying to fight with a severed leg.

Raibeart yelled, "Dragonheart! We have won!"

Then I heard Aðils Shape Shifter yell from the knoll, "Jarl Dragonheart! Eagle's Nest is under attack! It is Baggi Skull Splitter! He has come around the Water with many men. They are on horses and they have the witches with them."

The Norns had spun well. I had been deceived. My wonderful plan had been rendered useless. My family would all die and it would be my fault! I had known of the old Roman Road which travelled the high ground to the east of the Water but I had dismissed it. I now saw that the Danish army had been to fix my eye on my trap and allow Baggi and his witches to travel unmolested. I guessed they had been mounted.

"Ulfheonar to me!" I turned to Siggi the Tanner. He was tending to one of the wounded. "Go to Asbjorn the Strong. Tell him that I leave him in command. Tell him to finish off the Danes. I must go to my family."

"Aye jarl."

I saw that Erik Ulfsson had joined my other warriors in Valhalla. "Come Ulfheonar. Let us test our mettle against that of the Skull Takers." I picked up Ulf Olafsson's shield. It was well made and mine was shattered.

Erik Finnison followed Aðils, "Jarl let me come with you. I have lost my own family. It is right that I come to help you save yours."

Aðils Shape Shifter nodded, "He is good, Jarl Dragonheart. We might need his skill and he his fit."

"This is *wyrd*. Come with us Erik the Bowman."

Chapter 19

We set off up the path towards the Eagle's nest. That was our only advantage. The Danes had travelled across country and we would be able to use the path. We knew the path well. Snorri and Aðils ran ahead of us along with Beorn the Scout. They did so naturally. With two of my Ulfheonar in the Nest and Erik Ulfsson dead we were a small number and I prayed that we would be enough. I did not look behind me but I knew that the battle still raged below me. If I lost my family, then the outcome of the battle was irrelevant. I would have to make sure that the deaths of my men were not in vain.

The sounds of the battle below masked any signs of the conflict above. When we turned to pass the large boulder, I spied the Danes. They had surrounded the Eagle's Nest. The two rock traps had worked and ten Danes lay dead or dying beneath the man-made avalanche. It had slowed their attack, that was all. I saw that it was Baggi Skull Splitter's hearth-weru. There looked to be thirty of them. Other warriors were there too. The three witches stood behind them. I could see that they were using their magic. The battle had raged so long that the sun was setting behind Úlfarrberg. Our sacred mountain appeared to have a crown around it. But it also meant that we approached from the gloom in the east. With our wolf cloaks and black armour, we would be hidden.

The sounds of battle drifted to our ears along with the wailing chant of the witches. I could not make out faces on the fighting platform. I did not know if my son and grandson survived. I heard the sound of axes on wood. They were attempting to break into the stronghold. It was well made but it could not withstand Danish war axes for long. I forced my aching and tired legs to move faster. Olaf Leather Neck's wound had not stopped him from following us but it had slowed him down. I heard him struggling to catch us.

Suddenly Erik Finnison and Aðils Shape Shifter sprinted ahead of us. They were much younger than we were. I wondered if they had gone berserk. Then I realised what they intended. The both had the Saami bow. As we turned another bend I saw that they had halted two hundred paces from the Danes. Their bows bent as they put every piece of power they possessed into their arms. They released. Their arrows struck two of the Danish hearth-weru. It had an instantaneous effect. Every eye swivelled to see whence the attack had come. I

187

could not hear his words but I saw the skull bedecked figure of Baggi Skull Splitter turn and shout orders. I saw that they had managed to scale the walls! Even as I looked a defender fell to his death. It would not be long before the stronghold fell! We had no time to waste.

The three witches began to point at my archers. They began to mouth something which I guessed was a curse. The two archers were young and I feared that the power of the witches might be too much for them.

"Hurry! We must reach them before the witches do their worst."

I need not have feared for two arrows suddenly pitched into the two witches who flanked the bloated monstrosity that was Asta. The effect surprised even me. I saw Baggi shout orders and ten of his hearth-weru ran down the slope to form a shield wall before the one remaining Danish witch.

We reached my two archers. "That was well done, Aðils. I need you to fight with us. Erik keep your arrows flying!"

There were not many of us but we locked shields. Snorri took Olaf's place by my left and we locked shields to march towards the witches. We were too few to attack the rest of Baggi Skull Splitter's men but I hoped to draw more from the walls. I had to rely on my son, grandson and Aiden. If we could buy enough time, then the rest of my army could come to our aid.

The Danes we faced were as grotesque as the flat bloated witch. They had the skulls of animals hanging from their hair beneath their helmets. Each one had a human skull on their helmet. They had filed their teeth. They had bones hanging from their beards and moustaches. They hurled insults at us as we approached, "Your wolf skins will not stop our axes!"

"Are these all that you have left?"

"You will howl like a baby when we gut you!"

We ignored them. I heard Asta chanting behind them. I could not hear her words but I had faced a Norn and I feared no pustule ridden hag. I headed for the centre of the line of warriors. Baggi must have realised that we outnumbered his men for he detached another eight who hurried down the slope towards us. That was less for my family to fight.

The warrior I chose to fight had a red skull painted on his shield. He bared his teeth and roared, "I fear no sword of the gods for Asta has cast a spell of protection! I cannot be killed by mortal man! I am Horsten, Terror of the Night, and I will have your head to adorn my helmet!"

He must have worked himself up for he stepped forward, leaving the protection of the shield wall. He swung his long sword and I raised my shield although I never took my eyes from his face. Ulf's shield was well made and the sword sparked off my boss. His sword would be sharp while mine had lost its edge. I had to trust that the Allfather's power was still within it. I feinted to his left and he raised his shield. As he did so I stamped forward with my right leg and smashed my boot on his foot. As I had expected it did not hurt him but it made him step back. I punched my shield at his face. It smashed two of the bones which hung there and he roared in anger. While I had distracted him, I brought my sword over the top of his shield, for we were close and I used the guard to strike at his eye. Once again his head jerked back. It was a natural reaction. I had broken the line of the shields and Snorri and Haaken took advantage.

I heard the witch as she spat at us, "I curse you, Dragonheart and Snorri Witch Killer. I curse your seed and I curse your land. I curse your spirits and your warband!"

I saw that she had a crudely made stick doll and she was putting bone needles into it.

"By this token made of yew, you all will die you pathetic few, I take your hearts and drain your blood, I bathe and wash this ancient wood, I lit the fire to end your clan, you will die, a mortal man!"

Something snapped inside Snorri. Even as I raised my sword to kill the Dane I had maimed he swung his sword at the Dane he fought and knocked him to the ground. He ran to the witch and raising his sword, he stabbed her. Her claw like hands grabbed his cloak and pulled him closer to her. He stabbed her again. It was hard to find something vital beneath her layers of fat. I sank my sword into the Dane I fought as Snorri raised his sword to stab the witch again. She cursed and spat at him. The warrior Snorri had knocked to the ground stood and stabbed my scout in the back. I brought my sword over and took the Dane's head. Mortally wounded Snorri summoned up enough strength to swing his sword at the head of the witch. The grisly, pustule and wart covered skull flew through the air. The warriors Baggi had sent fell upon Snorri. Even as he slumped to the ground they began to hack at his body. I threw myself into them. I smashed my sword across the neck of one. My edge had gone but the blow was so hard that it broke his neck. Beorn the Scout was like a man possessed. His oldest friend lay dead at our feet and he recklessly hacked and chopped at the Danes around him. I saw one raise his sword to end Beorn's life too and then an arrow came from nowhere to throw him back. Cnut and Haaken led the charge to destroy the rest of the Danes. I knelt by Snorri. Life had left him but he had a smile upon his face.

I stood and raised my sword, "Baggi Skull Splitter, you have killed my men for the last time. Your witches are dead and you will join them. You cannot defeat the power of the Allfather!"

He still had many men with him and he roared at me defiantly, "This ends now, Dragonheart! I will kill you myself and tear your skull from your shoulders! I will make a goblet from it and drink your blood. I will spread the legs of the young witch and she will conjure no more!"

As they came towards us there was a roar as my gates opened and Ragnar led those who survived from the stronghold to fall upon the rear of the Danish line. The Skull Taker was right; this would end on this hillside beneath the Úlfarrberg.

Baggi Skull Splitter was a powerful warrior. He was far bigger than I was but he had a paunch on him. My sword was not sharp enough for me to end this swiftly. He had confidence for his helmet was not made of metal but a large human skull painted red. It would not stop a blow but I would struggle to be able to land one there. I forced myself to ignore those around me. If I fell then they would lose heart or, even worse, recklessly try to avenge me. I had to wear him down. His axe was not quite a two-handed axe. He could wield it one handed and he had a shield to defend against my sword. He brought the axe from far behind him. He had the slope in his favour. He brought the axe in an upward swing. It smashed into my shield and I began to fall backwards. I was only saved by the pressure of Olaf Leather Neck's shield. He had struggled to reach us but his very presence saved my life. I lunged forward as Olaf pushed me towards the Dane. My sword still had enough of an edge and point to stab the Dane in the knee. He roared in pain and swept his shield towards my head. I swivelled away from the blow. It missed my head by the width of a seax.

I was now standing sideways on the slope. If the Dane wished to continue to swing his axe he had to turn too. His wounded knee was on the downward slope. As he pulled back his axe to swing at me again I brought my sword backhanded across his right side. It smacked into his mail. Some of the links were severed and his arm flailed as he tried to recover his balance.

"You are Loki! You are the trickster! Fight like a warrior; beard to beard!"

"When I find a warrior, I will do so! You are a butcher of babies and not worth my spit!"

In answer, he brought the axe from behind him, over his head. Had I not moved then I would have been split in two. Holding my shield above me I stepped back. The move did not take me from his arc but he only hit the lower part of my shield. When a sliver of wood flew from it he gave a shout of joy. I feinted with my sword and then spun around, up the hill. I brought Ragnar's Spirit into the side of his mail again. My hand was guided for it found the place I had weakened the mail earlier. This time the blow hurt him. It might have little edge but my sword was heavy. Something broke within his body.

I now had the advantage of the slope. All around us the hearth-weru of the Danish jarl were fighting to the death. In the darkening evening, it was a battle fought face to face. None were dying easily. Like a wounded animal, they fought beyond reason, almost beyond life.

When Baggi next raised his axe to swing at me it was a little slower than it had been. This blow was a sideways one. I could not avoid it. I had to take the hit on my shield. Although weaker it still shivered my arm and cracked the shield. There was triumph on the Dane's face. I swung my sword low and connected with his shin. Not a killing blow it hurt. I saw blood on my blade. Undeterred he brought his axe overhand again. I was already far enough back that I did not need to step backwards and I leaned my body behind my shield. The pain up my arm was less but a hole appeared in the shield. It would not last much longer.

He was now warier of me. He watched my eyes and was ready for my feints and spins. I was running out of ways to defeat him. Had my sword been sharp then I could have used it on his legs. I did the only thing I could, I traded blows with his shield. He thought I was beaten for the sword did not even dent the shield. When next he swung, I knew what the outcome would be. My shield would be destroyed.

"This ends soon, Dragonheart and I will have that sword melted down and made into a drinking vessel!"

As soon as he said that I knew that the Allfather would not allow it. He swung his axe. It was slower and delivered with less power. He was tiring. His weight, his wounds and his exertions had sapped his energy. The shield shattered leaving just the boss in my hand. I threw the boss at his face as I whipped out my seax. As his right hand came up to protect his face I stabbed forward with the seax. It was sharp. I struck through the gap I had made in his mail. It grated against his ribs as it entered his body. I twisted as I pulled it out and I stepped back. The seax is broad bladed. Blood poured from the wound. He punched at me with his shield and I was forced on to the back foot. I saw him try to raise his axe again. It caused a greater outpouring of blood. I swung my sword high above his shield. I aimed at his skull covered helmet. He brought his axe up to block the blow. The force of my strike smashed his axe handle in two.

He threw the head at me and drew his own sword. I was tiring too but not as much as he was. I danced away from the scything sword which struck air. It tired him and caused more blood to flood from his body. I feinted with my seax. I could see that he feared it. He stepped back on his left leg and opened his body. "Allfather guide my hand!" I lunged at his throat. He was weak and he was tired. His left hand was too slow and Baggi Skull Splitter died as my sword entered his throat and went up through his skull. I twisted and tore upwards. His skull split in two. Brains, bone and blood erupted as I ended the life of the man who would have been king.

I whirled around and saw that we had been the last two to fight. Ragnar stood there his sword dripping with blood and his mail blood spattered. Olaf Leather Neck knelt. I had not lost any of the Ulfheonar but I saw that only Einar the Tall remained of those hearth-weru who had followed my son, Wolf Killer. I nodded to Ragnar, "Where are my daughter and her family?"

He gestured inside with his sword, "They are within," he hesitated, "they tend to Gruffyd."

My heart sank to my boots. The Norns, it seemed, had not finished punishing me. I sheathed my sword and ran through the gates. The battle around the gate had been fierce. The Danes had lost many men trying to gain entry. The door of the hall was open and I clambered up the ladder. Ylva and Kara were on either side of my son who lay, white as a sheet, save for a reddened bandage around his head. At his feet knelt Elfrida.

Aiden put his arm out, "He lives, jarl, but he is hovering between this world and the next. Ylva and Kara are bringing him back. Do not disturb them. It would be best."

I took out my sword. It was still bloody. Shaking off Aiden's arm I walked towards my son. Ylva and Kara had their eyes closed. I said nothing but I laid the sword along his body. "Allfather let your power flow through this sword and heal my son." The room was filled with silence. I saw Kara and Ylva stiffen and then my son began to breathe a little easier.

Kara, Elfrida and Ylva opened their eyes and stood. Kara said, quietly, "He was almost gone, father and then suddenly his spirit spoke to us. He will live!" She saw the sword and nodded, "This is *wyrd*."

"Is it over grandfather?"

I nodded, "It is although we have paid a heavy price. Snorri slew Asta but it was his last act. He is in Valhalla now."

"I am sorry. This is all my fault!" She threw herself in my arms and began to sob.

Cradling her I murmured in her ear, "That is like blaming the Land of the Wolf for being beautiful and making people desire it. The fault lies on others who wish to take what we have. The clan has paid a fearful price but we have kept the land safe. We have enemies to pursue but the threat is gone."

Aiden said, "Come, wife, come Elfrida, we have men to heal. Ylva, stay with Gruffyd."

I shook my head, "No, I shall be his healer. The Allfather has shown me the true power of the sword. My warriors need you. We shall be staying here this night."

After they had gone I pulled a chair over and sat next to Gruffyd's head. I laid one hand on the hilt of my sword and one on his head. I spoke quietly, "I have lost one son, Gruffyd. I could not live if I lost a second. I should have had you with my men. The Allfather has given me a second chance and I will not spurn it. I shall make you a warrior so powerful that none will dare face you. I will prepare you to be jarl when I am gone."

A breeze seemed to enter the room and he sighed. His breathing settled into the rhythm of someone asleep. Old Ragnar had always said that sleep was the best healer and I prayed so. I must have fallen asleep for I was shaken awake. I looked up and saw Haaken.

"Jarl Dragonheart, we have won. Asbjorn and Ketil destroyed the rest of the warband. Aðils and Beorn are now leading Ketil and his men to pursue them. They were forced to head north towards Ketil's land. He swore he would pursue them until they fell into the sea."

"And the butcher's bill?"

"We lost many men. I have never known a day when we lost three Ulfheonar." He shook his head and his voice caught, "I thought Snorri would outlive me. His wife has just had his first son. He had so much to live for."

"He had killed two witches. He felt cursed. When he saw the witch cursing our people it was too much for him. He died for his wife and his son. He could not allow his land to be cursed. It was a good death but I will grieve for him. Long after his son has grown up I will remember the greatest of scouts."

"Aye."

We sat in silence. It was comfortable. We needed no words. It was so quiet that when Gruffyd stirred we both jumped. His eyes opened and his hands went to the sword. He sat up, "I thought it was a dream."

"A dream?"

"Yes father. I was in a cave. It was the cave where we were trapped and the witch was coming for me. She took the form of a giant wyrme. Kara, Ylva and Elfrida came to protect me but the wyrme ate them. I ran as far into the cave as I could go. When I could go no further I turned to face my enemy. Suddenly I found I held Ragnar's Spirit and I smote the head from the wyrme."

Haaken touched his dragon, "Each time I think I understand the power of this sword I am surprised."

Gruffyd swung his legs from the table upon which he had been laid. He handed me the sword. "Is it over, father? Will the witch be coming again?"

I shook my head, "The battle was fought. I slew Baggi Skull Splitter. Snorri died bravely, he slew the Danish witch. The world is safer now without their spawn. And we have saved our own. Ylva is the Viking witch and she will only grow in power."

Epilogue

It was the middle of Mörsugur when we finally returned to Cyninges-tūn. We had many wounded to tend. We had dead to bury and enemies to burn. There was treasure and weapons to share and I had a jarl to appoint. Eystein the Brave had been one of Ulf's hearth-weru. He was the only one to survive and I knew he would be a good leader. When all was done, we headed home. The wounded rode and the rest of us walked. Olaf's wound was the worst he had suffered. He had to be brought back on a cart; he hated it.

There were homes without men. We had paid a heavy price. The wives, daughters and mothers accepted their loss. They knew that they would be cared for. That was the way of the clan but we mourned. We feasted too for that was our way. We sang songs to remember them and their loss. Snorri's wife and his son, Bjorn, were brought to live with Kara and her family. Ylva found the presence of the baby comforting. She was now a woman and her experiences both in meeting the witch and the events since had changed her. Snorri's son, Bjorn, was a means for her to adjust to her new life.

Ragnar had changed too. He had fought well but he had seen men die for him. That was always a humbling experience. On our way back to our home he had told me that he now knew that he could be a better leader. Einar would be his mentor and they would choose warriors to follow him. We had lost so many warriors that our training and practice was even more important. Ragnar was determined to help create as many new warriors as he could. It was *wyrd*.

Aðils and Beorn returned to tell us that Ketil had chased the survivors of the battle until there was no trace of them left. Beorn said, "We did not get them all but the ones who escaped us will never dare set foot in this land again."

He had then left to return to Úlfarrberg. He wished to pay his respects to Snorri who lay in the barrow with Ulla, Ulf and Erik. Brigid refused to allow Gruffyd out of her sight. I received dark looks. She blamed me for his wound. I summoned Aðils Shape Shifter as Þorri began. Ragnar and Einar the Tall were already in my hall, "We have a task to perform. I owe a duty to those who died to pay back those who betrayed us."

"But grandfather the witch and the Skull Takers are dead!"

"We had spies in our land and we go to find them. They thought that they had escaped us but they have not. I would have you three come with me. Many of my Ulfheonar would come but this is a task for a few and I chose you."

Einar said, "Speaking for myself, jarl, I am honoured."

Ragnar said, "As are we all."

"Then say farewell to your mother. We leave on the morrow."

After they had gone to prepare for our journey I went to Brigid to tell her what I intended. "But who are these spies? What good will it do to hunt them down? You could be killed and for what? Nothing! The spies, whoever they were, are gone! You know who they are and they will not return. The White Christ says to forgive."

"I am not of the White Christ and it is not nothing. These spies insinuated themselves into our land. They gained the confidence of our people. My task is necessary. It discourages others who would do the same and it warns my people of the dangers we face here, in the heart of the Land of the Wolf. We do not forgive and we never forget. You hurt us and we will remember. Unless my enemies prise Ragnar's Spirit from my dead hand I will fight them until there is no breath left in my body!"

She waved an irritated hand at me. "This is a nonsense. It is winter. The spies are long gone and you will not be able to follow a trail. I am not even certain that you know who they are!"

I looked at her and told her who the spies were. She blanched and her hand went to her cross. "Truly?"

"Have you ever known me to be foresworn? I have had it confirmed by Kara. I know where they will flee and I will find them."

"What will you do to them when you find them?"

"That is simple. I will take them somewhere quiet and tell them that they will die and then Ragnar's Spirit will take their lives."

"Both of them?"

"Both of them. Then I will return home and we will watch our land for other enemies. This land, the Land of the Wolf shall be the wolf's fortress. None shall harm us again."

The End

Glossary

Afon Hafron- River Severn in Welsh

Alpín mac Echdach – the father of Kenneth MacAlpin, reputedly the first king of the Scots

Alt Clut- Dumbarton Castle on the Clyde

An Lysardh - Lizard Peninsula Cornwall

Balley Chashtal -Castleton (Isle of Man)

Bardanes Tourkos- Rebel Byzantine General

Bebbanburgh- Bamburgh Castle, Northumbria also known as Din Guardi in the ancient tongue

Beck- a stream

Beinn na bhFadhla- Benbecula in the Outer Hebrides

Belesduna - Basildon

Blót – a blood sacrifice made by a jarl

Blue Sea- The Mediterranean

Bondi- Viking farmers who fight

Bourde- Bordeaux

Bjarnarøy –Great Bernera (Bear Island)

Byrnie- a mail or leather shirt reaching down to the knees

Caerlleon- Welsh for Chester

Caer Ufra -South Shields

Caestir - Chester (old English)

Càrdainn Ros -Cardross (Argyll)

Casnewydd –Newport, Wales

Cephas- Greek for Simon Peter (St. Peter)

Chape- the tip of a scabbard

Charlemagne- Holy Roman Emperor at the end of the 8th and beginning of the 9th centuries

Celchyth - Chelsea

Cherestanc- Garstang (Lancashire)

Corn Walum or Om Walum- Cornwall

Cymri- Welsh

Cymru- Wales

Cyninges-tūn – Coniston. It means the estate of the king (Cumbria)

Dùn Èideann –Edinburgh (Gaelic)

Din Guardi- Bamburgh castle

Drekar- a Dragon ship (a Viking warship)

Duboglassio –Douglas, Isle of Man

Dun Holme- Durham

Dún Lethglaise - Downpatrick (Northern Ireland)

Durdle- Durdle door- the Jurassic coast in Dorset

Dyrøy –Jura (Inner Hebrides)

Dyflin- Old Norse for Dublin

Ēa Lōn - River Lune

Ein-mánuðr - middle of March to the middle of April

Eoforwic- Saxon for York

Falgrave- Scarborough (North Yorkshire)

Faro Bregancio- Corunna (Spain)

Ferneberga -Farnborough (Hampshire)

Fey- having second sight

Firkin- a barrel containing eight gallons (usually beer)

Fret-a sea mist

Frankia- France and part of Germany

Fyrd-the Saxon levy

Garth- Dragon Heart

Gaill- Irish for foreigners

Galdramenn- wizard

Gesith- A Saxon nobleman. After 850 AD, they were known as thegns

Glaesum –amber

Gleawecastre- Gloucester

Gói- the end of February to the middle of March

Gormánuður- October to November (Slaughter month- the beginning of winter)

Grendel- the monster slain by Beowulf

Grenewic- Greenwich

Gulle - Goole (Humberside)

Hagustaldes ham -Hexham

Hamwic -Southampton

Haustmánuður - September 16th- October 16th (cutting of the corn)

Haughs- small hills in Norse (As in Tarn Hows)

Hearth-weru- The bodyguard or oathsworn of a jarl

Heels- when a ship leans to one side under the pressure of the wind

Hel - Queen of Niflheim, the Norse underworld.

Here Wic- Harwich

Hersey- Isle of Arran

Hersir- a Viking landowner and minor noble. It ranks below a jarl

Hetaereiarch – Byzantine general

Hí- Iona (Gaelic)

Hjáp - Shap- Cumbria (Norse for stone circle)

Hoggs or Hogging- when the pressure of the wind causes the stern or the bow to droop

Hrams-a – Ramsey, Isle of Man

Hwitebi - Norse for Whitby, North Yorkshire

Hywel ap Rhodri Molwynog- King of Gwynedd 814-825

Icaunis- British river god

Issicauna- Gaulish for the lower Seine

Itouna- River Eden Cumbria

Jarl- Norse earl or lord

Joro-goddess of the earth

kjerringa - Old Woman- the solid block in which the mast rested

Knarr- a merchant ship or a coastal vessel

Kyrtle-woven top

Lambehitha- Lambeth

Leathes Water- Thirlmere

Legacaestir- Anglo Saxon for Chester

Ljoðhús- Lewis

Lochlannach – Irish for Northerners (Vikings)

Lothuwistoft- Lowestoft

Lough- Irish lake

Louis the Pious- King of the Franks and son of Charlemagne

Lundenburgh- the fort in the heart of London (the former Roman fort)

Lundenwic - London

Maeresea- River Mersey

Mammceaster- Manchester

Manau/Mann – The Isle of Man(n) (Saxon)

Marcia Hispanic- Spanish Marches (the land around Barcelona)

Mast fish- two large racks on a ship designed to store the mast when not required

Melita- Malta

Midden- a place where they dumped human waste

Miklagård - Constantinople

Mörsugur - December 13th -January 12th (the fat sucker month!)

Nikephoros- Emperor of Byzantium 802-811

Njoror- God of the sea

Nithing- A man without honour (Saxon)

Odin - The "All Father" God of war, also associated with wisdom, poetry, and magic (The Ruler of the gods).

Olissipo- Lisbon

Orkneyjar-Orkney

Penrhudd – Penrith Cumbria

Þorri -January 13th -February 12th - midwinter

Portesmūða -Portsmouth

Pillars of Hercules- Straits of Gibraltar

Pyrlweall -Thirwell, Cumbria

Ran- Goddess of the sea

Roof rock- slate

Rinaz –The Rhine

Sabrina- Latin and Celtic for the River Severn. Also, the name of a female Celtic deity

Saami- the people who live in what is now Northern Norway/Sweden

Samhain- a Celtic festival of the dead between 31st October and1st November (Halloween)

St. Cybi- Holyhead

Scree- loose rocks in a glacial valley

Seax – short sword

Sennight- seven knights- a week

Sheerstrake- the uppermost strake in the hull

Sheet- a rope fastened to the lower corner of a sail

Shroud- a rope from the masthead to the hull amidships

Skeggox – an axe with a shorter beard on one side of the blade

South Folk- Suffolk

Stad- Norse settlement

Stays- ropes running from the mast-head to the bow

Strake- the wood on the side of a drekar

Streanæshalc- Saxon for Whitby, North Yorkshire

Suthriganaworc - Southwark (London)

Syllingar Insula, Syllingar- Scilly Isles

Tarn- small lake (Norse)

Tella- River Béthune which empties near to Dieppe

Temese- River Thames (also called the Tamese)

The Norns- The three sisters who weave webs of intrigue for men

Tilaburg - Tilbury

Thing-Norse for a parliament or a debate (Tynwald)

Thor's day- Thursday

Threttanessa- a drekar with 13 oars on each side.

Thrall- slave

Tinea- Tyne

Trenail- a round wooden peg used to secure strakes

Tynwald- the Parliament on the Isle of Man

Tvímánuður -Hay time-August 15th -September 15th

Úlfarrberg- Helvellyn

Úlfarrland- Cumbria

Úlfarr- Wolf Warrior

Úlfarrston- Ulverston

Ullr-Norse God of Hunting

Ulfheonar-an elite Norse warrior who wore a wolf skin over his armour

Vectis- The Isle of Wight

Volva- a witch or healing woman in Norse culture

Waeclinga Straet- Watling Street (A5) Windlesore-Windsor

Waite- a Viking word for farm

Werham -Wareham (Dorset)

Wintan-ceastre -Winchester

Withy- the mechanism connecting the steering board to the ship

Woden's day- Wednesday

Wulfhere-Old English for Wolf Army

Wyddfa-Snowdon

Wyrd- Fate

Wyrme- Norse for Dragon

Yard- a timber from which the sail is suspended

Ynys Enlli- Bardsey Island

Ynys Môn-Anglesey

Maps and drawings

Ulf Olafsson's Stronghold

Britannia 825 A.D.

The Land of the Wolf

STRATHCLYDE

NORTHUMBRIA

Stad on the Eden

Caer Ligra

Ketil's Stad

Myrdynn's Cave

Ulfarberg

Windar's Mere

Cyninges-tun

Dunum

Hwitebi

Ulfarston

Sigtrygg's Stad

Eoforwic

Fulford

Stamford

MERCIA

N

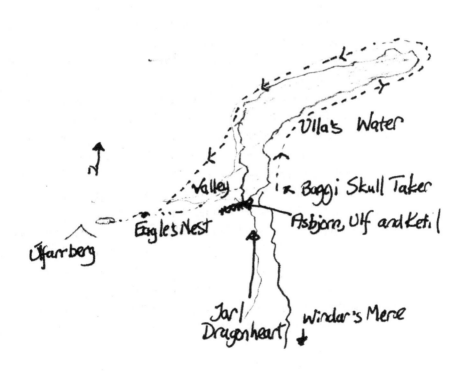

Ulla's Water

Valley

Baggi Skull Taker

Asbjorn, Ulf and Ketil

Eagle's Nest

Ulfarberg

N

Jarl Dragonheart

Windar's Mere

Historical note

The Viking raids began, according to records left by the monks, in the 790s when Lindisfarne was pillaged. However, there were many small settlements along the east coast and most were undefended. I have chosen a fictitious village on the Tees as the home of Garth who is enslaved and then, when he gains his freedom, becomes Dragon Heart. As buildings were all made of wood then any evidence of their existence would have rotted long ago, save for a few post holes. The Norse began to raid well before 790. There was a rise in the populations of Norway and Denmark and Britain was not well prepared for defence against such random attacks.

My raiders represent the Norse warriors who wanted the plunder of the soft Saxon kingdom. There is a myth that the Vikings raided in large numbers but this is not so. It was only in the tenth and eleventh centuries that the numbers grew. They also did not have allegiances to kings. The Norse settlements were often isolated family groups. The term Viking was not used in what we now term the Viking Age beyond the lands of Norway and Denmark. Warriors went a-Viking which meant that they sailed for adventure or pirating. Their lives were hard. Slavery was commonplace. The Norse for slave is thrall and I have used both terms.

The ship, '*The Heart of the Dragon*' is based on the Gokstad ship which was found in 1880 in Norway. It is 23.24 metres long and 5.25 metres wide at its widest point. It was made entirely of oak except for the pine decking. There are 16 strakes on each side and from the base to the gunwale is 2.02 metres giving it a high freeboard. The keel is cut from a piece of oak 17.6 metres long. There are 19 ribs. The pine mast was 13 metres high. The ship could carry 70 men although there were just sixteen oars on each side. This meant that half the crew could rest while the other half rowed. Sea battles could be brutal. The drekar was the most efficient warship of its day. The world would have to wait until the frigates of the eighteenth century to see such a dominant ship again. When the Saxons before Alfred the Great tried to meet Vikings at sea it ended in disaster. It was Alfred who created a warship which stood a chance against the Vikings but they never really competed. The same ships as Dragonheart used carried King William to England in 1066.

The Vikings raided far and wide. They raided and subsequently conquered much of Western France and made serious inroads into Spain. They even travelled up the Rhone River as well as raiding North Africa. The sailors and warriors we call Vikings were very adaptable and could, indeed, carry their long ships over hills to travel from one river to the next. The Viking ships are quite remarkable. Replicas of the smaller ones have managed speeds of 8-10 knots. The sea going ferries, which ply the Bay of Biscay, travel at 14-16 knots. The journey the 'Heart of the Dragon' makes from Santander to the Isles of Scilly in a day and a half would have been possible with the oars and a favourable wind and, of course, the cooperation of the Goddess of the sea, Ran! The journey from the Rhine to Istanbul is 1188 nautical miles. If the *'Heart of the Dragon'* had had favourable winds and travelled nonstop she might have made the journey in 6 days! Sailing during the day only and with some adverse winds means that 18 or 20 days would be more realistic.

Seguin I Lupo was Duke of Vasconia and he briefly rebelled against the Holy Roman Emperor. This was around the time my novel was set. After a few years, he was deposed, killed and the Dukedom absorbed back into the Empire. The wine trade at his capital, Bourde (Bordeaux) had been established by the Romans and would continue to draw trade to this region. The Asturias Kingdom was expanding west at this time too and gradually absorbed Galicia.

Nikephoros was Emperor from 802-811. Bardanes Tourkos did revolt although he did not attempt a coup in the palace as I used in my book. He was later defeated, blinded, and sent to a monastery. Nikephoros did well until he went to war with Krum, the Khan of Bulgaria. He died in battle and Krum made a drinking vessel from his skull!

I have recently used the British Museum book and research about the Vikings. Apparently, rather like punks and Goths, the men did wear eye makeup. It would make them appear more frightening. There is also evidence that they filed their teeth. The leaders of warriors built up a large retinue by paying them and giving them gifts such as the wolf pendant. This was seen as a sort of bond between leader and warrior. It also marked them out in battle as oathsworn. There was no national identity. They operated in small bands of free booters loyal to their clan leader. The idea of sword killing was to render a weapon unusable by anyone else. On a simplistic level this could just be a bend but I have seen examples which are tightly curled like a spring. Viking kings were rare it was not until the end of the ninth century that national identity began to emerge.

The length of the swords in this period was not the same as in the later medieval period. By the year 850 they were only 76 cm long and in the eighth century they were shorter still. The first sword Dragon Heart used, Ragnar's, was a new design, and was 75 cm long. This would only have been slightly longer than a Roman gladius. At this time the sword, not the axe was the main weapon. The best swords came from Frankia, and were probably German in origin. A sword was considered a special weapon and a good one would be handed from father to son. A warrior with a famous blade would be sought out on the battlefield. There was little mail around at the time and warriors learned to be agile to avoid being struck. A skeggox was an axe with a shorter edge on one side. The use of an aventail (a chain mail extension of a helmet) began at about this time. The highly decorated scabbard also began at this time.

A wedge was formed by having a warrior at the front and then two and so on. Sometimes it would have a double point, boar's snout. A wedge with twenty men at the rear might have over a hundred and fifty men. It would be hard to stop. The blood eagle was performed by cutting the skin of the victim by the spine, breaking the ribs so they resembled blood-stained wings, and pulling the lungs out through the wounds in the victim's back.

I have used the word saga, even though it is generally only used for Icelandic stories. It is just to make it easier for my readers. If you are an Icelandic expert, then I apologise. I use plenty of foreign words which, I know, taxes some of my readers. As I keep saying it is about the characters and the stories.

It was more dangerous to drink the water in those times and so most people, including children drank beer or ale. The process killed the bacteria which could hurt them. It might sound as though they were on a permanent pub crawl but in reality, they were drinking the healthiest drink that was available to them. Honey was used as an antiseptic in both ancient and modern times. It was also the most commonly available sweetener. Yarrow was a widely-used herb. It had a variety of applications in ancient times. It was frequently mixed with other herbs as well as being used with honey to treat wounds. Its Latin name is Achillea millefolium. Achilles was reported to have carried the herb with him in battle to treat wounds. Its traditional names include arrowroot, bad man's plaything, bloodwort, carpenter's weed, death flower, devil's nettle, eerie, field hops, gearwe, hundred leaved grass, knight's milefoil, knyghten, milefolium, milfoil, millefoil, noble yarrow, nosebleed, old man's mustard, old man's pepper, sanguinary, seven year's love, snake's grass, soldier, soldier's woundwort, stanchweed, thousand seal, woundwort, yarroway, yew. I suspect Tolkien used it in The Lord of the Rings books as Kingsfoil, another ubiquitous and often overlooked herb in Middle Earth.

The Vikings were not sentimental about their children. A son would expect nothing from his father once he became a man. He had more chance of reward from his jarl than his father. Leaders gave gifts to their followers. It was expected. Therefore, the more successful you were as a leader the more loyal followers you might have. A warrior might be given battle rings by his jarl. Sometimes these were taken from the dead they had slain. Everything would be recycled!

The word lake is a French/Norman word. The Norse called lakes either waters or meres. They sometimes used the old English term, tarn. The Irish and the Scots call them Lough/lochs. There is only one actual lake in the Lake District. All the rest are waters, meres, or tarns. When they talk of the Water they mean Coniston Water in Cumbria.

The Bangor I refer to (there were many) was called Bangor is-y-coed by the Welsh but I assumed that the Vikings would just use the first part of the place name. From the seventeenth century, the place was known as Bangor of the Monks (Bangor Monachorum). Dolgellau was mined for gold by people as far back as the Romans and deposits have been discovered as late as the twenty first century. Having found gold in a stream at Mungrisedale in the Lake District I know how exciting it is to see the golden flecks in the black sand. The siege of the fort is not in itself remarkable. When Harlech was besieged in the middle ages two knights and fifteen men at arms held off a large army.

Anglesey was considered the bread basket of Wales even as far back as the Roman Invasion; the combination of the Gulf Stream and the soil meant that it could provide grain for many people. In the eighth to tenth centuries, grain was more valuable than gold. The Viking raids began in the early ninth century and plagued the inhabitants thereafter.

When writing about the raids I have tried to recreate those early days of the Viking raider. The Saxons had driven the native inhabitants to the extremes of Wales, Cornwall, and Scotland. The Irish were always too busy fighting amongst themselves. It must have come as a real shock to be attacked in their own settlements. By the time of King Alfred almost sixty years later they were better prepared. This was also about the time that Saxon England converted completely to Christianity. The last place to do so was the Isle of Wight. There is no reason to believe that the Vikings would have had any sympathy for their religion and would, in fact, have taken advantage of their ceremonies and rituals not to mention their riches.

There was a warrior called Ragnar Hairy-Breeches. Although he lived a little later than my book is set I could not resist using the name of such an interesting sounding character. Most of the names such as Silkbeard, Hairy-Breeches etc. are genuine Viking names. I have merely transported them all into one book. I also amended some of my names- I used Eric in the earlier books and it should have been Erik. I have now changed the later editions of the first two books in the series.

Bothvar Bjarki was a famous berserker and the Klak brothers did exist. I did not make either name up! Guthrum was also a Dane who lived in East Anglia.

Seguin I Lupo was Duke of Vasconia which broke away from the Empire briefly at the start of the ninth century.

Slavery was far more common in the ancient world. When the Normans finally made England their own they showed that they understood the power of words and propaganda by making the slaves into serfs. This was a brilliant strategy as it forced their former slaves to provide their own food whilst still working for their lords and masters for nothing. Manumission was possible as Garth showed in the first book in this series. Scanlan's training is also a sign that not all of the slaves suffered. It was a hard and cruel time- it was ruled by the strong.

The word 'testify' comes from Anglo-Saxon. A man would clutch his testicles and swear that the evidence he was giving was the truth. If it was not, then he would lose his testicles. There was more truth in the Anglo-Saxon courts than there is these days!

The Vikings did use trickery when besieging their enemies and would use any means possible. They did not have siege weapons and had to rely on guile and courage to prevail. The siege of Paris in 845 A.D. was one such example.

The Isle of Man(n) is reputed to have the earliest surviving Parliament, the Tynwald although there is evidence that there were others amongst the Viking colonies on Orkney and in Iceland. I have used this idea for Prince Buthar's meetings of Jarls. The Isle of Man(n) was one of the first places settled by Norsemen. The names on the island reflect their long Viking history. The world's first parliament, the Tynewald was held there. The Calf of Man is a small island off the south-western coast. The three legs of Man which makes up their flag still came from an early Jarl on the island. I have used Jarl Erik as that warrior. It is, of course, fiction of my own creation.

The blue stone they treasure is aquamarine or beryl. It is found in granite. The rocks around the Mawddach are largely granite and although I have no evidence of beryl being found there, I have used the idea of a small deposit being found to tie the story together.

There was a famous witch who lived on one of the islands of Scilly. According to Norse legend Olaf Tryggvasson, who became King Olaf 1 of Norway, visited her. She told him that if he converted to Christianity then he would become king of Norway.

The early ninth century saw Britain converted to Christianity and there were many monasteries which flourished. These were often mixed. These were not the huge stone edifices such as Whitby and Fountain's Abbey; these were wooden structures. As such their remains have disappeared, along with the bones of those early Christian priests. Hexham was a major monastery in the early Saxon period.

I do not know it they had warriors to protect the priests but having given them a treasure to watch over I thought that some warriors might be useful too.

I use Roman forts in all of my books. Although we now see ruins when they were abandoned the only things which would have been damaged would have been the gates. Anything of value would have been buried in case they wished to return. By 'of value' I do not mean coins but things such as nails and weapons. Many of these objects have been discovered. A large number of the forts were abandoned in a hurry. Hardknott fort, for example, was built in the 120s but abandoned twenty or so years later. When the Antonine Wall was abandoned in the 180s Hardknott was reoccupied until Roman soldiers finally withdrew from northern Britain. I think that, until the late Saxon period and early Norman period, there would have been many forts which would have looked habitable. The Vikings and the Saxons did not build in stone. It was only when the castle builders, the Normans, arrived that stone would be robbed from Roman forts and those defences destroyed by an invader who was in the minority. The Vikings also liked to move their homes every few years; this was, perhaps, only a few miles, but it explains how difficult it is to find the remains of early Viking settlements.

The place names are accurate and the mountain above Coniston is called the Old Man. The river is not navigable up to Windermere but I have allowed my warriors to carry their drekar as the Vikings did in the land of the Rus when travelling to Miklagård. The ninth century saw the beginning of the reign of the Viking. They raided Spain, the Rhone, Africa, and even Constantinople. They believed they could beat anyone!

King Egbert was a real king who did indeed triumph over King Coenwulf. He founded the power base upon which Alfred the Great built. When he defeated the Mercians he became, de facto, High King of Britain. It was also at this time that the Danes came to take over East Anglia and Yorkshire. The land became, over the next 50 years, Danelaw. Its expansion was only halted by Alfred and was finally destroyed when King Harold defeated his brother and King Harald Hadrada at Stamford Bridge in 1066. Until Alfred the Danes were used as hired swords. They fought for gold. It was a mistake for more often than not, as with the first Angles invited over, Hengist and Horsa, they stayed and conquered. So, it would prove with the Danes. Eardwulf was king of Northumbria twice: first from 796-806 and from 808-810. The king who deposed him was Elfwald II. This period was a turbulent one for the kings of Northumbria and marked a decline in their fortunes until it was taken over by the Danes in 867. This was the time of power for Mercia and East Anglia. Coenwulf ruled Mercia. Wessex had yet to rise.

I have made up Elfrida and Egbert's marriage to her but the kings of that time had many liaisons with many women. Some kings sired up to twenty illegitimate children and many legitimate ones. The practice continued into the late middle ages. Wives were frequently taken for political reasons. The inspiration for the abduction comes from the story of the Welsh Princess Nest (Nesta) who, in the 12th century had two children by King Henry 1st and was then married to one of his friends. She was abducted by a Welsh knight who lived with her until her husband recaptured her and killed her abductor. Harald Klak became King of Denmark in 826 but I made up his brother.

The Danish raids on the east coast began in the late 700s. However, the west coast and Hibernian were raided by Norse and Rus warriors who also went on to settle Iceland. There is less recorded evidence of their raids, attacks and settlements. The records we have are the Anglo-Saxon Chronicles and they tend to focus on the south and east of what was England. The land that is now the Lake District was disputed land between Northumbria and Strathclyde however the Norse influence on the language and its proximity to the Isle of man and Dublin make me think that the Norse there would not have been part of what would become Danelaw.

There were many Viking raids on London in the ninth century. They increased dramatically after 825. Dragonheart's raid is one of the first. 842 and 851 saw the largest raids. One was reputed to have 350 drekar! It was in the ninth century when the Danes finally conquered what is now East Anglia, Essex and, of course, Northumbria. They were not uniquely Danes. Some were Norse from Norway while others were the Rus or Swedes. However, Denmark and the lands of the Low Countries were the closest and they had the majority of the raiders. Rising sea levels at this time meant that much of their own lands were becoming submerged. The warriors came first; made homes and then brought their families.

Carhampton was a royal hunting estate of King Egbert. The Vikings attacked it in force in 838 bringing 25 ships.

The blood ceremony was taken from Mark Harrison's book, 'Viking Hersir'. I adapted it from the clan ceremony. I also used some of the elements from the fortress of Trelleborg from the same publication.

The Vikings had two seasons: summer and winter. As with many things a Viking lived simply and his world was black or white! There was no room for grey or any shades save the dead!

I used shadow raven website for the Norse months http://shadowraven.net/calendar/norse.html.

Saint-Valery is a small port at the mouth of the Somme. The bones of the saint were buried beneath the monastery and abbey there. They were built in the seventh century. In the eighth and ninth century, they were raided and devastated by Viking raids. The policy of the French Kings was to buy off the Vikings. The Mayor of Frisia did hire Danes to stop raids by other Vikings. Eventually the Danes were hired in East Anglia too.

The coast lines were different in the eighth and ninth centuries. The land to the east of Lincoln was swamp. Indeed, there had been a port just a few miles from Lincoln in the Roman age. Now Lincoln is many miles from the sea but this was not so in the past. Similarly, many rivers have been straightened. We can thank the Victorians for that. The Tees had so many loops in it that it took as long to get from Yarm to the sea as it did to get down to London! Similarly, many place names and places have changed. Some had Saxon names which became Norse. Some had Old English names. Some even retained their Latin names. It was quite common for one place to be known by two names.

Windar's Mere is actually Ambleside. The Romans chose its location and Dragonheart is too clever a warrior to ignore its defensive potential.

The Vikings did not have a religion in the way that we do. There was no organisation. They had no priests or mullahs. They had beliefs. The gods and the spirits were there. You did not worship them. You asked them for help, perhaps, but you could equally curse them too.

I used the following books for research

- Vikings- Life and Legends -British Museum
- Saxon, Norman and Viking by Terence Wise (Osprey)
- The Vikings (Osprey) -Ian Heath
- Byzantine Armies 668-1118 (Osprey)-Ian Heath
- Romano-Byzantine Armies 4th-9th Century (Osprey) -David Nicholle
- The Walls of Constantinople AD 324-1453 (Osprey) -Stephen Turnbull
- Viking Longship (Osprey) - Keith Durham
- The Vikings in England Anglo-Danish Project
- Anglo Saxon Thegn AD 449-1066- Mark Harrison (Osprey)
- Viking Hersir- 793-1066 AD - Mark Harrison (Osprey)
- Hadrian's Wall- David Breeze (English Heritage)

Griff Hosker November 2016

Other books

by

Griff Hosker

If you enjoyed reading this book, then why not read another one by the author?
Ancient History
The Sword of Cartimandua Series (Germania and Britannia 50A.D. – 130 A.D.)
Ulpius Felix- Roman Warrior (prequel)
Book 1 The Sword of Cartimandua
Book 2 The Horse Warriors
Book 3 Invasion Caledonia
Book 4 Roman Retreat
Book 5 Revolt of the Red Witch
Book 6 Druid's Gold
Book 7 Trajan's Hunters
Book 8 The Last Frontier
Book 9 Hero of Rome
Book 10 Roman Hawk
Book 11 Roman Treachery
Book 12 Roman Wall
Book 13 Roman Courage

The Aelfraed Series (Britain and Byzantium 1050 A.D. - 1085 A.D.
Book 1 Housecarl
Book 2 Outlaw
Book 3 Varangian

The Wolf Warrior series (Britain in the late 6th Century)
Book 1 Saxon Dawn
Book 2 Saxon Revenge
Book 3 Saxon England
Book 4 Saxon Blood
Book 5 Saxon Slayer
Book 6 Saxon Slaughter
Book 7 Saxon Bane
Book 8 Saxon Fall: Rise of the Warlord
Book 9 Saxon Throne

Book 10 Saxon Sword

The Dragon Heart Series
Book 1 Viking Slave
Book 2 Viking Warrior
Book 3 Viking Jarl
Book 4 Viking Kingdom
Book 5 Viking Wolf
Book 6 Viking War
Book 7 Viking Sword
Book 8 Viking Wrath
Book 9 Viking Raid
Book 10 Viking Legend
Book 11 Viking Vengeance
Book 12 Viking Dragon
Book 13 Viking Treasure
Book 14 Viking Enemy
Book 15 Viking Witch
Bool 16 Viking Blood
Book 17 Viking Weregeld
Book 18 Viking Storm
Book 19 Viking Warband
Book 20 Viking Shadow
Book 21 Viking Legacy

The Norman Genesis Series
Hrolf the Viking
Horseman
The Battle for a Home
Revenge of the Franks
The Land of the Northmen
Ragnvald Hrolfsson
Brothers in Blood
Lord of Rouen
Drekar in the Seine

The Anarchy Series England 1120-1180
English Knight
Knight of the Empress

Northern Knight
Baron of the North
Earl
King Henry's Champion
The King is Dead
Warlord of the North
Enemy at the Gate
Fallen Crown
Warlord's War
Kingmaker
Henry II
Crusader
The Welsh Marches
Irish War
Poisonous Plots
Princes' Revolt
Earl Marshal

Border Knight 1190-1300
Sword for Hire
Return of the Knight
Baron's War
Magna Carta

Struggle for a Crown England 1367-1485
Blood on the Crown

Modern History
The Napoleonic Horseman Series
Book 1 Chasseur a Cheval
Book 2 Napoleon's Guard
Book 3 British Light Dragoon
Book 4 Soldier Spy
Book 5 1808: The Road to Corunna
Waterloo

The Lucky Jack American Civil War series
Rebel Raiders
Confederate Rangers

The Road to Gettysburg

The British Ace Series
1914
1915 Fokker Scourge
1916 Angels over the Somme
1917 Eagles Fall
1918 We will remember them
From Arctic Snow to Desert Sand
Wings over Persia

Combined Operations series 1940-1945
Commando
Raider
Behind Enemy Lines
Dieppe
Toehold in Europe
Sword Beach
Breakout
The Battle for Antwerp
King Tiger
Beyond the Rhine

Other Books
Carnage at Cannes (a thriller)
Great Granny's Ghost (Aimed at 9-14-year-old young people)
Adventure at 63-Backpacking to Istanbul

For more information on all of the books then please visit the author's web site at http://www.griffhosker.com where there is a link to contact him. Or you can Tweet me at @HoskerGriff

Made in the USA
Middletown, DE
09 March 2021